TOEFL

李英松／著

托福文法與構句

中冊

自序

　　托福考試有關文法部份，Part A 是全部未完成的，要應考者在四個答案當中，選擇一個正確的答案，將句子完成且要符合文法規則和整個句子的意義。這些答案有可能是單字，有可能是片語，也有可能是子句。至於它們擺放的位置也許在句子的前段，也許在句子的尾段，或許在句子的中段，通常這些題目有十五題之多。

　　Part B 是通通已經完成的句子，但是要應考者在整個句子的四個地方，找出哪個地方出了問題，是不符合文法規則呢？還是它們的意義不合乎邏輯呢？一般來說這些題目共有二十五題，每個題目都只有一個地方出了問題，不是單字就是片語，應考者只要指出地方而已不必改正，似乎比較 Part A 容易一些些。

　　講到出題的範圍，真是五花八門千變萬化，Part A 加上 Part B 總共有四十道題目，而應考者要在短短的二十五分鐘之內作答完畢，應考者如何展現功力，就要想想古人所言，「工欲善其事，必先利其器」。

　　我們所研讀過的英文八大詞類除了驚嘆詞之外，其餘的名詞、動詞、冠詞、形容詞、介詞、連接詞、副詞再加上片語、子句、不定詞、動名詞、分詞和標點符號等等都是出題的內容。我們如何準備？如何充實應考的能力？這就是一門很大的功課。

　　筆者在準備托福考試時和之後所收集資料編著成書的過程中，意識到萬物不離其宗，因而歸納出考題依據之準則，以供讀者參考。諸如，專有名詞的大寫和單複數，動詞的時態和語態，冠詞的不定和特定，形容詞的變化和比較，介詞的種類和用法，動名詞和現在分詞區別與用法，句子的平行和倒裝，標點符號如何使用，等等問題，一切的一切均在本系列書〈托福文法與構句〉前冊書中舉例詳細說明過。

　　讀者在研讀文法規則之後，不斷的練習作答，必能融會貫通，從容面對托福考試。

目錄

自序   **3**

第 十九 章   托福文法考古題解析   **5**

                   〈從四個答案當中，選擇一個有錯誤的答案〉

第十九章 ｜ 托福文法考古題解析

〈 從四個答案當中，選擇一個有錯誤的答案 〉

1. <u>Each</u> of the <u>buses</u> <u>run</u> on a <u>different</u> schedule.
    A   B   C   D

    ＜解答＞ C：runs

2. Please <u>don't</u> <u>play</u> the radio so <u>loud</u> when <u>I'm</u> on the telephone.
               A   B   C   D

    ＜解答＞ C：loudly

3. In order to reach the new <u>Cozy</u> <u>Company</u> factory, one must travel <u>North</u>
                             A   B   C

    on the <u>Parkway</u> for several miles.
               D

    ＜解答＞ C：north

4. Because Moria Martine, my neighbor, began jury duty . I am substituting
                     A   B   C

    for whom at work .
               D

    ＜解答＞ C：,

5. The injured bird <u>flew</u> to the ground, <u>letting</u> his <u>broken</u> wing <u>lain</u> at his side.
                 A   B   C   D

    ＜解答＞ D：lay

6. We <u>seen</u> the lights which <u>shined</u> in the distance, and we <u>began</u> to <u>walk</u>
      A   B   C   D

toward them.

<解答> A：saw

7. Upon seeing the young child <u>fall</u> into the lake, Eric <u>sprung</u> to his feet <u>ran</u>
                                 A   B   C

and <u>dived</u>.
        D

<解答> B：sprang

8. Because I had <u>forgotten</u> my driver's license, the policeman <u>forbiddend</u> me
                A   B

to <u>drive</u> any <u>farther</u>.
    C   D

<解答> B：forbade

9. Because Teddy had frequently <u>fallen</u> asleep on the job, he was not <u>payed</u>
                              A   B

the full <u>amount</u> that had been <u>written</u> into his contract.
         C   D

<解答> B：paid

10. Once their leader had <u>fallen</u>, the young soldiers did not <u>know</u> how to
                    A   B

continue,so they <u>fled</u> in many directions and were never <u>seen</u> again.
            C   D

<解答> C：fled

11. If you <u>chose</u> to <u>rise</u> within the company, you <u>must</u> <u>raise</u> your level of work.
         A   B   C   D

<解答> A：choose

12. The <u>armed</u> man <u>slayed</u> the innocent victim, <u>stole</u> his watch, and <u>ran</u> down
         A   B   C   D

the alley.

<解答>　B：slew

13.　The guest <u>arrived</u> unexpectedly, <u>shaked</u> everyone's hand, <u>ate</u>, and <u>left</u> as
　　　　　　　　　　A　　　　　　　　　　B　　　　　　　　　C　　　　　D

　　unexpectedly as he had arrived.

　　<解答>　B：shook

14.　Maxine <u>waked</u> me early this morning, and I <u>ate</u> my eggs, <u>drunk</u> my juice,
　　　　　　　　A　　　　　　　　　　　　　　　　B　　　　　　C

　　and <u>left</u>.
　　　　　D

　　<解答>　C：drank

15.　A shopping trip <u>makes</u> me angry. Prices <u>soar</u> each week. Meat prices
　　　　　　　　　　　A　　　　　　　　　　B

　　<u>changes</u> almost daily. Oranges, apples, and bananas <u>cost</u> more than ever.
　　　　C　　　　　　　　　　　　　　　　　　　　　　　　　　D

　　<解答>　C：change

16.　In the spring the honeysuckle <u>drops</u> over the hillside. Its sweet <u>smells</u>
　　　　　　　　　　　　　　　　　　　A　　　　　　　　　　　　　　　B

　　<u>hangs</u> heavily in the air outside. It floats into the room when the doors
　　　　C

　　<u>are open</u>.
　　　　D

　　<解答>　B：smell

17.　Tom <u>jogs</u> each morning. Macon and Gary <u>join</u> him on Mondays and
　　　　　　A　　　　　　　　　　　　　　　B

　　Thursdays.The Robinson twins <u>likes</u> jogging too. Jogging now <u>replaces</u>
　　　　　　　　　　　　　　　　C　　　　　　　　　　　　　　D

　　basketball as the neighborhood pastime.

　　<解答>　C：like

18.　Each year local artists <u>participate</u> in an art show. The Community Center
　　　　　　　　　　　　　A

<u>offers</u> a perfect gallery. One artist <u>wins</u> in each of five categories.

    B   C

The winning artists <u>displays</u> their works in the Town Hall.

                        D

＜解答＞ D：display

19. A hummingbird <u>dives</u> daily in and out of the honeysuckle. He <u>bombs</u> <u>past</u>

                A   B   C

the doors with his heavy load and <u>balanced</u> on a branch of the little olive tree.

                               D

＜解答＞ D：balances

20. The farmer and his hired men <u>gathers</u> the corn. The farmer, along with his

                            A

hired men, <u>harvests</u> the wheat. Neither the corn nor the wheat is <u>neglected</u>.

        B   C

The farmer's wife and daughter <u>argue</u> a great deal.

                        D

＜解答＞ A：gather

21. A teenage driver <u>causes</u> one out of every three automobile accidents.

                A

Many <u>accuse</u> teen drivers of not concentrating on the road. Three out of

       B

six parents <u>interviewed</u> <u>fears</u> for their children's safety.

             C   D

＜解答＞ D：fear

22. The delegate and <u>his</u> alternate <u>votes</u> at <u>each</u> <u>monthly</u> meeting.

              A   B   C   D

＜解答＞ B：vote

23. The electrician and his assistant <u>always</u> <u>shuts</u> off the electricity <u>before</u>

                        A   B   C

《TOEFL 托福文法與構句 中冊》勘誤表

頁數	題數	訂正說明
P24	132	spenish → Spanish
P24	132	crystal → Crystal
P32	184	ex-roommate 兩個字要劃底線
P51	323	htan → than
P53	336	perple → people
P85	538	like many people supposec 全都要劃底線
P95	593	it cause → it causes
P98	609	abso dot → also dot
P104	645	句首 the → The
P105	650	Put → put 小寫並加劃底線
P110	680	句首 some → Some
P131	816	propsals → proposals
P133	831	〈解答〉univerally → universally
P134	886	coate → coats
P141	943	〈解答〉we haver to → we have to
P174	1099	countrolled → controlled
P177	1122	句首 Chcikens → Chickens
P181	1140	〈解答〉enphaized → emphasized
P186	1172	the is a likly → she is a likly
P205	1295	out experience → our experience
P206	1302	on hundred years → one hundred years

P214	1349	pepresentative → representative
P217	1365	〈解答〉 he boosted → be boosted
P232	1457	bilieve → believe
P239	1500	peopls → people
P242	1517	tor the purpose → for the purpose
P245	1537	we connot hope → we cannot hope
P250	1569	for seceral → for several
P254	1594	are voaluable → are valuable

beginning <u>work</u>.

     D

 ＜解答＞ B：shut

24. Martin and his brother <u>walks</u> to <u>work</u> <u>each</u> morning and <u>take</u> the bus home

         A   B C   D

  each evening.

 ＜解答＞ A：walk

25. If a person <u>maintains</u> a good historical perspective, he <u>understands</u> the

        A   B

  <u>present</u> and <u>predicted</u> the future.

   C   D

 ＜解答＞ D：predicts

26. The late Louis Braille, <u>inventor</u> of the Braille alphabet, <u>pioneered</u> in his

          A   B

  own right and <u>contributes</u> to <u>aids</u> for the handicapped.

        C   D

 ＜解答＞ C：contributed

27. <u>One</u> of those packages <u>belong</u> to the <u>tall</u> man at the end of the <u>long</u> line.

   A   B   C   D

 ＜解答＞ B：belongs

28. Although I <u>can't</u> <u>see</u> you, I can <u>hear</u> you <u>good</u>.

      A B   C   D

 ＜解答＞ D：well

29. As food prices continue to <u>rise</u>, more and <u>more</u> people turn to farming and

              A   B

  <u>almost</u> of them <u>enjoy</u> it.

   C   D

 ＜解答＞ C：most

30. A book of food <u>stamps</u> <u>fall</u> <u>onto</u> the counter in the supermarket and several

         A   B C

people <u>reached</u> for it.

       D

＜解答＞　B：fell

31. The <u>plumbers</u> union, along with <u>several</u> other unions in the area, <u>choose</u>

      A   B   C

not to <u>work</u> on Saturdays.

       D

＜解答＞　C：chooses

32. Some of the finest modern artists cannot <u>sketch</u> <u>accurate</u> nor <u>reproduce</u> a

                                    A   B   C

likeness <u>well</u>.

       D

＜解答＞　B：accurately

33. The superintendent and his wife <u>argues</u> <u>frequently</u> and the neighbors <u>listen</u>

                             A   B   C

<u>attentively</u>.

  D

＜解答＞　A：argue

34. We <u>spent</u> a perfect day at the beach because the ocean was <u>real</u> calm and

      A   B

the sun <u>wasn't</u> <u>too</u> hot.

      C   D

＜解答＞　B：really

35. Robert pace <u>designed</u> a unique method of piano instruction which <u>combines</u>

         A   B

<u>classical</u>, <u>romance</u>, and contemporary music.

  C   D

＜解答＞　D：romantic

36. The team <u>played</u> <u>clumsy</u> and, therefore, <u>lost</u> the <u>game</u>.

      A   B   C   D

<解答> B：clumsily

37. Before anyone <u>makes</u> a decision, he <u>weighs</u> all of the alternatives and
                     A   B

   <u>chose</u> the <u>best</u>.
      C   D

   <解答> C：chooses

38. During the <u>recent</u> blackout, <u>many</u> refrigerators <u>defrosted</u> and the food <u>spoils</u>.
                    A   B   C   D

   <解答> D：spoiled

39. Perry <u>enters</u> the <u>crowded</u> movie theater, <u>buys</u> popcorn, and <u>looked</u> for a
              A   B   C   D

   seat.

   <解答> D：looks

40. Because <u>she</u> <u>enjoys</u> the exercise, Patricia, <u>alongs</u> with several of her friends,
                 A   B   C

   <u>skates</u> every Friday evening.
      D

   <解答> C：along

41. Maria and her <u>best</u> friend, Lucy, <u>goes</u> to <u>adult</u> school twice each week and
                      A   B   C

   <u>study</u> together.
      D

   <解答> B：go

42. Don't <u>rise</u> your hand at the meeting unless you <u>plan</u> to <u>speak</u> in <u>favor</u> of
              A   B   C   D

   the proposal.

   <解答> A：raise

43. Because <u>few</u> money is available, we are <u>faced</u> with the problem of providing
                 A   B

<u>better</u> education at <u>lower</u> cost.

       C   D

＜解答＞　A：less

44. The tools <u>in</u> the storage chest <u>accomplishes</u> <u>most</u> of the <u>necessary</u> tasks.

             A   B   C   D

＜解答＞　B：accomplish

45. <u>Please</u> <u>take</u> the <u>tape</u> recorder with you and tape the evening's <u>discussion</u>.

     A   B   C   D

＜解答＞　B：bring

46. The <u>more</u> they <u>grapple</u> with the problem, the <u>less</u> the members of the

        A   B   C

legislature <u>understands</u> it.

           D

＜解答＞　D：understand

47. The <u>tiles</u> in the bathroom <u>shows</u> <u>signs</u> of <u>wear</u>.

      A   B   C   D

＜解答＞　B：show

48. A carton of eggs <u>smash</u> on the floor at <u>least</u> <u>once</u> a week in <u>that</u> store.

              A   B C   D

＜解答＞　A：smashes

49. Of <u>all</u> the <u>downtown</u> merchants, I <u>like</u> Mr. Mitchell <u>more</u>.

     A   B   C   D

＜解答＞　D：most

50. Of all the people I <u>know</u>, Manuel <u>works</u> <u>most</u> <u>efficient</u>.

            A   B   C   D

＜解答＞　D：efficiently

51. The radio and the TV <u>play</u> so <u>loud</u> <u>that</u> I have trouble <u>reading</u>.

          A   B   C   D

＜解答＞　B：loudly

52. Mr. Ricardi <u>played</u> basketball <u>so</u> <u>good</u> that the men <u>asked</u> him to be the
　　　　　　　A　　　　　　B　C　　　　　　　　D

center on the neighborhood team.

　　＜解答＞　C：well

53. Buddy <u>listens</u> to instructions <u>attentively</u>, but cannot <u>remember</u> them <u>clear</u>.
　　　　　　　A　　　　　　　　　B　　　　　　　　C　　　　　　　D

　　＜解答＞　D：clearly

54. One of the women <u>on</u> the bus <u>talk</u> <u>incessantly</u> and <u>annoys</u> the driver.
　　　　　　　　　　A　　　　　B　　C　　　　　　D

　　＜解答＞　B：talks

55. Several doses of that medicine <u>makes</u> me <u>feel</u> tired and <u>react</u> <u>slowly</u>.
　　　　　　　　　　　　　　　A　　　　　B　　　　　　C　　D

　　＜解答＞　A：make

56. I would not <u>have</u> <u>rang</u> your doorbell if I didn't <u>have</u> an <u>important</u> message.
　　　　　　　A　　B　　　　　　　　　　　C　　　D

　　＜解答＞　B：rung

57. Ecology <u>is</u> <u>emerging</u> into an exact science. At last, the function of waste
　　　　　A　　B

products <u>are</u> <u>being</u> discovered.
　　　　　C　　D

　　＜解答＞　C：is

58. Now, as their multiple functions <u>are</u> gradually <u>been</u> <u>studied</u>, their importance
　　　　　　　　　　　　　　　A　　　　　B　　C

<u>is</u> more apparent than ever before.
D

　　＜解答＞　B：being

59. Each local ecology group through its efforts, <u>have</u> <u>been</u> <u>instrumental</u>, in
　　　　　　　　　　　　　　　　　　　　A　　B　　C

recent years, in identifying and <u>solving</u> solid waste problems.
　　　　　　　　　　　　　　D

<解答> A：has

60. Glass, plastic, and paper finally <u>has</u> <u>been</u> <u>recognized</u> as reusable and <u>are</u>
                                                 A B   C   D

    being recycled.

    <解答> A：have

61. Finally, man's <u>belief</u> that his own actions, at least in past, <u>control</u> his destiny
                        A   B

    <u>are</u> <u>being</u> justified.

     C   D

    <解答> C：is

62. The chairman of one local organization <u>believes</u> that the advent of recycling
                                                    A

    waste products <u>are</u> just beginning. The same <u>is</u> true of non-polluting detergents,
                       B   C

    which <u>may</u> perhaps be even more important.

             D

    <解答> B：is

63. We <u>had traveled</u> extensively <u>before</u> we <u>had</u> <u>bought</u> our summer home.
             A   B   C D

    <解答> C：cancel

64. For the past year, <u>however</u>, we <u>were</u> <u>inclined</u> to <u>stay home</u>.
                        A   B C   D

    <解答> B：have been

65. Perhaps <u>by the time</u> our children <u>are grown</u>, <u>we have decided</u> to <u>travel</u> again.
                A   B   C   D

    <解答> C：we will have decided

66. During the <u>past</u> <u>several</u> years, the children's <u>increasing</u> activities <u>hampered</u>
                A   B   C   D

    our independence.

    <解答> D：have hampered

67. Before we <u>started</u> a family, we <u>did not travel</u> as much as we <u>should</u> <u>have</u>.
        　　　　　　　A　　　　　　　　　B　　　　　　　　　C　　D
    ＜解答＞ B：had not traveled

68. As soon as they <u>become</u> independent of us, <u>we will</u> <u>have</u> <u>become</u> independent
        　　　　　　　　　　A　　　　　　　　　　　B　　C　　D
    of them.
    ＜解答＞ C：cancel

69. Travel <u>became</u> so expensive over the <u>past</u> few years that we <u>can</u> no longer
        　　　　A　　　　　　　　　　　B　　　　　　　　　　C
    <u>afford</u> it.
    　D
    ＜解答＞ A：has become

70. We <u>traveled</u> in Europe and Asia <u>before</u> we <u>went</u> to <u>South</u> America.
        　　A　　　　　　　　　　B　　　C　　D
    ＜解答＞ A：had traveled

71. <u>He</u> and <u>his</u> brother strenuously object to <u>me</u> <u>smoking</u>.
    A　　　B　　　　　　　　　　　　　C　　D
    ＜解答＞ C：my

72. Sam finds <u>my</u> signing offensive, but <u>he</u> enjoys <u>me</u> playing <u>the</u> piano.
        　　　A　　　　　　　　　B　　C　　　　D
    ＜解答＞ C：my

73. If you are wondering <u>who</u> it was <u>who</u> called <u>you</u> earlier in the week, it was
        　　　　　　　　A　　　B　　　C
    <u>him</u>.
    　D
    ＜解答＞ D：he

74. Would <u>you</u> please buy tickets for the basketball game <u>for</u> <u>him</u> and <u>I</u> ?
        　　A　　　　　　　　　　　　　　　　　　B　C　　D
    ＜解答＞ D：me

75. Don wanted <u>us</u>, John and <u>I</u>, to help <u>him</u> build <u>his</u> new garage.

                   A   B   C   D

    ＜解答＞ B：me

76. Jane and <u>me</u> invited <u>our</u> husbands and <u>them</u> to join <u>our</u> physical fitness class.

              A   B   C   D

    ＜解答＞ A：I

77. <u>He</u> invited Jim and <u>she</u> to join <u>his</u> car pool <u>that</u> day.

   A   B   C   D

    ＜解答＞ B：her

78. Although <u>he</u> plays tennis better than <u>I</u> do, <u>I</u> played chess better than <u>him</u>.

               A   B   C   D

    ＜解答＞ D：he

79. The man <u>who</u> you called is out and <u>his</u> assistant insists <u>that</u> <u>he</u> will not

           A   B   C   D

return again today.

    ＜解答＞ A：whom

80. Although <u>her</u> is interesting and <u>she's</u> witty, I don't think that <u>she</u> is the right

              A   B   C

girl for <u>my</u> friend.

          D

    ＜解答＞ A：she

81. The <u>angry</u> man <u>ran</u> <u>hurriedly</u> into the crowded room and shouted <u>loud</u> at

          A   B   C   D

the guest.

    ＜解答＞ D：loudly

82. <u>What</u> <u>is</u> the <u>social</u> implications of the <u>small</u> car ?

   A   B   C   D

    ＜解答＞ B：are

83. There again, I must <u>insist</u> that I <u>do</u> not like <u>you</u> smoking in <u>my</u> home.

                       A   B   C   D

　　＜解答＞　C：your

84. Without <u>fail</u>, Carlo and <u>she</u> <u>attends</u> <u>monthly</u> board of education meeting.
　　　　　　　A　　　　　B　　C　　　　D
　　＜解答＞　C：attend

85. <u>Somehow</u> a misunderstanding about <u>this</u> situation <u>has developed</u> between
　　　A　　　　　　　　　　　　　　　　B　　　　　　　　C

　　you and <u>I</u>.
　　　　　　D
　　＜解答＞　D：me

86. Airman Donald G. Farrell <u>grimaced</u> as <u>him</u> <u>squeezed</u> into the simulated
　　　　　　　　　　　　　　　A　　　　B　　C

　　space cabin <u>which was</u> to be his home for seven days.
　　　　　　　　　D
　　＜解答＞　B：he

87. Although Jan <u>worked</u> all day, she <u>did</u> not <u>feel</u> <u>good</u>.
　　　　　　　　A　　　　　　　　　B　　C　D
　　＜解答＞　D：well

88. Just between <u>we</u> two, I <u>believe</u> Jim did not <u>write</u> the contract <u>properly</u>.
　　　　　　　A　　　　　B　　　　　　　C　　　　　　　　D
　　＜解答＞　A：us

89. Neither the congressman <u>nor</u> the people <u>whom</u> he <u>represents</u> <u>approves</u>
　　　　　　　　　　　　　　A　　　　　　　B　　　　C　　　　D

　　of this bill.
　　＜解答＞　D：approve

90. Soft drinks <u>satisfy</u> the appetite, <u>offer</u> absolutely nothing toward building health,
　　　　　　　A　　　　　　　　B

　　<u>taking</u> up valuable space, and particularly <u>crowd</u> out milk needed for growth
　　　C　　　　　　　　　　　　　　　　　　　　D

　　and normal bone and teeth structure.
　　＜解答＞　C：take

91. Personal health educators would be people who know the basic facts of

nutrition, food buying, cooking, physical fitness, how to motivate people,
 A   B   C   D

and interviewing.

<解答> D：motivation

92. Doctors are doing very little health education. They are not orinted or trained
      A   B

to be health educators, cannot make money dispensing health education, and
         C

there is no interest in being health educators.

   D

<解答> D：are not interested

93. Men are bent intently over chessboards. They are men of all ages, but most
                A   B

are closer to life's twilight than its dawn. They are in battle with one
               C

another, the chessboard is their battlefield.

  D

<解答> D：① another; the ② another, and the ③ another. The

94. Yet, it boasts not a single authentic chess master. Is this sad ? No, it's irrelevant.
 A   B

For, if a man is seeking out excellence in chess he would do well to stay away
 C   D

from St. James Park.

<解答> D：chess, he

95. Good chess is not being played in St. James Park, out life is being played.
                A

Here sits Liebowitz, he has escaped again from his wife. She will be along
     B

about 7 o'clock to remind him loudly that he is a married man with children.
" Your supper is cold again, Liebowitz ! " She has never called him Liebowitz
anywhere in the <u>world but</u> in St. James Park. It is the circumstances, the men
                                                     C

there, the <u>lateness</u> of the hour.
                D

＜解答＞ B：Liebowitz; he

96. What he would find here is <u>grimness, determination</u>, <u>anguish</u>, wisdom after
                               A   B

<u>the fact</u>, bitterness under the breath, and <u>there are a number of accidental</u>
    C   D

<u>brilliances.</u>

＜解答＞ D：a mumber of accidental brilliances

97. The sun is <u>hot. Never</u> mind. Sometimes a dizzle <u>begins. Never</u> mind. This is not
                     A   B

some silly pastime to idle time <u>away, this</u> is <u>chess ! This</u> outdoor chess
                                   C   D

congregation is the only one of its kind in the borough.

＜解答＞ C：① away; this ② away. This

98. Mrs. Romano exclaimed<u>, Frankie,</u> the parakeet has disappeared <u>! "</u>
                         A   B   C   D

＜解答＞ B：, " Frankie

99. The presiden<u>t's</u> desk was covered with all sorts of business paper<u>s; </u>invoices,
              A   B

recipts, minutes of his last meeti<u>ng,</u> and projected plans for the new buil<u>ding</u>.
                                 C   D

＜解答＞ B：papers:

100. Frankie answere<u>d, "</u> Mom <u>,</u> I don't know why <u>;</u> it was there when I tried to
                            A   B   C

clean it with the vacucum cleaner .

                                        D

＜解答＞　D：. "

101. We expect to arrive at Kennedy Airport at 8;15 P.M. on Thursday , June 8, 1976 .

                                          A   B   C   D

＜解答＞　A：8:15 P.M.

102. " You will never catch me. " shouted Batman . The pursuers vowed to catch him.

    A   B   C   D

＜解答＞　B：! "

103. Although we had met only once, he recognized me immediately and began to

                                        A

regale me with the following : he had just arrived in town ; he had bought a

                                B   C

house; and he had just been promoted within his company.

        D

＜解答＞　A：re-cognized

104. The student said, that he now understands the theory behind these problems.

                    A   B

He said , " Suddenly, everything falls into place. "

            C   D

＜解答＞　A：cancel

105. Do you really believe that you were a different person at twenty nine from

                A   B

the one you are at thirty ?

                C D

＜解答＞　B：twenty-nine

106. The author said. " You can learn to write only through writing. " He said

                A   B

that one can never learn to write by reading how-to books.

                                      C   D

<解答> A：,"

107. If you are planning to send a present to Laur<u>ie,</u> go to the <u>half-yearly</u> sale in
                                        A   B

    the childre<u>ns,</u> departmen<u>t.</u>
               C   D

    <解答> C：children's

108. Alice told Marison <u>she was</u> to stay at home and be a babysi<u>tter.</u> Marison
                       A   B

    exclaime<u>d, "</u> wha<u>t</u> a shame<u>! "</u>
               C   D

    <解答> C：," What

109. <u>Dont,</u> forget to write two <u>r's</u> in <u>"deferred. "</u>
    A   B   C   D

    <解答> A：Don't

110. "<u> </u>Clean your room <u>;</u> take the laundry to the basement <u>;</u> and wash the car <u>."</u>
    A   B   C   D

    instructed Mother.
    <解答> D：, "

111. When I arrived (<u>after a four hour drive</u>), I found that my <u>cousin's</u> <u>weren't</u>
                          A   B   C

    at <u>home.</u>
       D

    <解答> B：cousins

112. <u>Aftet</u> you till the soi<u>l, add</u> some plant food and water. Then You'll be ready
    A   B

    to plant the flower<u>s, "</u> concluded the garde<u>ner.</u>
                      C   D

    <解答> A：" After

113. The <u>ex Senator</u> hoped that his <u>protege's</u> bill would pass the <u>two-thirds</u> ma<u>rk.</u>
           A   B   C   D

<解答> A：ex-Senator

114. <u>Was</u> it Eisa who sai<u>d</u>, "<u>Our</u> sales meeting begains at 9:30 A.M. <u>sharp" ?</u>
      A   B   C   D

<解答> D：? "

115. Although Septemb<u>er, June,</u> and April have thirty <u>day's</u> December and January
                            A   B   C

have <u>thirty-one</u> days.
            D

<解答> C：days,

116. At <u>11:45</u> A.M. the <u>commuter's</u> <u>train</u> pulled them into the <u>jam-packed</u> station.
            A   B   C   D

<解答> B：commuters'

117. "<u>I</u> know when I will arrive on t<u>ime,</u> " answered Marie. "<u>it</u> will be when my
      A   B   C

alarm clock is finished beibg <u>repaired.</u> "
                                          D

<解答> C：. " It

118. He replied encouragingly <u>,</u> " Remember that Ted said <u>,</u> " <u>Let</u> Irene wait.
                                    A   B   C

I'll interview her as soon as I return <u>.</u> ' "
                                              D

<解答> C：' Let

119. After the vicious dog had attacked the trespasser, the dog's owner

<u>said, "</u> <u>Didn't</u> you see the sign which reads <u>,</u> <u>Beware of Dog</u> , before you
      A   B   C

entered my properyt <u>? ".</u>
                          D

<解答> D：? "

120. The show is called <u>"</u> Day after Day <u>; "</u> it starts at <u>2:30</u> <u>P.M.</u>
                          A   B   C   D

　　＜解答＞　B：" ;

121. After having read the third chapter , entitled " Spring-time Planting ", I felt
　　　　　　　　　　　　　　　　　　　A　　　　B　　　　　　　　C

　　that I was ready to tackle the gardening job.
　　　　　　　　　　　　　　　　　　　D

　　＜解答＞　C：, "

122. Our History course this semester highlights civilization of the East.
　　　A　　B　　　　　　　　　　　　　　　　　C　　　　　　　D

　　＜解答＞　B：history

123. My family plans to move to cypress street in Millville, Ohio.
　　　A　　　　　　　　　　　　　　B　　　　　　C　　　D

　　＜解答＞　B：Cypress Street

124. The Thompkins' plans for Labor day include a visit to the beach.
　　　　　A　　　　　　　　B　　　　　　　C　　　　　D

　　＜解答＞　B：Labor Day

125. I asked father to lend me the Chevrolet so that we can drive to the
　　　　　　　A　　　　　　　　　　　B

　　Rosemont club which is on the east side of town.
　　　　　　　C　　　　　　　　　D

　　＜解答＞　A：Father

126. This September, both of my children, Bob and Ronny, will be attending Cedar
　　　　　A　　　　　　　　　　　　　　　　　　　　　　　　　　　　　　　B

　　High school.
　　　C　　D

　　＜解答＞　D：School

127. " Why don't you read the Winston Item, " said mother, " and check for sales
　　　　A　　　　　　　　　　B　　　　　　　　　　C　　　D

　　on air conditioners ? "

　　＜解答＞　C：Mother

128. I've already crossed the <u>Atlantic ocean</u> by air; but this summer, in <u>July</u>, I hope

          A B   C

 to make the crossing on an <u>Italian</u> freighter.

            D

  ＜解答＞ B：Ocean

129. You recall <u>Reverend</u> <u>Hempsteal</u> saying that he will study <u>religious</u> philosphies

        A   B   C

 of the <u>east</u>.

     D

  ＜解答＞ D：East

130. Including <u>caucasians</u> , <u>Blacks</u>, and <u>Orientals</u>, the population of <u>Winfield</u>,

        A   B   C   D

 Pennsylvania has grown to one and a half million.

  ＜解答＞ A：Caucasians

131. The Ridgedale <u>Garden</u> <u>club</u> developed a hybrid <u>rose</u> and named it

        A B   C

 <u>Everlasting Beauty</u>.

     D

  ＜解答＞ B：Club

132. <u>More</u> and more elementary <u>schools</u> are teaching in <u>spenish</u> in order to meet

   A   B   C

 the needs of the <u>community</u>.

          D

  ＜解答＞ C：Spanish

133. <u>Uncle</u> John and my <u>father</u> are going to <u>crystal Lake</u> on <u>saturday</u> to try out

   A   B   C   D

 their new fishing gear.

  ＜解答＞ D：Saturday

134. Waiting for the <u>Twenty-second Street</u> bus, we had time to admire the

            A

arrow shirts displayed in Stone's Haberdashery.
　　　　B　　　　　　　　　　C　　　　D
　＜解答＞ B：Arrow

135. Speaking to the town's Community Action Council, Dr. J.l. Raio suggested
　　　　　　　　　　　A　　　　　　B　　　　　　　　C

revamping mental health services.
　　　　　　　　　　　　D
　＜解答＞ C：Dr. J.L. Raio

136. He speaks as though he knows everything.
　　　A　　B　　　C　　　D
　＜解答＞ C：knew

137. Proced two blocks North to the traffic light, and turn right onto Rumson Lane.
　　　A　　　　　　　B　　　　　　　　　　　　　　　　　　C　　　D
　＜解答＞ B：north

138. " If you plan to see the entire art exhibit, " Joan said, " Be sure to arrive at
　　　A　　　　　　　　　　　　B　　　　　C　　　D
10 A. M. "
　＜解答＞ D：be

139. The guide led us to a straight path through the woods and to a lovely veil.
　　　　　　A　　　　　　B　　　　C　　　　　　　　　　　　　D
　＜解答＞ D：vale

140. Because I was anxious to avoid another argument, I accepted Roy's apology.
　　　　　　　　A　　　　　　　　　　　　　　　　B
His story seemed credible so there was no point in carrying the argument
　　　　　　　　C
any further.
　　　D
　＜解答＞ A：eager

141. The principal members of the committee decided to lead a discussion about
　　　A　　　　　　　　　　　　　　　　　　　　B

the peace <u>movement</u> and the <u>type of a</u> person attracted to it.

        C   D

<解答> D：type of

142. My neighbor <u>dies</u> her <u>hair</u> <u>two</u> times every <u>week</u>.

       A   B C   D

<解答> A：dyes

143. Sue left the elevator and <u>proceeded</u> to the <u>personal</u> office. The cold, efficient

           A   B

interviewer lowered Sue's <u>morale</u>, but she was <u>eager</u> to obtain the job.

           C   D

<解答> B：personnel

144. Many of the <u>minors</u> in the audience began to <u>lose</u> <u>there</u> tempers because the

        A   B C

discussion <u>seemed</u> partisan.

        D

<解答> C：their

145. We had <u>already</u> planned our vacation to an unknown <u>isle</u> when our friends

      A   B

said that they were <u>all ready</u> to come <u>along to</u>.

          C   D

<解答> D：along too

146. The <u>effect</u> of the unusual visitor on the family was starting. Mother <u>adopted</u>

   A   B

Mr. Chuggley's speech habits; father <u>altered</u> his smoking habits to suit

               C

Mrs.Chuggley's allergy; and I found myself <u>continuously</u> saying, " yes, Ma'am. "

                   D

<解答> D：continually

147. The chairman <u>tryed</u> <u>to</u> explain that the <u>principle</u> of freedom to pursue one's

         A B   C

beliefs was not the <u>main</u> issue.

D

　＜解答＞　A：tried

148. You are <u>all together</u> mistaken about <u>their</u> decision <u>to write</u> to the newspaper.
A　　　　　　　　　　B　　　　C　D

　＜解答＞　A：altogether

149. The <u>course</u> of action determined by the city <u>counsel</u> at its last meeting has
A　　　　　　　　　　　　　　　B

<u>already</u> begun to <u>affect</u> us.
C　　　　　　D

　＜解答＞　B：council

150. It was not the committe's intention to <u>persecute</u> anyone but rather to make <u>plain</u>
A　　　　　　　　　　　　　　　　　　B

the <u>already</u> divergent viewpoints and to <u>precede</u> to bring them together.
C　　　　　　　　　　　　D

　＜解答＞　D：proceed

151. Ira Swanson <u>writes</u> about the religious <u>rights</u> of the Indians who inhabit the
A　　　　　　　　B

island <u>right</u> off the coast <u>of</u> Japan.
C　　　　　D

　＜解答＞　B：rites

152. Family gatherings are <u>always</u> interesting. Grandpa is usually <u>angry with</u>
A　　　　　　　　　　　　　　　　B

Aunt Jean. Rhoda insists upon sitting <u>besides</u> Grandma. Mother tries to
C

divide her attention equally <u>among</u> all of the guests.
D

　＜解答＞　C：beside

153. The <u>main</u> effect of the chairman's speech was <u>to quiet</u> the audience so that the
A　　　　　　　　　　　　　　B　C

discussion could continue <u>farther</u>.
　　　　　　　　　　　　　D

　＜解答＞　D：further

154. The <u>capital</u> of each state is the <u>cite</u> of the <u>capitol building</u> of that state and
　　　　　A　　　　　　　　　B　　　　　　C

main attraction for <u>sightseers</u>.
　　　　　　　　　D

　＜解答＞　B：site

155. I was <u>altogether</u> shocked when Sam returned the ice bucket which he had
　　　　　　A

<u>borrowed from</u> us last spring. When I <u>complemented</u> him for returning it
　　　B　　　　　　　　　　　　　　　C

so promptly, Sam's red face told me that he understood my <u>implied</u> sarcasm.
　　　　　　　　　　　　　　　　　　　　　　　　　D

　＜解答＞　C：complimented

156. The next speaker <u>waisted</u> more time by expressing anger with the young people
　　　　　　　　　A

<u>present</u> rather than <u>formally</u> addressing the <u>issues</u> at hand.
　　B　　　　　　　C　　　　　　　　D

　＜解答＞　A：wasted

157. Because the <u>currant</u> was <u>strong</u>, we had <u>great</u> difficulty reaching <u>shore</u>.
　　　　　　　　　A　　　　B　　　　　C　　　　　　　　D

　＜解答＞　A：current

158. Please put the change <u>into</u> your pocket before you lose it. It's hard enough
　　　　　　　　　　　A

to keep pace with today's prices without carelessly <u>losing</u> money. That <u>kind</u>
　　　　　　　　　　　　　　　　　　　B　　　　　　C

of carelessness makes me <u>loose</u> my temper.
　　　　　　　　　D

　＜解答＞　D：lose

159. I am certain that the committee <u>learned</u> a lesson about discussing <u>volatile</u> issues.
A   B

  Next time it will <u>altar</u> <u>its</u> presentation so that speakers will be more to the point.
C D

  ＜解答＞ C：alter

160. I, for one, <u>didn't</u> <u>appreciate</u> the <u>manor</u> in <u>which</u> she answered.
A B   C D

  ＜解答＞ C：manner

161. The <u>minor</u> <u>led</u> his <u>team</u> into the shaft. After several hours of dangerous work,
A B C

  they <u>ascended</u> jubilantly.
D

  ＜解答＞ A：miner

162. That way, <u>less</u> misunderstandings will occur. The Lakeview Town <u>Council</u>
A   B

  had planned a <u>similar</u> discussion, but changed <u>its</u> program.
C   D

  ＜解答＞ A：fewer

163. We <u>truly</u> felt that the <u>exorbitant</u> <u>expenditure</u> was a <u>waist</u>.
A   B C   D

  ＜解答＞ D：waste

164. I am <u>formally</u> engaged in a program of good nutrition. I always eat a <u>healthy</u>
A   B

  breakfast. I consume <u>fewer</u> sweets and I spend <u>less</u> time stalking the
C   D

  refrigerator for snacks.

  ＜解答＞ B：healthful

165. It will have a speaker on the new <u>adoption</u> laws. Many people need <u>advise</u> on
A   B

this topic. It <u>plainly</u> will be less controversial than the <u>peace</u> movement was.
                          C   D

　＜解答＞　B：advice

166. We <u>wade</u> both <u>arguments</u>, and we decided in <u>favor</u> of the <u>contract</u>.
         A   B   C   D

　＜解答＞　A：weighed

167. Sue asked if she <u>might</u> go swimming at the pool. Although Sue <u>can</u> swim <u>quite</u>
                        A   B   C

well, her mother refused permission. Sue was angry and said she was being
<u>prosecuted</u>.
   D

　＜解答＞　D：persecuted

168. The council has <u>all ready</u> advertised in local papers and <u>expects</u> a long <u>number</u>
                 A   B   C

of people to be <u>eager</u> to attend.
                  D

　＜解答＞　A：already

169. The <u>members</u> of the <u>panel</u> were asked to leave <u>there</u> jackets in the <u>outer</u> office.
        A   B   C   D

　＜解答＞　C：their

170. We <u>heard</u> Pete <u>moan</u>, and we saw that he <u>had become</u> deadly <u>pail</u>.
        A   B   C   D

　＜解答＞　D：pale

171. The <u>nutritious</u> food, the fine <u>weather</u>, and the <u>exercise</u> made us feel <u>grate</u>.
        A   B   C   D

　＜解答＞　D：great

172. "Would you like to record the song you wrote ? ", the conductor asked
A   BCD

the singer.

　＜解答＞　D：cancel

173. <u>Sue</u> <u>Simpson</u>, the lead in The Glass <u>menagerie,</u> is a really competent <u>actress</u>.

     A   B   C   D

<解答>　C：menagerie (comma 取消)

174. Please <u>leave</u> Marie go to the movies <u>with</u> me because I <u>may</u> not go to town

             A   B   C

<u>alone</u>.

    D

<解答>　A：let

175. If you wish<u>,</u> you may pick some flowers <u>=</u> only those along the side of the

            A   B

house <u>=</u> for your centerpiece <u>. "</u>

       C   D

<解答>　D：. (" 取消)

176. <u>When</u> you leave <u>School</u> today, take a <u>bus</u> and meet me in New York <u>City</u>.

     A   B   C   D

<解答>　D：school

177. If you don't <u>want</u> to <u>build</u> shelves for me, <u>then</u> <u>learn</u> me how to build them

                  A   B   C   D

myself.

    <解答>　D：teach

178. "My favorite book<u>,</u> " said Meliessa " is Animal Farm<u>. "</u>

    A   B   C   D

<解答>　C：,

179. <u>Our</u> <u>course</u>, <u>history IA</u> , will include discussion of the settlement of the

    A   B   C

<u>American</u> colonies.

     D

<解答>　C：History IA

180. Because this is a <u>real</u> problem in <u>our</u> community, we need a <u>real</u> dedicated

                  A   B   C

group of citizens <u>to</u> study possible solutions.

         D

<解答>　C：very

181. The show (<u>for which</u> you have tickets) begins <u>promptly</u> at <u>7:45</u> and ends

      A   B   C

<u>believe it or not</u> at 11:00.

     D

<解答>　D：(believe it or not)

182. <u>Remember</u> that <u>Ellie</u> said we should meet <u>Her</u> for lunch on <u>Tuesday</u>.

    A   B   C   D

<解答>　C：her

183. Many reports indicate that sugar-coated <u>serials</u> are not <u>healthful</u>; <u>therefore</u>,

                 A   B   C

more nutritious breakfast foods <u>are</u> appearing on the market.

             D

<解答>　A：cereals

184. Last Sunday , I met my <u>ex</u> roommate (<u>whom</u> I haven't seen for twelve <u>years</u>)

      A   B   C   D

in the supermarket.

  <解答>　B：ex-roommate

185. <u>On</u> <u>Twenty-second</u> <u>street</u> there's a charming restaurant called <u>Lou's</u>.

 A   B   C   D

<解答>　C：Street

186. When Sturt gives the signal, <u>everyone</u> must <u>rise</u> to his feet, <u>raise</u> his hands

              A   B   C

above his head, at <u>set</u> down.

       D

<解答>　D：sit

187. "<u>After</u> you've practiced writing Y's ," said Miss Green , go right on to S's ."

 A   B   C   D

　　＜解答＞　C：, "

188. <u>Mr. Goren</u> reminded <u>us</u>, " <u>all</u> lights must be turned off in the laboratory at
　　　A　　　B　　　　　　C　　D

the end of the work day. "
　　＜解答＞　D：All

189. Because so <u>many</u> campers had cut down tress, <u>there</u> were <u>less</u> trees this year
　　　　　　　A　　　　　　　　　　　　　　　　B　　　　　　C

<u>than</u> ever before.
　　D
　　＜解答＞　C：fewer

190. The <u>Brownies</u> annual party was at the home of Jane <u>Simpson</u> on Friday<u>, at</u>
　　　　　A　　　　　　　　　　　　　　　　　　　　　B　　　　　　C

<u>4:15P.M.</u>
　D
　　＜解答＞　A：Brownies'

191. The <u>lieutensant</u> asked <u>captain</u> <u>John Forbes</u> to cut the ribbon at the ceremonies
　　　　　A　　　　　　　B　　　　　C

marking the opening of <u>Fort Titan.</u>
　　　　　　　　　　　　　D
　　＜解答＞　B：Captain

192. Mr. Smith <u>taught</u> the science <u>class</u> the <u>affect</u> of radiation <u>upon</u> cells.
　　　　　　　A　　　　　　　B　　　C　　　　　　　D
　　＜解答＞　C：effect

193. <u>Two thirds</u> of the membership voted <u>—</u> despite last year<u>'s</u> increase—the <u>dues</u>
　　　A　　　　　　　　　　　　　　　B　　　　　　　C　　　　　　　D

for the next fiscal year.
　　＜解答＞　A：Two-thirds

194. <u>This</u> <u>October,</u> <u>halloween</u> falls on <u>a</u> Tuesday.
　　　A　　B　　　C　　　　　D
　　＜解答＞　C：Halloween

195. That <u>author</u> carries the <u>principle</u> of free will <u>farther</u> than any <u>previous</u> author.

               A   B   C   D

<解答> C：further

196. The painter called this morning to say <u>"</u> that he <u>won't</u> be able <u>to</u> begin

                                          A   B   C

working until next <u>weekend</u>.

                    D

<解答> A：cancel

197. <u>"</u> We can learn much , " said <u>Edith</u>, " <u>from</u> the cultures of the <u>east</u>. "

A   B C   D

<解答> D：East

198. Mrs. Kelly Warren, <u>formally</u> Miss Kelly O'Rourke, <u>emigrated</u> <u>from</u> Ireland

                         A   B   C

this <u>past</u> year.

          D

<解答> A：formerly

199. Please <u>take</u> that envelope (<u>the</u> one on the hall <u>table</u>) across the street to

                A   B   C

Mrs. <u>Jone's</u>.

          D

<解答> D：Jones

200. <u>One</u> of the earliest and most significant <u>British</u> <u>documents</u> is the <u>magna carta</u>.

  A   B   C   D

<解答> D：Magna Carta

201. <u>Its</u> an <u>illusion</u> to expect that <u>course</u> of action to have a positive <u>effect</u> on our

A   B   C   D

long-range plan.

<解答> A：It's

202. No <u>two</u> <u>cities</u> in <u>this</u> country <u>is</u> identical.

          A   B   C   D

<解答> D：are

203. A carton of cigarettes <u>has</u> <u>been</u> <u>laying</u> on this counter <u>all</u> week.
                                       A   B   C   D

<解答> C：lying

204. <u>One</u> of the <u>necessary</u> prerequisites for change <u>are</u> <u>open-mindedness</u>.
  A   B   C   D

<解答> C：is

205. Taxes and <u>laughter</u> <u>is</u> always <u>present</u> in our <u>American</u> way of life.
                 A   B   C   D

<解答> B：are

206. Mario <u>is</u> a much <u>more</u> <u>efficient</u> bartender than <u>him</u>.
           A   B   C   D

<解答> D：he

207. <u>Each</u> of the choices <u>are</u> <u>equally</u> unappealing to <u>me</u>.
  A   B   C   D

<解答> B：is

208. One of <u>those</u> women <u>speak</u> <u>as</u> well <u>as</u> a professional lecture.
              A   B C   D

<解答> B：speaks

209. The Township Committee <u>had</u> not <u>realized</u> that so many residents <u>was</u>
                                A   B   C

<u>concerned</u> about the new zoning law.
  D

<解答> C：were

210. I <u>noticed</u> that older women <u>walk</u> <u>more</u> <u>graceful</u> than teen-age girls.
    A   B   C   D

<解答> D：gracefully

211. When I must <u>speak</u> to a <u>large</u> group of people, I always speak <u>too</u> <u>soft</u>.
                  A   B   C D

<解答> D：softly

212. <u>Any</u> of the women in that office <u>may</u> express <u>their</u> opinion at <u>any</u> time.
  A   B   C   D
 <解答> C：her

213. <u>The boys</u> <u>were waiting</u> for the <u>headmaster</u> <u>come</u> in.
  A B   C D
 <解答> D：to come

214. Either Charlie or <u>I</u> will <u>call</u> you or <u>he</u> when the order <u>is</u> ready.
      A B   C   D
 <解答> C：him

215. <u>Was</u> <u>it</u> Mr. Farrar <u>whom</u> <u>called</u> you ?
 A B   C   D
 <解答> C：who

216. Eileen and <u>me</u> <u>are</u> <u>working</u> on <u>the</u> night shift with them.
     A B C   D
 <解答> A：I

217. The problem of <u>too</u> many people <u>require</u> <u>immediate</u> attention by world leaders
       A   B   C

 <u>as well as</u> scientists and environmentalists.
   D
 <解答> B：requires

218. Because his lawyer <u>strongly</u> <u>adviced</u> him to do <u>so</u>, Mr. Rodriguez <u>offered</u>
        A   B   C   D

 his wife a generous settlement.
 <解答> B：advised

219. <u>Your</u> supervisor <u>does</u> not appreciate <u>you</u> walking in <u>consistently</u> at 9:10.
  A   B   C   D
 <解答> C：your

220. The <u>principle</u> reason for <u>my</u> not borrowing <u>your</u> credit card is that I'm afraid
     A   B   C

I'll <u>lose</u> it.

      D

＜解答＞　A：principal

221. After many months <u>of</u> <u>arguing</u>, Congress finally <u>adapted</u> the bill <u>into</u> law.

               A   B   C   D

＜解答＞　C：adopted

222. Fifteen minutes <u>are</u> all that I <u>can</u> <u>spare</u> to listen to <u>your</u> problems.

             A   B C   D

＜解答＞　A：is

223. I <u>am</u> <u>always</u> at the bus stop <u>earlier</u> than <u>him</u>.

    A   B   C   D

＜解答＞　D：he

224. Romeo and Juliet <u>are</u> one of my favorite plays, but <u>I've</u> never <u>seen</u> <u>it</u> performed.

             A   B   C D

＜解答＞　A：is

225. Eisenhower <u>was</u> president before Kennedy <u>was</u>, and Nixon <u>served</u> after

            A   B   C

Kennedy <u>had</u>.

        D

＜解答＞　A：had been

226. Either the executive <u>or</u> members of his staff <u>was</u> <u>responsible</u> for <u>breaking</u>

             A   B   C   D

the law.

＜解答＞　B：were

227. The mail carriers <u>each</u> <u>has</u> <u>their</u> own <u>personal</u> gripes.

             A   B C   D

＜解答＞　B：have

228. <u>Each</u> of the contestants <u>hope</u> to <u>win</u> the <u>grand</u> prize.

  A   B   C   D

＜解答＞　B：hopes

229. <u>Either</u> the subway or the <u>buses</u> <u>is</u> <u>crowed</u> at this time of day.
　　　A　　　　　　　　　　　B　C　　D
　　　＜解答＞ C：are

230. The dishes in the box <u>is</u> <u>on</u> sale this week only <u>and</u> will be <u>sold</u> for more
　　　　　　　　　　　　A　B　　　　　　　　　　C　　　　　　D
　　　next week.
　　　＜解答＞ A：are

231. Before the alarm <u>had stopped</u> <u>ringing</u>, Vera <u>had</u> <u>pulled</u> up the shade.
　　　　　　　　　　　A　　　　　　B　　　　　C　　D
　　　＜解答＞ A：stopped

232. Elissa <u>types</u> <u>much quicker</u> <u>than</u> any <u>other</u> woman in the office.
　　　　　　　A　　　　B　　　　C　　　D
　　　＜解答＞ B：more quickly

233. Everyone must <u>realize</u> <u>their</u> own potential and <u>try</u> to <u>achieve</u> it.
　　　　　　　　　　A　　　B　　　　　　　　C　　　D
　　　＜解答＞ B：his

234. Manuel and <u>me</u> <u>travel</u> to <u>work</u> together each <u>week-day</u> morning.
　　　　　　　　　A　　B　　　C　　　　　　　　D
　　　＜解答＞ A：I

235. <u>Either</u> of those two congressmen <u>will</u> <u>vote</u> against the President's
　　　A　　　　　　　　　　　　　　　　B　　C
　　　<u>proposing</u> bill.
　　　　D
　　　＜解答＞ D：proposed

236. <u>Any</u> of the local merchants <u>are</u> <u>willing</u> to <u>support</u> the United Fund.
　　　A　　　　　　　　　　　B　C　　　　D
　　　＜解答＞ B：is

237. Greast men <u>throughout</u> history <u>hardly</u> <u>never</u> avoided some minor <u>scandal</u>.
　　　　　　　　A　　　　　　　B　　C　　　　　　　　　D
　　　＜解答＞ C：ever

238. Lady Bird Johnson <u>scarcely</u> <u>never</u> <u>missed</u> an opportunity <u>beautify</u> America.
　　　　　　　　　　　A　　　B　　　C　　　　　　　　　D

　　＜解答＞　B：ever

239. Manny <u>was</u> shocked when Alfred <u>raised</u> his voice; no one had <u>never</u> <u>spoken</u> to
　　　　　　A　　　　　　　　　　　　B　　　　　　　　　　　C　　　D

　　him in that tone of voice.

　　＜解答＞　C：ever

240. A wise consumer <u>carefully</u> <u>reads</u> the labels and doesn't <u>never</u> <u>buy</u> unmarked
　　　　　　　　　　　　A　　　　B　　　　　　　　　　　　　C　　　D

　　products.

　　＜解答＞　C：cancel

241. Some scientists <u>they</u> believe <u>that</u> one of the long-range <u>effects</u> of food additives
　　　　　　　　　　　A　　　　　B　　　　　　　　　　　　C

　　<u>is</u> hyperactivity in children.
　　D

　　＜解答＞　A：cancel

242. If you really <u>had</u> <u>wanted</u> to, you could <u>of</u> <u>prevented</u> that misunderstanding.
　　　　　　　　　A　　B　　　　　　　　C　　D

　　＜解答＞　C：have

243. The sun <u>it</u> <u>is</u> 865,000 miles in diameter and <u>has</u> a surface temperature of
　　　　　　A　B　　　　　　　　　　　　　　C

　　<u>about</u> 10,000 F°.
　　　D

　　＜解答＞　A：cancel

244. The <u>sightseeing</u> trip on the sightssing bus <u>was</u> <u>one of</u> the highlights of our <u>much</u>
　　　　　A　　　　　　　　　　　　　　　　B　　C　　　　　　　　　　　　D

　　deserved vacation.

　　＜解答＞　A：cancel

245. If you <u>had</u> called ahead <u>of</u> time, I could <u>of</u> <u>been</u> ready when you arrived.
　　　　　　A　　　　　　　B　　　　　　　　C　　D

＜解答＞　C：have

246. My brother <u>he</u> never <u>calls</u> before <u>visiting</u> <u>us</u>.
　　　　　　　　A　　　　　　B　　　　　　　C　　　D

＜解答＞　A：cancel

247. According to historians <u>,</u> when the people in power cannot keep the governed <u>,</u>
　　　　　　　　　　　　　A　　　　　　　　　　　　　　　　　　　　　　　　　　　　　B

content <u>,</u> <u>revolution</u> is a possibility.
　　　　C　　　D

＜解答＞　B：cancel

248. Great literature <u>,</u> as well as great art <u>:</u> is a part of the <u>American</u> <u>tradition</u>.
　　　　　　　　　　A　　　　　　　　　　　B　　　　　　　　　　　C　　　　D

＜解答＞　B：,

249. During their first few years on the American <u>continent</u> <u>,</u> the pioneers lived off
　　　　　　　　　　　　　　　　　　　　　　　　　A　　　B

the animals in the woods <u>,</u> and stole corn from the <u>natives</u>.
　　　　　　　　　　　　C　　　　　　　　　　　　　　D

＜解答＞　C：cancel

250. The <u>Virginians</u> needed their own leader <u>,</u> Jefferson <u>,</u> <u>Sam</u> Adams was not
　　　　　A　　　　　　　　　　　　　　　　　B　　　　C　　D

their type.

＜解答＞　C：;

251. There are those who would say that <u>"</u> John Kennedy was the greatest
　　　　　　　　　　　　　　　　　　　　　A

<u>president</u> to date <u>,</u> and others would say that he has been <u>idealized</u>.
　　B　　　　　　C　　　　　　　　　　　　　　　　　　　　　D

＜解答＞　A：cancel

252. The Declaration of Independence states , <u>" ......</u> that all men are created
　　　　　　　　　　　　　　　　　　　　　　　　A

equal <u>,</u>that they are endowed by their Creator with certain inalienable
　　　　B

rights ; that among these are Life , Liberty , and the pursuit of Happiness " .
           C   D

＜解答＞ D：. "

253. The pioneers were a hardy , brave group of people , who would look in disbelief
         A   B

on the comforts of today's middle class.
       C   D

＜解答＞ B：cancel

254. They traveled with the bare necessities : food , water , warm clothing , tools ,
            A B   C   D

and weapons.

＜解答＞ A：:

255. Many say George Washington was a competent general , and a good president;
                 A   B

however , some historians would disagree.
   C D

＜解答＞ A：cancel

256. A flower consists of a calyx , a corolla , a staman and pistils.
 A   B   C D

＜解答＞ D：a stamen

257. Had anyone asked him , Barrow could of told the investigators some
  A   B   C   D

useful details about the robbery.

＜解答＞ C：could have

258. He has been sitting at the table for several hours and drank considerably more
    A   B   C

wine than is good for his health.
    D

＜解答＞ B：① has drunk ② has been drinking

259. In pre-paring for the test to be given next week, you should review each

      A   B   C

assignment and do the things which suggested below.

                                    D

<解答> D：① whick are suggested ② suggested

260. To think of the future in relation at the present is essential to civilization.

      A   B   C   D

<解答> C：to

261. The direction for this kind of exercise at first glance seen needless complex.

            A   B   C   D

<解答> D：needlessly

262. Cowboys in movies never seem to have any trouble to draw guns out of

            A   B   C   D

their holsters.

<解答> C：in drawing

263. In this city is to be found both the most renowned scholars and the scoundrels

 A   B   C   D

of the country.

<解答> B：are

264. William the Conqueror built the Tower of London to protect himself from

                           A   B

them he had conquered.

  C   D

<解答> C：those

265. Plants of these type grow best in places where there is a great deal of shade.

             A   B   C   D

<解答> A：this

266. Every doctor must know both medical theory and technique so that he can

                  A   B

apply <u>it</u> <u>in helping</u> his patients.
        C   D

＜解答＞ C：them

267. In his book <u>on</u> sculpture called " Aratra Pentelici, " Ruskin describes <u>an</u>

          A   B

experience <u>in which</u> many of <u>us students</u> would enjoy.
                C   D

＜解答＞ C：which

268. <u>By</u> the time the thief was <u>finally</u> captured, he had spent <u>most</u> all the money

A   B   C

he <u>had stolen</u>.
        D

＜解答＞ C：almost

269. <u>Althougth</u> aging improves some foods, fish must be handled <u>prompt and careful</u>

     A   B

from the <u>moment of</u> the catch <u>until final processing</u>.
              C   D

＜解答＞ B：promptly and carefully

270. Unfortunately, <u>two of the</u> boys <u>has been bit</u> by snakes the <u>last time</u> the family

                          A   B   C

camped <u>in</u> the valley.
        D

＜解答＞ B：were bitten

271. The danger is <u>when</u> there <u>is</u> a series of care that <u>are</u> ready to cross an

              A   B   C

<u>obstructed</u> area.
       D

＜解答＞ A：that

272. Every candidate who <u>has swam</u> the length of the pool will be given a certificate

                    A   B

stating that <u>he</u> has <u>proved</u> his competence.

　　　　　　　　C　　　　D

　　＜解答＞　B：swum

273. <u>Whether</u> you agree of <u>not</u>, this was the <u>most perfect</u> arrangement for <u>him</u> and

　　　　A　　　　　　　B　　　　　　　　C　　　　　　　　　D

Paul under the circumstances.

　　＜解答＞　C：perfect

274. She spoke so <u>indistinct</u> that we dial not know <u>whether</u> we were to <u>precede</u> <u>or</u>

　　　　　　　A　　　　　　　　　　　B　　　　　　C　　D

follow the procession.

　　＜解答＞　A：indistinctly

275. I read in the paper <u>that</u> the killer and his accomplises <u>are</u> to be <u>hung</u> at noon

　　　　　　　　　　A　　　　　　　　　　　　B　　　　　C

<u>by order of</u> the governor.

　　　　D

　　＜解答＞　C：hanged

276. Is there no one among you to <u>whom</u> I can turn <u>to</u> for <u>advice</u> and <u>comfort</u> ?

　　　　　　　　　　　　　　　A　　　　　　B　　　C　　　　D

　　＜解答＞　B：cancel

277. You should <u>bring</u> the results to Mr. Taylor's office so that the <u>council</u> <u>can</u>

　　　　　　A　　　　　　　　　　　　　　　　　　　　B　　　C

examine the details for <u>themselves</u>.

　　　　　　　　　　　　D

　　＜解答＞　A：take

278. <u>Whether</u> or not Marx's understanding of social conflicts <u>are</u> in any way

　　A　　　　　　　　　　　　　　　　　　　　　　　B

" scientific " <u>remains</u> <u>a vexing question</u>.

　　　　　　C　　　　　D

　　＜解答＞　B：is

279. <u>Of course</u>, we <u>shall</u> have to agree <u>with</u> you when you say that Henry is taller

        A   B   C

    than <u>any boy</u> in his class.

            D

    ＜解答＞ D：any other boy

280. I am <u>positive</u> that the cat had not <u>drank</u> all of <u>its</u> milk before the alarm <u>was</u>

              A   B   C   D

    sounded.

    ＜解答＞ B：drunk

281. One of the workers <u>has</u> <u>hung</u> the curtains that <u>had</u> been <u>laying</u> on the floor.

                         A   B   C   D

    ＜解答＞ D：lying

282. The first three <u>millennia</u> of written history <u>were strewn with</u> the wreckage of

               A   B

    <u>falling</u> empires and <u>extinct</u> civilizations.

      C   D

    ＜解答＞ C：fallen

283. <u>Few</u> living things <u>are linked</u> <u>together</u> as intimately <u>than</u> bees and flowers.

    A   B   C   D

    ＜解答＞ D：as

284. My son was <u>closer</u> to <u>my husband and I</u> on <u>that last day</u> of his life than

               A   B   C

    <u>he had been</u> for a long time.

        D

    ＜解答＞ B：my husband and me

285. <u>Only</u> about one <u>of</u> twelve of the young <u>men and women</u> of this country

    A   B   C

    <u>receive</u> a college education.

      D

    ＜解答＞ D：receives

286. After the program <u>had began</u>, he left his seat <u>so quietly</u> that no one <u>complained</u>
                             A   B   C

that <u>his</u> leaving disturbed the speaker.
     D

 ＜解答＞ A：had begun

287. It was <u>considerable</u> <u>of</u> you not to play <u>the piano</u> while your brother had <u>a bad</u>
             A   B   C   D

headache.

 ＜解答＞ A：considerate

288. Anyone <u>which</u> breaks the law <u>should be prepared</u> to accept the consequences
             A   B

<u>of</u> <u>his action</u>.
 C   D

 ＜解答＞ A：who

289. With John and <u>my</u> <u>helping</u> him, Mr. Fisher <u>began</u> to build <u>a stone</u> wall around
                A   B   C   D

the garden.

 ＜解答＞ A：me

290. The quiet <u>weekends</u> <u>one</u> has looked forward <u>are</u> often <u>jarred</u> by the noise of
          A   B   C   D

lawn mowers.

 ＜解答＞ C：to are

291. <u>From</u> the time a driver enters a car <u>until</u> he leaves it, he must be careful;
  A   B

a <u>moment's careless</u> may be his <u>last</u>.
       C   D

 ＜解答＞ C：moment's carelessness

292. We are not <u>particular</u> aware <u>of</u> idioms until we <u>begin</u> <u>to study</u> a foreign
           A   B   C   D

language.

　　＜解答＞　A：particularly

293. When visiting New York City, the tourist should take a boat ride arround
　　　　　A　　　　　　　　　　　　　　　B

Manhattan to familiarize yourself with the city.
　　　　　　　C　　　　D

　　＜解答＞　D：himself

294. It is easier to learn to do something when there is not necessary of first
　　　　　A　　　　　B　　　　　　　　　　　　　　C

" unlearning " present way of doing it.
　　　　　　　　　　　　　D

　　＜解答＞　C：no

295. There have been many revolutions in the history of the world, but only few
　　　　A　　　　　　　　　　　　　　　　　　　　　　　　B　C　D

were successful.

　　＜解答＞　C：only a

296. Without consulting Margie or us, Jane asserted that every one unless her had
　　　　　　　　　　　　　　A　　　　　　　　　　　　　　　　B

to contribute one-tenth of his earnings to the fund.
　　　　　　　C　　　　D

　　＜解答＞　B：except

297. Neither of the drivers who are being held by the police knows to whom to
　　　　　　　　　　　　　　A　　　　　　　　　　　B　　C

blame for his.
　　　　　　D

　　＜解答＞　C：whom

298. If you would have asked me I would have told you the whole story.
　　　A　　　B　　　　　　　C　　　　　　　D

　　＜解答＞　B：had asked

299. Among the three boys I would judge Tom to be the more intelligent, especially
　　　　A　　　　　　　　　　　　　　B　　　　　　　C

where abstract concepts <u>are</u> concerned.

                D

＜解答＞ C：most intelligent

300. Neither John <u>and</u> his father was able <u>to wake up</u> <u>early enough</u> <u>to catch</u> the

         A   B   C   D

morning train.

＜解答＞ A：nor

301. If you <u>had told</u> me <u>just that</u> I was to do, they <u>would never have found</u> fault

     A   B   C

with <u>my</u> handling of the case.

     D

＜解答＞ B：just what

302. <u>Being</u> tired, Herb listened <u>heedlessly</u> to the words that had sounded so

  A   B

<u>meaningfully</u> to him <u>only</u> a brief two hours before.

   C   D

＜解答＞ C：meaningful

303. <u>Being that</u> he is sensible, <u>we are</u> going to find that it is <u>he</u> who <u>will</u> assume

  A   B   C   D

most of the responsibility.

＜解答＞ A：Because

304. The more <u>one knows</u> <u>about</u> Elizabethan England, <u>the more</u> you understand

      A   B   C

the <u>importance of</u> the British navy.

     D

＜解答＞ A：you know

305. My roommate lives in a small town in <u>central</u> Missouri, a quiet town <u>which</u>

             A   B

I would like <u>to live</u> <u>myself</u>.

      C   D

<解答> B：in which

306. When Edison died, it was proposed <u>that</u> the American people <u>turned off</u>
A B

<u>all power</u> in their homes, streets, and factories for several minutes <u>in honor of</u>
C D

their great man.

<解答> B：turn off

307. This year, <u>as the past</u>, the oil company <u>will sponsor</u> a television series <u>based on</u>
A B C

<u>major</u> literary works.
D

<解答> A：as in the past

308. <u>At</u> school Paul ran <u>into</u> many new problems, such as <u>handling</u> his pocket money
A B C

and <u>to choose</u> his friends.
D

<解答> D：choossing

309. <u>It</u> is often easier <u>to select</u> a particular tool <u>than to</u> <u>use them</u> correctly.
A B C D

<解答> D：use it

310. Apparently <u>angry</u> by several <u>recent</u> thefts Mr. Jones <u>hired</u> two more <u>watchmen</u>.
A B C D

<解答> A：angered

311. The members of the children's orchestra were told that when one was

<u>asked</u> to play <u>more softly</u>, <u>you</u> should <u>not play</u> loudly.
A B C D

<解答> C：① one ② he

312. The news of the loss <u>suffered</u> by our troops <u>were</u> <u>much worse</u> than we
A B C

had expected.

       D

＜解答＞ B：was

313. Because of the accident, grandmother will forbid my brother and me
     A   B

from swimming in the river unless someone agrees to watch us.
       C   D

＜解答＞ C：to swim

314. Although professor Grant's lectures usually ran over the fifty-minute period,
                                   A

but not any of his students ever objected.
   B   C   D

＜解答＞ B：not only

315. When Rhodesia declared their independence from England, few thought that
                    A   B

the new government would last even a month.
                  C   D

＜解答＞ A：① its ② her

316. Writing in a terce, lucid style, the book describes the author's childhood
     A   B   C

experiences in Lousiana just before the outbreak of the Civil War.
                 D

＜解答＞ A：Written

317. Not doing your assignments consistently will make learning the material
     A   B   C

less easier for you.
   D

＜解答＞ D：difficult

318. It is surprising that Marquesne is such a fine writer, for he has not read only
      A   B   C

a few books <u>other than</u> his own.

               D

　＜解答＞　C：read

319. If Greg <u>had tried</u> <u>harder</u> to reach the <u>opposing</u> shore, we would not have <u>had</u>
         A   B   C   D

　to pick him up in the boat.

　＜解答＞　C：opposite

320. My hat was <u>blown</u> <u>off</u> by the wind <u>while walking</u> down <u>a narrow</u> street.
            A   B   C   D

　＜解答＞　C：while I was walking

321. He <u>enjoyed</u> <u>the</u> coffee so much <u>just</u> because it tasted so <u>deliciously</u>.
        A   B   C   D

　＜解答＞　D：delicious

322. <u>Had</u> they had enough cash <u>on</u> hand, they <u>would buy</u> this fancy <u>furniture</u>.
  A   B   C   D

　＜解答＞　C：would have bought

323. The good statesman, <u>like</u> all sensible human beings, always <u>learns</u> <u>more</u> from
                   A   B   C

　<u>their</u> opponents htan from his supporters.

   D

　＜解答＞　D：his

324. It is an <u>accepted</u> custom in our country <u>for</u> men <u>to remove</u> their hats when
          A   B   C

　a woman <u>entered</u> the room.

        D

　＜解答＞　D：enteres

325. The bond issue, proposed <u>as</u> a way <u>of financing</u> <u>a centennial celebration,</u>
                     A   B   C

　<u>failed</u> <u>in</u> a narrow margin.

   D

<解答>　D：by

326. The prophets <u>charged</u> the villagers <u>with guilty of</u> <u>confusing</u> the appearance

                        A   B   C

of religion <u>with</u> its substance.

            D

<解答>　B：with being guilty

327. Today divorce is <u>not longer</u> regarded <u>as</u> a disgrace, <u>nor</u> a tragedy, <u>not even</u>

                        A   B   C   D

a failure.

<解答>　A：no longer

328. The landlady <u>suspicioned</u> that someone <u>must</u> have broken <u>into</u> the house

                        A   B   C

which she <u>was watching</u> the T. V. show.

             D

<解答>　A：suspected

329. <u>Seeing</u> the trouble he had <u>caused</u>, he promised to be more <u>carefully</u> in the

    A   B   C

future.

<解答>　C：careful

330. Neither Richard nor I <u>was</u> able to recall when Mary had <u>last</u> <u>spoke</u> to us in

                        A   B C

<u>so friendly</u> a manner.

         D

<解答>　C：spoken

331. Children, she believes, are <u>supposed</u> to answer <u>politely</u> when <u>spoke</u> to by

                                A   B   C

<u>an</u> adult.

   D

<解答>　C：spoken

332. Apparently <u>angered</u> by several <u>loud</u> interruptions, the speaker <u>shooked</u> his
            A   B   C

    fist at the crowd <u>in the auditorium</u>.
                            D

    ＜解答＞ C：shook

333. There has been <u>hardly no sign of</u> agreement <u>as yet</u> <u>between</u> mangement and
                         A   B   C

    the union <u>in their dispute</u> over wages and working conditions.
                    D

    ＜解答＞ A：no sign of

334. <u>As</u> every <u>other</u> member of the team, Klaus <u>wore</u> an official uniform <u>in</u> the
    A   B   C   D

    victory parade.
    ＜解答＞ A：Like

335. Electric power had become <u>a so important</u> part of <u>American life</u> that a complete
                              A   B

    shut-down <u>for even</u> a few seconds would have created <u>chaos</u>.
               C   D

    ＜解答＞ A：so important a

336. The expert estimates that more than half a billion perple go to bed <u>hungrily</u>
                                                        A

    every night and <u>some</u> million children die before they <u>reach the age of</u> five
                       B   C

    because they do not <u>get enough</u> to eat.
                       D

    ＜解答＞ A：hungry

337. The <u>very</u> destructiveness of war on <u>both friend and foe</u> has rendered it
       A   B

    <u>uselessly</u> <u>as a means of</u> settling international disputes.
       C   D

<解答> C：useless

338. <u>The only way</u> to influence <u>others</u> is to talk about <u>that</u> they want and show

        A   B   C

them how to get <u>it</u>.

            D

<解答> C：what

339. The prices of the <u>works</u> of art are <u>so</u> high that <u>most museums</u> cannot afford

                 A   B   C

<u>buying</u> them.

  D

<解答> D：to buy

340. <u>After</u> a <u>great deal</u> of <u>initial</u> confusion, the antiwar demonstrators decided

   A   B   C

<u>protesting</u> inside the administration building instead of in the gymnasium.

    D

<解答> D：to protest

341. The runner, who was <u>about</u> <u>to compete</u> for the first time in a <u>major</u> track meet,

               A   B   C

waited <u>patient</u> in the starting blocks.

    D

<解答> D：patiently

342. When science, business, and art <u>learn</u> something of <u>each others'</u> methods and

                A   B

goals, the world <u>will have come</u> <u>closer to</u> cultural harmony.

              C   D

<解答> B：each other's

343. <u>Before</u> he died, the old man who <u>lives</u> next door to the drugstore used

    A   B

<u>to feed</u> the pigeons <u>three times</u> a day.

  C   D

＜解答＞　B：lived

344. It is difficult <u>to classify</u> mathematics <u>as simply</u> an art or a science because
　　　　　　　　　　　A　　　　　　　　　　B

　　　<u>they contain</u> elements <u>of both</u>.
　　　　　C　　　　　　　　D

　　＜解答＞　C：it contains

345. It usually takes much <u>less</u> time to fly from one country <u>to another</u> than
　　　　　　　　　　　A　　　　　　　　　　　　　　　B

　　　<u>traveling</u> <u>by train</u>.
　　　　C　　　D

　　＜解答＞　C：to travel

346. People are often suprised <u>when they</u> find <u>out</u> <u>about</u> the complex <u>serial</u> of
　　　　　　　　　　　　　　A　　　　　B　　C　　　　　　　D

　　　processes that are involved in the manufacture of paper.

　　＜解答＞　D：series

347. You will <u>not be</u> able to pass your examination <u>except</u> you study <u>harder</u> than you
　　　　　　　A　　　　　　　　　　　　　B　　　　　　C

　　　<u>do</u> now.
　　　D

　　＜解答＞　B：unless

348. Modern business and industry <u>demand</u> that young men <u>and</u> women <u>can speak</u>
　　　　　　　　　　　　　　A　　　　　　　　B　　　　C

　　　and write <u>clearly</u>.
　　　　　　　D

　　＜解答＞　C：speak

349. A carefully <u>trained</u> observer can <u>discover</u> details very <u>easy</u> although others
　　　　　　　A　　　　　　　　B　　　　　　　C

　　　<u>never</u> see them.
　　　D

　　＜解答＞　C：easily

350. <u>Because</u> he was <u>very</u> sick, he <u>laid</u> in bed waiting <u>for</u> the doctor to come.

     A   B   C   D

     ＜解答＞ C：lay

351. To Mrs. Foster and Miss Rocen the advice sounded <u>wrong</u>, but every <u>else</u>

                                                        A   B

     at the meeting <u>consider</u> it <u>perfect</u>.

                    C   D

     ＜解答＞ C：considered

352. Although he <u>knew</u> the teacher wanted <u>a</u> exact answer, he <u>was unable</u> to

                  A   B   C

     supply <u>it</u>.

            D

     ＜解答＞ B：an

353. The students were all <u>obedient</u> <u>and</u> did <u>that</u> the teacher had <u>told</u> them to do.

                           A   B   C   D

     ＜解答＞ C：what

354. As a result of having <u>on</u> a wet shirt for quite <u>a</u> while, he had one of <u>the worse</u>

                           A   B   C

     colds he had <u>ever</u> had.

                  D

     ＜解答＞ C：the worst

355. The tourists got <u>to</u> the resort so early <u>therefore</u> the clerk <u>there</u> wasn't even <u>up</u> yet.

                      A   B   C   D

     ＜解答＞ B：that

356. Ellen <u>would prefer</u> <u>going to</u> the theater more frequently, but her schedule

           A   B

     <u>prevents</u> her <u>attending at</u> more than one play a month.

     C   D

     ＜解答＞ D：attending

357. My sons <u>left</u> the farm for they <u>had lost</u> interest <u>to farm</u> and sought their
                A   B   C

fortunes in <u>the city</u>.
                D

　＜解答＞　C：in farming

358. <u>Despite</u> all the snow <u>in</u> the valley, the cabin <u>remained</u> warm and <u>comfortably</u>.
     A   B   C   D

　＜解答＞　D：comfortable

359. The librarian insists that John <u>will take</u> no more <u>books</u> from the library before
                                       A   B

he <u>returns</u> all the books he <u>has borrowed</u>.
        C   D

　＜解答＞　A：take

360. He felt so <u>bad</u> after that Ethel and I had to ask <u>whoever</u> we met <u>to do</u> the work
               A   B   C

<u>for</u> him.
D

　＜解答＞　B：whomever

361. The man <u>was asked</u> to pay <u>a</u> extra sum of money <u>on account of</u> the
               A   B   C

unpredictable <u>spendings</u>.
                D

　＜解答＞　B：an

362. It <u>has been estimated</u> that the efforts of <u>only</u> one per cent of the <u>world's</u>
            A   B   C

population <u>moves</u> civilization forward.
            D

　＜解答＞　D：move

363. Traditionally, <u>only a senior</u> can be elected <u>captain</u> of the football team, <u>but</u>
                      A   B   C

any player is <u>applicable</u> for the honor.
D

＜解答＞ D：① eligible ② quatified

364. I knew that without <u>they</u> to help me, it was <u>going to be </u>difficult for me

                A   B

<u>to repair</u> the roof and <u>paint</u> the front porch.

   C   D

＜解答＞ A：them

365. Long before his death, Goethe was recognized both <u>in Germany and France</u>

                                              A

<u>as one of</u> the <u>really</u> great <u>figure</u> of world literature.

   B   C   D

＜解答＞ D：figures

366. <u>Aside of</u> the resolution to have more ecumenical conferences, the <u>greatest</u>

   A   B

accomplishment of the group <u>was that</u> it met <u>at all</u>.

                       C   D

＜解答＞ A：Aside from

367. No one, <u>at any rate</u> no English writer, <u>has written</u> better about <u>childhood</u>

         A   B   C

<u>than have</u> Charles Dickens.

   D

＜解答＞ D：than has

368. <u>When in childhood</u>, Mozart seemed to have <u>few</u> interests <u>part from</u> music,

        A   B   C

<u>about which</u> he had an insatiable curiosity.

   D

＜解答＞ A：In childhood

369. <u>After achieving</u> success <u>in domesticating</u> the dog, neolithic man would logically

      A   B

turn his attention <u>to other</u> animals, especially to <u>that</u> he used for food.

        C   D

 ＜解答＞ D：those

370. The law requires that a husband <u>pays</u> the debts of his wife <u>until</u> formal notice

            A   B

 <u>is given</u> that he no longer has to pay <u>them</u>.

  C   D

 ＜解答＞ A：should pay

371. The offices, laboratory, and museum <u>are</u> situated at the top of the hill <u>in which</u>

             A   B

 <u>they command</u> a <u>fine view</u>.

   C   D

 ＜解答＞ B：on which

372. Many members of the Historical Society <u>though</u> that last month's lecture on

               A

 acient civilizations <u>were</u> among the most <u>interesting</u> they had <u>ever attended</u>.

        B   C   D

 ＜解答＞ B：was

373. The watchman does his routine <u>every night</u>, <u>trying</u> every door, walking

            A   B

 <u>through</u> every hall and <u>listens</u> for any unusal sounds.

  C   D

 ＜解答＞ D：listening

374. Jacques-Yves Consteau <u>has estimated</u> that <u>only</u> one third to one half as many

         A   B

 fish and other forms of marine life <u>live in</u> the oceans now <u>that</u> lived there

              C   D

 twenty years ago.

 ＜解答＞ D：as

375. Paul often <u>doubted</u> his brother's loyalty to the organization, but the <u>carefulness</u>
              A   B

he <u>took</u> in carrying out his assignments was <u>beyond</u> question.
     C   D

<解答> B：care

376. The more Robert <u>tried to please</u> his mother through more flattery, <u>the greater</u>
                     A   B

he <u>succeeded</u> <u>in</u> annoying her.
     C   D

<解答> B：greatly

377. A singular characteristic of New Zealand's kiwi bird <u>is its</u> nostrils are <u>at</u> the
                                        A   B

<u>tip of</u> its beak.
  C D

<解答> A：is that its

378. <u>After</u> he <u>finishes</u> his duty, he often occupies <u>hisself</u> <u>by fishing</u>.
    A   B   C   D

<解答> C：himself

379. The Duke <u>has not spoke</u> to the Queen <u>once</u> <u>ever since</u> the accident <u>occurred</u>.
                A   B   C   D

<解答> A：has not spoken

380. The mammoth, <u>which</u> <u>once roamed</u> in Asia, Europe, and North America,
                 A   B

<u>were</u> <u>covered with</u> a long, shaggy outercoat.
  C   D

<解答> C：was

381. Joe <u>stepped on</u> the brakes to make a stop <u>in time</u> <u>to be avoiding</u> <u>hitting</u> a boy.
       A   B   C   D

<解答> C：to avoid

382. Joe grinned and winked at <u>his visitor</u>, <u>thinking he</u> to be <u>slightly</u> insane <u>but</u>
           A   B   C   D

harmless.
 <解答>　B：thinking him

383. Having summoned <u>us</u> loard members, the president stated that he wanted
        A

to talk <u>serious</u> about <u>the plans for</u> the <u>future of</u> the company.
    B   C   D
 <解答>　B：seriously

384. Sargasso Sea takes <u>its name</u> from the patches of seaweed <u>that cover</u> <u>an oval</u>
        A   B   C

area two-thirds as large <u>than</u> the continental United States.
         D
 <解答>　D：as

385. People in Minnesota, who <u>take pride</u> in their <u>rugged</u> houses, <u>actively</u> <u>engaging</u>
          A   B   C   D

<u>in</u> cultural pursuits.
 <解答>　D：engage in

386. <u>Born and reared</u> in New York, Henry <u>became</u> interested <u>in</u> music and opera at
    A   B   C

<u>a very little age</u>.
    D
 <解答>　D：a very young age

387. Nicholas finds <u>these kind of assignments</u> <u>unpleasant</u>, but the does say that he
       A   B

<u>has had</u> little <u>practice</u> writing about the books he read.
 C   D
 <解答>　A：this kind of assignments

388. The Hoenes <u>appear</u> friendly and <u>peaceful</u>, but they are <u>deeply</u> suspicious of
      A   B   C

<u>another</u> tribes.

       D

<解答> D：other

389. Most people know <u>that</u> it is like <u>to have</u> their blood pressure taken but few

                  A   B

<u>understand</u> the meaning of the number <u>used to record</u> blood pressure.

      C   D

<解答> B：what

390. Our <u>art professor</u> is not only one of the <u>towering figures</u> of modern art

         A   B

<u>and also</u> a visionary who <u>has not lost</u> his sense of humor.

    C   D

<解答> C：but also

391. If George had <u>left earlier</u> he <u>will be</u> able to <u>arrive in</u> Brussels before Martha <u>did</u>.

              A   B   C   D

<解答> B：would had been

392. Mrs. Grimm does not look forward to travelling by train, <u>why</u> the schedules

                                        A

are <u>too</u> irregular and the service <u>is</u> <u>usually poor</u>.

     B   C   D

<解答> A：because

393. If you ask <u>you</u> <u>what you</u> really want to do, you <u>can</u> solve your problem <u>quickly</u>.

           A   B   C   D

<解答> A：① yourself ② yourselves

394. Bacteria, <u>forze</u> for <u>at least</u> 10,000 years, have <u>multiplied</u> <u>when exposed to</u>

          A   B   C   D

light and air.

<解答> A：frozen

395. Since <u>no other</u> students <u>volunteered</u>, Cecily <u>took</u> the responsibility <u>to collect</u>

          A   B   C   D

papers for the teacher.

<解答> D：① for collecting ② for the collection of

396. Long term results <u>can hardly</u> <u>be expected</u> <u>to be achieved</u> <u>in brief a time</u>.
         A   B   C   D

<解答> D：① in a brief time ② in so short time

397. <u>Many</u> of the bones and artifacts <u>recently, found</u> in Central Africa are <u>similarly</u>
  A   B   C

to <u>those found</u> in Eastern Asia and Australia.
    D

<解答> C：similar

398. The white settlers of North America <u>began signing</u> treaties <u>with</u> the Indians
              A   B

in the seventeenth century and continued <u>to do them</u> <u>through</u> the nineteenth
                 C   D

century.

<解答> C：① to do so ② to sign them

399. <u>Because</u> his limited resurces Robert knew he <u>had to</u> choose between <u>buying</u>
  A   B   C

a winter coat <u>and spending</u> a week at the seashore.
      D

<解答> A：Because of

400. The oriental fruit fly causes <u>extensive damage</u> to grapefruit, lemons, and
             A

oranges, <u>but does not harm</u> to the trees <u>on which</u> fruit <u>grows</u>.
      B   C   D

<解答> B：① does not harm ② does no harm

401. Although many intelligent and determined women <u>do rise to</u> positions of
                 A

authority <u>but</u> these women <u>remain</u> merely <u>a minority</u>.
    B   C   D

<解答> B：cancel

402. The professor <u>insisted to publish</u> his results of experiments <u>even though</u> it
　　　　　　　　　　　A　　　　　　　　　　　　　　　　　　B

　　<u>could not be</u> confirmed by researches <u>conducted</u> by others.
　　　　C　　　　　　　　　　　　　　D

　　<解答> A：insisted on publishing

403. This should be a <u>committee decision</u> but it <u>might best he</u> made <u>at the basic of</u>
　　　　　　　　　A　　　　　　　　　　B　　　　　　　C

　　experts, <u>opinions</u>.
　　　　　　D

　　<解答> C：on the basis of

404. Mrs. Swanson, <u>a member of</u> <u>the social committee</u>, is <u>the only</u> woman <u>which</u>
　　　　　　　　　A　　　　　B　　　　　　　　C　　　　　D

　　has a new car.

　　<解答> D：① that ② who

405. <u>On</u> August 3, 1719, the ship, <u>under the command of</u> John Rogers,
　　　A　　　　　　　　　　　　　B

　　<u>having reached</u> Southampton <u>with</u> 18 men alive.
　　　C　　　　　　　　　　　D

　　<解答> C：reached

406. <u>Members of</u> the party <u>were surprised</u> by <u>Johnson</u> winning <u>the election</u>.
　　　A　　　　　　　　B　　　　C　　　　　　　D

　　<解答> C：Johnson's

407. The World Wildife Funds <u>supports</u> scientific research and conservation projects
　　　　　　　　　　　　A

　　designed <u>to save</u> endangered animals <u>by preserving</u> <u>its</u> natural habitats.
　　　　　　B　　　　　　　　　　　　C　　　　D

　　<解答> D：their

408. The prison inmates <u>have protested</u> such conditions <u>as</u> contaminated food,
　　　　　　　　A　　　　　　　　　　　　B

brutal environment, and <u>condition is</u> <u>unsanitary</u>.

                C   D

<解答>　D：unsanitary condition

409. <u>Missing</u> the class of geography because his watch <u>stops</u>, Morris <u>went to</u> the

     A   B   C

teacher and <u>asked for</u> the assignment.

                  D

<解答>　B：stopped

410. Fireworks, <u>which</u> <u>originated</u> <u>century ago</u> in Chian, <u>were brought</u> to Europe by

             A   B   C   D

Marco Polo.

<解答>　C：① centuries ago ② a century ago

411. Virian didn't <u>go to the movies</u> last night <u>because</u> she was so busy <u>to prepare</u>

                   A   B   C

for her <u>trip</u> to Brazil and Chile.

          D

<解答>　C：preparing

412. <u>That</u> the intelligence test <u>actually gives</u> a measurement <u>of intelligence</u> of

   A   B   C

individuals <u>are</u> questioned by eminent psychologists.

            D

<解答>　D：is

413. Since <u>a nation's banks</u> provide the support <u>for</u> its economy <u>and</u> any hint as

             A   B   C

to insolvency <u>causes</u> great concern.

             D

<解答>　C：cancel

414. Neither of these reasons <u>justifies</u> <u>our</u> allowing him <u>to pass</u> after he did <u>so poor</u>

                        A   B   C   D

in the physics examination.

<解答> D：so poorly

415. While living in the country as girl, Martha was used to walk through the
　　　A　　　　　　　　　　B　　　　　　　　C

woods behind her house.
　　　　D

<解答> C：used to

416. Mr. Chu did not know how to organize the party because he did not know
　　　　　　　　　　　　A　　　　　　　　　　　　　　　B

how many people they would be.
　　C　　　　　　D

<解答> D：there

417. Many people are afraider of appearing to be socially awkward than of being
　　　　　　　A　　　　　　　　　　　B

inconsiderate to their fellow human beings.
　　C　　　　　　D

<解答> A：are more afraid

418. The new legislation is intended to eliminate unemployment by guaranteing
　　　　　　　　　　　A　　　B　　　　　　　　　　　C

a job to every person who wants them.
　　　　　　　　　　　D

<解答> D：it

419. In the production of prunes, the fruit is gathered dipped in a bye solution
　　　　　　　　　　　　　　　　A

to prevent fermentation, and then they dry them in the sun or in large ovens.
　　B　　　　　　　　　　　　　C　　　　　　　D

<解答> C：dried

420. Ganymede, the largest of the moon of Jupiter, has a very rough surface
　　　　　　　　　　A　　　　　　　　　B

composed of rocky or metallic materials embedded in ice.
　　C　　　　　　　　　　　　　　D

<解答>　A：of the moons

421. Hannibal <u>he crossed</u> the Alps <u>with</u> me, elephants, and equipment <u>with</u> the

      A   B   C

intention <u>of attacking</u> Rome.

      D

 <解答>　A：crossed

422. <u>The first time</u> that Gertrude <u>went skiing</u>, she bruised one of her <u>legs</u> and

    A   B   C

broke <u>another</u>.

   D

 <解答>　D：the other

423. The river of West Pakistan supplies water <u>to the nearly tillers</u> living on the

                 A

river basin but <u>they</u> can not irrigate <u>the famine areas</u> 200 miles <u>away</u>.

     B   C   D

 <解答>　B：it

424. The <u>highly significant</u> discovery of <u>the origins</u> of primitive man <u>have been</u>

     A   B   C

made <u>on the eastern shore</u> of Lake Turkana.

    D

 <解答>　C：has been

425. The study of geometry is an aspect of <u>mathematic</u> which <u>is extremely</u>

            A   B

important <u>in the field of</u> <u>surveying</u>.

    C   D

 <解答>　A：mathematics

426. Mccarthy was <u>not overly scrupulous</u> in the method <u>of conducting</u> investigations

       A   B

and <u>by obtaining</u> admission of guilt through <u>intimidation of witnesses</u>.

   C   D

<解答>　C：of obtaining

427. The president of the United States <u>is usually elected</u> for a <u>four years term</u>
　　　　　　　　　　　　　　　　　　　　　　　　A　　　　　　　　　　　　　B

of office and he <u>may choose</u> to <u>run for</u> another term.
　　　　　　　　　C　　　　　　D

<解答>　B：four-year-term

428. <u>At</u> <u>its</u> last meeting, the city council <u>was decided</u> to open future meeting to
　　　A　B　　　　　　　　　　　　　　　　　　C

representatives <u>of all</u> the minority groups in the community.
　　　　　　　　　D

<解答>　C：decided

429. The <u>only way</u> to reach <u>the edge of</u> the forest was <u>to take</u> the narrow dirt path
　　　　　A　　　　　　　　B　　　　　　　　　　　　C

<u>in the front of</u> us.
　　　D

<解答>　D：in front of

430. He wrote <u>at least</u> ten novels, but only two <u>out the ten</u> that <u>are now known</u>
　　　　　　　A　　　　　　　　　　　　　　　B　　　　　　C

were published <u>during his lifetime</u>.
　　　　　　　　　　　D

<解答>　B：out of the ten

431. <u>Even though</u> Sadat <u>has been studying</u> English for three years before he
　　　A　　　　　　　　B

<u>came to the United States</u>, it is still difficult <u>for him</u> to express himself.
　　　　　　C　　　　　　　　　　　　　　　　　D

<解答>　B：had been studying

432. Work <u>on</u> the two new hotel for tourists <u>were begun</u> <u>immediately after</u> the
　　　　A　　　　　　　　　　　　　　　　　B　　　　C

new mayor <u>took office</u>.
　　　　　　　D

<解答> B：was begun

433. Sir Winston Churchill <u>was</u> British Prime Minister from 1940 <u>to</u> 1945,
          　　　　　　　　　　A　　　　　　　　　　　　　　　　B

    <u>during that time</u> the <u>played</u> a decisive role in the conduct of the Second
          　　　　C　　　　　　　D

    World War.

    <解答> C：during which time

434. <u>As soon as completing</u> his examination <u>of</u> the patient, the doctor offered his
          　　　　A　　　　　　　　　　　　　　　B

    <u>judgment</u> of <u>her</u> condition.
          　　C　　　　D

    <解答> A：Upon completing

435. No sooner had the words <u>been spoken</u> <u>when</u> he <u>realized</u> that he
          　　　　　　　　　　　　A　　　　B　　　　C

    <u>should have remained</u> silent.
          　　　　　D

    <解答> B：than

436. Mr. Johansen felt <u>hurriedly</u> <u>as</u> he tried to <u>make his way</u> through the crowds to
          　　　　　　　　A　　　　B　　　　　　　　C

    the ticket window only five minutes before the bus <u>was to leave</u>.
          　　　　　　　　　　　　　　　　　　　　　　　　　　　　　D

    <解答> A：hurried

437. I <u>know of</u> <u>no woman</u> in the neighborhood <u>who is</u> more generous than <u>her</u>.
          　A　　　B　　　　　　　　　　　　C　　　　　　　　　　D

    <解答> D：she

438. Arriving <u>for</u> the concert early is better than <u>to take</u> the chance <u>of being</u> <u>late</u>.
          　　　A　　　　　　　　　　　　　　　B　　　　　　　　C　　　D

    <解答> B：taking

439. The law <u>I am referring to</u> requires that everyone <u>who</u> <u>owns</u> a car <u>has</u> accident
          　　　　　A　　　　　　　　　　　　　　　　B　　C　　　　　D

insurance.

　　＜解答＞　D：have

440. The company's decision <u>to finance</u> college educations <u>for qualified</u> employees
　　　　　　　　　　　　　　　　A　　　　　　　　　　　　　　　B

was <u>based on</u> a desire to increase efficiency, divert excess taxable income,
　　　C

and <u>the improvement of</u> moral.
　　　　　　　　　　D

　　＜解答＞　D：improve

441. It is possible that Indians originally <u>have migrated</u> to the Western Hemisphere
　　　　　　　　　　　　　　　　　　　　　　　A

<u>over</u> a bridge of land that <u>once existed</u> <u>between</u> Siberia and Alaska.
　B　　　　　　　　　　　　C　　　　　D

　　＜解答＞　A：migrated

442. The United States in <u>composed of</u> fifty states, two <u>of those</u> are <u>separated from</u>
　　　　　　　　　　　　A　　　　　　　　　　　B　　　　　　C

<u>the others</u> by land or water.
　D

　　＜解答＞　B：of which

443. <u>Nobody</u> would give him a chance <u>to produce</u> the movie <u>he knew</u> he was
　　　A　　　　　　　　　　　　　B　　　　　　　　C

capable <u>to create</u>.
　　　　D

　　＜解答＞　D：of creating

444. Only <u>those</u> applicants who show promise <u>to success</u> <u>will be called</u> for
　　　　A　　　　　　　　　　　　　　　B　　　　　C

<u>an interview</u>.
　D

　　＜解答＞　B：of

445. Inhabitants of the valley of Vilcabamba in Ecuador <u>are</u> <u>remarkably</u> long-lived,

                                              A   B

    a phenomenon doctors <u>attribute to</u> their frugal diet and <u>tranquility</u> way of life.

                               C   D

    ＜解答＞ D：tranquil

446. Many modern skyscrapers, though <u>visually pleasing</u>, <u>they have</u> heating and

                                      A   B

    cooling systems that require <u>closed</u> windows and consequently <u>waste</u> energy.

                               C   D

    ＜解答＞ B：have

447. Anyone <u>which</u> breaks the law <u>should be prepared</u> to accept the consequences

             A   B

    <u>of his</u> action.

    C D

    ＜解答＞ A：who

448. <u>Ever since</u> the Civil War, the <u>status of</u> women <u>was</u> <u>a live</u> social issue in this

        A   B   C   D

    country.

    ＜解答＞ C：has been

449. The international Law of the Sea conference is an attempt <u>resolving</u>

                                                     A

    <u>major differences</u> among countries <u>with</u> <u>conflicting</u> interests.

        B   C   D

    ＜解答＞ A：to resolve

450. While <u>some of</u> lawyers would endorse <u>the opposite</u> view, <u>most</u> would

               A   B   C

    probably agree that freedom of the press <u>is not absolute</u>.

                                                 D

    ＜解答＞ A：① some of the ② some

451. The <u>effects of</u> the imbalance <u>among</u> world population and food supply

      A   B

<u>may well</u> have a serious <u>impact on</u> the developed nations.

    C   D

＜解答＞ B：between

452. Neither the federal <u>or</u> the state government <u>was willing</u> <u>to contribute</u> funds

               A   B   C

<u>to help</u> the city operate its bus system.

    D

＜解答＞ A：nor

453. Because <u>its</u> decisions are <u>anonymous made</u> bureaucratic government makes

      A   B

<u>many</u> abuses of power <u>possible</u>.

   C   D

＜解答＞ B：anonymously made

454. Senator White <u>always</u> speaks <u>more forceful</u> than <u>any of</u> the members of

         A   B   C

the opposition party.

    D

＜解答＞ B：forcefully

455. Whether we make the trip <u>or not</u>, it will be <u>advisable</u> for us <u>to be renewing</u>

        A   B   C

our passparts <u>as soon as possible</u> in order to avoid any complications.

      D

＜解答＞ C：to renew

456. The angry workmen, <u>learning</u> the decision of the court, <u>threw</u> down <u>their</u> tools

      A   B   C

and <u>proclaim</u> a general strike.

    D

＜解答＞ D：proclaimed

457. It is <u>remarkable</u> <u>how much</u> a scientist <u>can learn about</u> the structure and history
             A   B   C

 of the moon <u>by</u> a sample of lunar soil.
            D

 ＜解答＞ D：by studying

458. Japan <u>has experienced</u> a <u>remarkable</u> economic <u>growing</u> in <u>the past decade</u>.
            A   B   C   D

 ＜解答＞ C：growth

459. The thief must <u>have entered</u> by <u>the kitchen window</u> and <u>stole</u> <u>the silver</u> while
             A   B   C   D

 the family was asleep.

 ＜解答＞ C：stolen

460. The reason for the exhaust systems <u>in American automobiles</u> <u>are</u> the
                                 A   B

 <u>severe level</u> of <u>air</u> pollution in urban areas.
        C   D

 ＜解答＞ B：is

461. You will never succed <u>to get</u> at the truth <u>if</u> you think you know, <u>ahead of</u> time,
                    A   B   C

 what the truth <u>should be</u>.
           D

 ＜解答＞ A：in getting

462. His <u>latest</u> proposal <u>was</u> neither a new idea <u>and not</u> a <u>sound one</u>.
        A   B   C   D

 ＜解答＞ C：nor

463. Good historians are the scarcest <u>of all</u> writers <u>because</u> <u>they</u> combine good
                             A   B   C

 style, thorough information, and <u>being impartial</u>.
                               D

 ＜解答＞ D：impartiality

464. Although it was still <u>somewhat</u> early, he <u>bagan</u> to speak to those <u>which</u>
                                    A   B   C

    <u>had already gathered</u> in the auditorium.
                D

    ＜解答＞ C：who

465. While <u>remaining accountable</u> to the administration <u>as well as</u> to those individuals
                     A   B

    <u>who submit</u> complaints, an arbitrator must decide each case on <u>their</u> own merits.
        C   D

    ＜解答＞ D：its

466. <u>Because</u> he was <u>greatly</u> <u>troubled by</u> his conscience, Hamlet was incapable <u>to kill</u>
     A   B   C   D

    the king.

    ＜解答＞ D：of killing

467. The young politician created a <u>split in</u> his party <u>when he spoke</u> to the
                                  A   B

    convention about his <u>sympathy to</u> the <u>outspoken</u> radicals.
                            C   D

    ＜解答＞ C：sympathy with

468. A <u>detailed</u> map of the mining camp was handed out, and the directions
        A

    <u>for getting</u> <u>there</u> were repeated <u>very clear</u>.
        B   C   D

    ＜解答＞ D：very clearly

469. <u>Opposite</u> to <u>popular</u> belief, the ostrich does not hide <u>its</u> head in the sand
      A   B   C

    <u>when frightened</u>; it runs.
             D

    ＜解答＞ A：Contrary

470. <u>Although</u> two battalions <u>were guarding</u> the base, underwater swimmers

　　　　A　　　　　　　　　　B

<u>were being able</u> to sabotage <u>several</u> warships.

　　　　　C　　　　　　　　D

＜解答＞ C：were able

471. The news <u>coming from</u> <u>different</u> parts of the world <u>are</u> often

　　　　　　　　　A　　　B　　　　　　　　C

<u>extremely discouraging</u> these days.

　　　　　D

＜解答＞ C：is

472. It is <u>hoped that</u> the rate of inflation <u>will continue</u> to <u>be reduced about</u> from its

　　　　　A　　　　　　　　　　　　B　　　　　　C

peak <u>of</u> three months ago.

　　　D

＜解答＞ C：be reduced

473. In 1937, <u>when</u> she was seventy-seven and could <u>not longer</u> <u>run</u> her farm,

　　　　　　A　　　　　　　　　　　　　　　B　　　C

Grandma Moses <u>began</u> to paint.

　　　　　　　　D

＜解答＞ B：no longer

474. <u>As one nears</u> the bridge, you come to <u>a narrow rocky valley</u>, <u>the site</u> of several

　　　A　　　　　　　　　　　　　　B　　　　　　C

<u>historic</u> battles.

　　D

＜解答＞ A：① When you near ② As you near

475. The degree <u>to which</u> taxation <u>should be used</u> to redistribute income, <u>not</u> pay

　　　　　　A　　　　　　B　　　　　　　　　　　　C

for governmental expenses, <u>is debatable</u>.

　　　　　　　　　　　D

＜解答＞ C：not to

476. Whether <u>or not</u> Vounegut's novels <u>are</u> good, <u>their popularity</u>, especially <u>toward</u>
           A   B   C   D

      young readers, is undemiable.

      ＜解答＞ D：with

477. The speaker announced that <u>there was</u> a small fire and directed <u>them</u> <u>nearest</u>
                                     A   B   C

      the door <u>to leave first</u>.
                 D

      ＜解答＞ B：those

478. <u>Although</u>, in all probability, new deposits of oil <u>will be</u> found, <u>but sooner</u> or
      A   B   C

      later the world's <u>supply will be</u> exhausted.
                         D

      ＜解答＞ C：sooner

479. <u>After writing</u> poetry unsucessfully for several years, he <u>was not certain</u>
      A   B

      <u>whether</u> to quit or <u>if he should continue</u> with his art.
      C   D

      ＜解答＞ D：to continue

480. <u>Early in August</u> many of <u>we boys</u> sent letters <u>asking for</u> money <u>from home</u>.
           A   B   C   D

      ＜解答＞ B：us boys

481. <u>Absurdly</u> is <u>one of</u> the most <u>prominent</u> themes of <u>twentieth-century</u> drama.
      A   B   D   D

      ＜解答＞ A：Absurdity

482. Some find seimming <u>more enjoyable</u> <u>than</u> <u>to sit</u> at home <u>reading</u>.
                          A   B C   D

      ＜解答＞ C：sitting

483. The farmer <u>has ruined</u> <u>the soils</u> <u>by planting</u> the same crop <u>every year</u>.
                A   B   C   D

<解答>　B：the soil

484. He <u>insists</u> that <u>your are</u> on time <u>for</u> the appointment <u>you made</u>.
   A   B   C   D

  <解答>　B：be

485. If someone <u>were to</u> <u>look through</u> the window, <u>they</u> would see <u>only an</u>
      A   B   C   D

empty room.

  <解答>　C：he

486. Neither Russia <u>nor</u> the United States <u>have been</u> able to convince <u>the other</u> that
       A   B   C

its social system is <u>the better</u> of the two.
       D

  <解答>　B：has been

487. The columnist <u>feels sure</u> <u>who</u> wins the election <u>will have</u> the support of
       A B   C

the parties.
  D

  <解答>　B：whoever

488. <u>Only then</u> <u>he became</u> aware of <u>the fact</u> that there were more difficulties ahead
    A   B   C

<u>than</u> he had expected.
  D

  <解答>　B：did he become

489. The philosopher's influence <u>over</u> men's minds became <u>far greater</u> <u>after</u> his
         A   B C

death <u>than his life</u>.
    D

  <解答>　D－than in his life

490. In the United States, Thanksgiving, <u>in spite of</u> <u>its</u> religious association, often
                A   B

had a <u>distinct</u> secular <u>flavour</u>.
             C   D

＜解答＞ C：distinctly

491. <u>If</u> you stay <u>over</u> four years in the United States, you will <u>have to have</u> your
     A   B   C

    visa <u>extend to</u> one more year.
              D

＜解答＞ D：extended to

492. <u>Not long after</u> Galileo's time, Sir Isaac Newton invented <u>another kind of</u>
         A   B

    telescope <u>which he used</u> mirrors <u>instead of</u> lenses.
                  C   D

＜解答＞ C：in which he used

493. Treasure Island, the book <u>that made</u> Robert Louis Stevenson <u>famous</u>,
                         A   B

    <u>has became</u> a best seller for readers <u>young and old</u>.
        C   D

＜解答＞ C：has become

494. In spite of <u>its small size</u>, Europe <u>has</u> a greater <u>impact on</u> world history than
                   A   B   C

    <u>any other</u> continent.
         D

＜解答＞ B：has had

495. <u>Among</u> the most remarkable eyes are <u>those of the dragonfly</u>, <u>for this insect</u>
      A   B   C

    has compound eyes <u>make up</u> of tiny eyes.
                      D

＜解答＞ D：made up

496. <u>By watching</u> sunspots, great storms <u>which rage</u> on the surface of the sun,
        A   B

scientists discovered <u>whether</u> the sun <u>spins on</u> its axis.
                             C   D

<解答> C：that

497. It is not known <u>exactly when</u> the first immigrants <u>arrived in</u> the New World,
                        A   B

but where <u>did that event occur</u> <u>is certain</u>.
                         C   D

<解答> C：that event occurred

498. Although the Indians <u>lacking animals</u>, they <u>had the ability</u> <u>to cultivate</u> plants
                             A   B   C

<u>suitable for</u> daily use.
        D

<解答> A：lacked animals

499. In the New World <u>as in</u> Europe, each region developed <u>its own</u> distinct pattern
                       A   B

of culture <u>adapted to</u> local conditions <u>and influential</u>.
                    C   D

<解答> D：and influences

500. This region of the Andes, <u>where</u> tin <u>was mixed</u> with copper to make bronze,
                          A   B

was <u>the greater</u> <u>center of</u> metallurgy.
                 C   D

<解答> C：the greatest

501. The natives, who were <u>used to get</u> most of <u>their living</u> from the sea,
                         A   B

<u>seldom if ever</u> ventured inland <u>to search for</u> food.
               C   D

<解答> A：used to getting

502. Our civilization is <u>so commonplace</u> to us <u>that</u> rarely <u>we stop</u> to think about
                           A   B   C

its complexity.
　　　　　D

＜解答＞　C：do we stop

503. Through the study of <u>trees rings</u>, <u>which originated</u> in Arizona, the houses
　　　　　　　　　　　　　　　A　　　　　　　　　B

　　in which the Anasazi lived can <u>accurately be dated</u>.
　　　C　　　　　　　　　　　　　　　D

　　＜解答＞　A：tree rings

504. The composer Verdi <u>has written</u> the opera Aida <u>to celebrate</u> <u>the opening of</u>
　　　　　　　　　　　　A　　　　　　　　　　　　B　　　　C

　　the Suez Canal, but the opera <u>was not performed</u> until 1871.
　　　　　　　　　　　　　　　　　　　D

　　＜解答＞　A：wrote

505. <u>Ever since</u> the world <u>began</u>, nations <u>have difficulty</u> <u>in keeping</u> peace with their
　　　A　　　　　　　　　B　　　　　　C　　　　　　　D

　　neighbors.

　　＜解答＞　C：have had difficulty

506. <u>From</u> archeological evidence, we know that the Egyptians were
　　　A

　　<u>highly organized</u>, civilized, and <u>they were skillful</u> <u>in using</u> crafts.
　　　B　　　　　　　　　　　　　　　　C　　　　　D

　　＜解答＞　C：skillful

507. A virus, which is <u>too small</u> <u>to be seen</u> <u>except with</u> a powerful microsecope,
　　　　　　　　　　A　　　　B　　　　C

　　<u>is causing</u> measles.
　　　D

　　＜解答＞　D：① causes ② is the cause of

508. The findings of Gregor Mendel <u>were published</u> in 1866, but scientists paid
　　　　　　　　　　　　　　　　　　A

little attention <u>to it</u> <u>for about</u> fifty years.
        B   C   D

＜解答＞ C：to them

509. When <u>a spider catches</u> an insect, it releases some poison <u>into an insect</u> with
             A   B

its fangs, but the poison of most spiders <u>is</u> <u>harmless to</u> man.
                                      C   D

＜解答＞ B：into the insect

510. Statesmen are people who <u>have attained</u> fame <u>because of</u> <u>which they have</u>
                             A   B   C

<u>achieved</u> in the field of government.
   D

＜解答＞ C：what they

511. William Pitt <u>urged that</u> the English colonists <u>were given</u> the some
                A   B

constitutional rights <u>to which</u> other English subjects <u>were entitled</u>.
                  C   D

＜解答＞ B：be given

512. Sir Winston Churchill, <u>as</u> the British Prime Minister, <u>leads</u> his country
                A   B

<u>to victory</u> during <u>the Second World War</u>.
  C   D

＜解答＞ B：led

513. Since 1975, the economy <u>has been growing</u> <u>steadily</u>, and today the country
                    A   B

ranks <u>as a one</u> of the world's <u>most rapidly</u> developing nations.
      C   D

＜解答＞ C：as one

514. Ships <u>which use</u> <u>to have to sail</u> around Africa <u>to get to</u> India from Europe can
       A   B   C

now <u>pass through</u> the Suez Canal.
　　　　　　　D

　　＜解答＞　A：which used

515. Sir James Dewar invented the thermos in 1892 <u>to keep</u> heat <u>away from</u> the
　　　　　　　　　　　　　　　　　　　　　　　　　A　　　　　　　B

　　liquefield gas <u>with which</u> he <u>was experiment</u>.
　　　　　　　　　　C　　　　　　D

　　＜解答＞　D：was experimenting

516. The vibrations <u>that make</u> musical sounds are <u>more pleasanter</u> than <u>those</u>
　　　　　　　　　　A　　　　　　　　　　　　B　　　　　　　　C

　　<u>causing</u> noise.
　　　　D

　　＜解答＞　B：more pleasant

517. Bats <u>are able</u> <u>to guide them</u> by producing sound waves <u>too high</u> for us <u>to hear</u>.
　　　　　A　　　B　　　　　　　　　　　　　　　C　　　　　　D

　　＜解答＞　B：to guide themselves

518. The captial city <u>is noted for</u> its many modern improvements, but in other parts
　　　　　　　　　　A

　　of the country, <u>lack of</u> <u>enough good</u> roads <u>have delayed</u> progress.
　　　　　　　　　　B　　　C　　　　　　D

　　＜解答＞　D：has delayed

519. Before <u>an explorer Norwegian</u> reached the South Pole in 1911, many other
　　　　　　　　A

　　explorers <u>had tried</u> <u>to reach it</u> and <u>failed</u>.
　　　　　　　B　　　C　　　D

　　＜解答＞　A：a Norwegian explorer

520. Plantation life in South Carolina <u>lasted until</u> the Civil War, <u>after which</u> most
　　　　　　　　　　　　　　　　　A　　　　　　　　　　B

　　of the state <u>suffering</u> <u>badly</u>.
　　　　　　　　C　　　D

　　＜解答＞　C：suffered

521. From the chart <u>shown</u> <u>on</u> page 115, one <u>can easily see</u> how large each
　　　　　　　　　　A　　B　　　　　　　　　　　C

　　country is and how many inhabitants <u>does it have</u>.
　　　　　　　　　　　　　　　　　　　　　　　　D

　　＜解答＞　D：it has

522. <u>Between</u> the two rivers, where Charleston <u>now stands</u>, <u>the first English</u>
　　　A　　　　　　　　　　　　　　　　　　B　　　　　　　　C

　　settlement <u>there was</u> established in 1680.
　　　　　　　　　　D

　　＜解答＞　D：was

523. The Taj Mahal, <u>that</u> took twenty-two years <u>to construct</u>, <u>is possibly</u> the most
　　　　　　　　　　A　　　　　　　　　　　　　B　　　　　C

　　beautiful building <u>in the world</u>.
　　　　　　　　　　　　D

　　＜解答＞　A：which

524. Every one of us <u>has read</u> that <u>any</u> substance burns, <u>that it</u> <u>unites with</u> oxygen.
　　　　　　　　　　A　　　　　B　　　　　　　　　C　　　D

　　＜解答＞　C：it

525. Cortes, <u>who conquered</u> Mexico City and <u>destroyed it lately</u>, considered
　　　　　　　A　　　　　　　　　　　　　　　B

　　Mexico <u>to be</u> the most beautiful city <u>he had ever seen</u>.
　　　　　　　C　　　　　　　　　　　　　　D

　　＜解答＞　B：destroyed it later

526. <u>Unless</u> we polish metals <u>frequently</u>, they <u>rust or tarnish</u> <u>when exposure</u> to air.
　　　A　　　　　　　　　B　　　　　　　C　　　　　D

　　＜解答＞　D：① when exposed ② when they are exposed

527. <u>Someone who</u> has ever tried <u>to pick up</u> spilled mercury will <u>agree that</u> this
　　　A　　　　　　　　　　　　B　　　　　　　　　　　　C

element is hard to handle.
                        D

<解答>　A：Anyone who

528. The medical science began with the Greek Hippocrates, who earned
            A   B

for himself the title of Father of Medicine.
        C   D

<解答>　A：Medical science

529. A person on a diet should keep in mind that the worst time to eat heavy is just
                A   B   C   D

before bedtime.

<解答>　D：to eat heavily

530. Sulfuric acid is used so exlensively in manufacturing that thousands of
                            A   B

factories would go out of business if this acid is unattainable.
                        C   D

<解答>　D：were unattainable

531. The dense Belgian fogs, like the most inland fogs, are caused by the cooling
                            A   B

of humid surface air to a relatively low temperature.
        C   D

<解答>　A：like most

532. That touching toads causes warts are still one of the most widely believed
                                    A   B

superstitions in America; however, no reputable authority supports this theory.
                    C   D

<解答>　A：is

533. Generally, Europe and Asia are regarded as being distinct continents, but they
        A   B

are <u>simply vast geography</u> divisions of the larger land mass <u>known as Eurasia</u>.
C   D

＜解答＞ C：simply vast geographic

534. <u>Because of</u> the large <u>amount</u> of salt, the specific <u>of the water</u> in Great Salt Lake,
A   B   C

Utah, is so great that one cannot sink or <u>completely submerging oneself</u> in it.
D

＜解答＞ D：completely submerge oneself

535. <u>Bothered by</u> the heavy traffic <u>along interstates highways</u>, some travelers prefer
A   B

<u>the more tranguil</u> routes of older, <u>two-lane</u> roads.
C   D

＜解答＞ B：along interstate highway

536. The eggs of eagles <u>are covered with</u> a natural mucilaginous coating
A

<u>what delays</u> the entrance of <u>harmful</u> germs <u>into the egg's interior</u>.
B   C   D

＜解答＞ B：① which delays ② that delays

537. Mountains have helped <u>to protest</u> the Swise <u>from invaders</u>, and, indeed,
A   B

Switzerland has remained <u>at peace</u> while other European nations
C

<u>engaging in war</u>.
D

＜解答＞ D：① engage in war ② have engaged

538. <u>The backbone</u> of the <u>single-humped</u> camel is not curved <u>upward in the middle</u>,
A   B   C

like <u>many people suppose</u>.
D

＜解答＞ D：as many people suppose

539. During <u>election campaigns</u>, politicians <u>frequently often</u> hold <u>debates</u> with
         A   B   C

other candidates <u>about</u> major issues.
                   D

＜解答＞ B：① frequently ② often

540. Popping in corn occurs whenever there is <u>an explosion caused by</u>
                                              A

<u>the expansion under pressure</u> of moisture <u>in</u> the starch grains
         B   C

<u>during the kernal</u> is dry heated.
         D

＜解答＞ D：when the kernal

541. Proper lighting is a <u>necessary for good eyesight;</u> <u>however</u>, human night vision
                              A   B

<u>can be temporarily</u> impaired <u>by extreme flashes of light</u>.
         C   D

＜解答＞ A：necessity

542. Hand grenades, round shells <u>filled with powder</u> and ignited
                                      A

<u>by means of a fuse,</u> <u>were</u> first used <u>in warfare during fifteenth century</u>.
         B   C   D

＜解答＞ D：in warfare during the fifteenth century

543. Fish <u>are</u> unable to sleep, but sometimes a fish in <u>an aquarium</u> will lie on
         A   B

<u>their side</u> and appear to be <u>completely unaware of</u> everything around it.
         C   D

＜解答＞ C：its side

544. <u>Even though</u> he has already been around <u>the earth</u> once on a bicycle, Lloyd
         A   B

Summer <u>is currently off</u> <u>on a seven-continents</u> marathon.
          C   D

<解答> D：on a seven-continent

545. One of the most serious human tragedies in the world <u>continue to unfold</u>
                                                                A

in some nations, where famine, conflict, and <u>severe drought</u> <u>have brought</u>
     B   C   D

millions of people close to starvation.

<解答> A：continues to unfold

546. <u>During the 1940's</u>, as a result of nuclear research, Dr. W.F. Eibby discovered
          A

carbon 14, <u>based on</u> radioactive rays <u>present in</u> <u>all plants living</u> and animals.
               B   C   D

<解答> D：all living plants

547. They were ready <u>to suffer</u> <u>death</u> <u>for the sake of</u> <u>his</u> country.
                         A   B   C   D

<解答> D：their

548. <u>Each year,</u> tourists from <u>all over the world</u> travel to Poland <u>to visit</u> <u>a birthplace</u>
         A   B   C   D

of Frederic Chopin.

<解答> D：the birthplace

549. The <u>most important</u> cause of <u>the War of 1812</u> <u>it was</u> the impressment of of
              A   B   C

American seamen <u>by the British</u>.
                         D

<解答> C：was

550. <u>Laying the foundation</u> for world-wide radio, Marconi <u>transmitted</u> long-wave
              A   B

signals without wires in 1895 <u>when only he was</u> <u>twenty one years old</u>.
                                       C   D

＜解答＞　C：when he was only

551. The second sentence <u>the Declaration of Independence</u> established
A

<u>the foundation</u> for the <u>civil rights</u> now enjoyed by every <u>United States</u> citizen.
B   C   D

＜解答＞　A：in the Declaration of Independence

552. <u>Great amounts of</u> energy are required <u>for the massive movements</u> of the air
A   B

<u>in the atmosphere</u> and for the exchange of heat and <u>moist between the</u>
C   D

atmosphere and the earth's land and water surfaces.

＜解答＞　D：moisture between the atmosphere

553. A perennial is a plant <u>that grows</u> for <u>more than</u> two <u>consecutive</u> seasons
A   B   C

<u>without be replanted</u>.
D

＜解答＞　D：without being replanted

554. For thousands of years, <u>man</u> has created <u>sweet-smelling</u> substances from
A   B

wood,herbs, and flowers <u>and using them</u> for perfume <u>or</u> medicine.
C   D

＜解答＞　C：① and has used them ② and used them

555. The cockroach <u>spreads disease</u> and is a serious meance <u>to public health</u>, <u>since</u>
A   B   C

it seeks out bakeries restaurant kitchens, and <u>it looks for food factories</u>.
D

＜解答＞　D：food factories

556. Although caffeine is a <u>moderately habit-forming drug</u>, coffee is not
A

regarded as harmfully to the average healthy adult.
　　　　　B　　　　　　C　　　　　　　　　D

＜解答＞ C：harmful to

557. Scientific prediction of earthquakes remains primitive and haphazard; however,
　　　　　　　　　　　　　　　　　　　　A

scientists can make general predictions after monitor magnetic changes
　　　　　　　B　　　　　　　　　　　　　　　　C

along principal faults.
　　　　D

＜解答＞ C：monitoring magnetic changes

558. According to a study of firstborn children, children whose mothers expert
　　　　A　　　　　　　　　　　　　　　　　　　　　　　B

them to learn very little as infants develop more slow than children whose
　　　　　　　　　　　　　　　　　　　　C

mothers expect them to begin learning immediately.
　　　　　　　　　　　　　　　　　　D

＜解答＞ C：more slowly than

559. Societes from the primitive to the highly civilzed have used food,
　　　　　　　　　　　　　　　A　　　　　　B

their most essential resource in social bonding celebrations of all kind and in
　　　　　　　　C　　　　　　　　　　　　　　　　　　　　D

sacred rituals.

＜解答＞ D：of all kinds

560. Recent trends seem to indicate that American may come to follow the example
　　　　　　　A　　　　　　　　　　　　　　B

of those other nations where the bicycle it is an important means of
　　　　C　　　　　　　　　D

transportation.

＜解答＞ D：the bicycle is

561. <u>Between</u> the mountains and the plateau <u>lies</u> the Great Valley, <u>which is rich in</u>
      A   B   C

     fertile crop lands and <u>apples orchards</u>.
                                D

    ＜解答＞ D：apple orchards

562. <u>Since</u> fireworks <u>are danger</u>, many cities have laws <u>preventing</u> businesses
     A   B   C

    <u>from selling them</u>.
        D

    ＜解答＞ B：are dangerous

563. <u>During World War II</u>, many Eskimos served <u>in the Army or Navy</u>; <u>another</u>
          A   B   C

    worked on airfields or supplied meat <u>to the armed forces</u>.
                                      D

    ＜解答＞ C：others

564. <u>There is</u> no doubt that the successful late eighteenth-century improvements
       A

    <u>in spinning and weaving methods</u>, resulting in increased production of fabrics,
                   B

    <u>have a great effect</u> on the invertors of <u>the sewing machine</u>.
          C   D

    ＜解答＞ C：had a great effect

565. Encephalitis, the only mosquito borne human disease <u>in this country now</u>
                                            A

    active, can kill <u>its victims</u> <u>or</u> cause them <u>permanent brain damage</u>.
                     B   C   D

    ＜解答＞ A：now active in this country

566. Often, <u>when</u> a new era began in history, a myth for that era <u>springs up</u> at the
          A   B

same time; the myth usually <u>contained useful advice</u> for <u>coping with</u> the times
                                                            C   D

ahead.

＜解答＞　B：sprang up

567. Every day, at least eight Americans <u>choke to death</u> when food or <u>other objects</u>
                                                          A   B

become <u>lodging</u> in <u>their throats</u>.
              C   D

＜解答＞　C：lodged

568. Every city <u>in the United States</u> has <u>traffic</u> problems because <u>the amount</u> of cars
                        A   B   C

<u>on American streets</u> and highways is increasing every year.
                            D

＜解答＞　C：the number

569. Thirteen hundred medical professionals, <u>all of which</u> have been trained <u>to treat</u>
                                                                  A   B

drug dependency, <u>attended</u> the annual convention <u>sponsored by</u> the Society to
                            C   D

Prevent Drug Abuse.

＜解答＞　A：all of whom

570. <u>Despite the disappearance</u> of the Mayan enpire, <u>there are still</u> Mayans in the
                A   B

region <u>in which</u> <u>they once inhabited</u>.
              C   D

＜解答＞　C：which

571. <u>To be good for</u> agricultural purposes, soil <u>must have</u> <u>in it</u> the minerals
                A   B   C

<u>plants required</u>.
              D

＜解答＞　D：plants require

572. Because the farms of Europe <u>produce</u> <u>less food</u> than <u>the people</u> need, some
                                     A   B   C

    producuts must be <u>to bring</u> from other lands.
                         D

    ＜解答＞ D：brought

573. The <u>police investigation</u> <u>revealed that</u> the thieves <u>have planned</u> the robbery
                 A   B   C

    <u>carefully</u> before they stole the jewelry.
       D

    ＜解答＞ C：had planned

574. <u>These early</u> people did not learn <u>how to make</u> bronze until 1500 B.C., but
       A   B

    <u>they have done</u> <u>excellent work</u> with other metals.
         C   D

    ＜解答＞ C：they did

575. <u>Unlike</u> many other people, the <u>America Indians</u> <u>had to discover</u> agriculture
    A   B   C

    <u>for themselves.</u>
       D

    ＜解答＞ B：American Indians

576. <u>The element</u> uranium, which is <u>a hard, silvery</u> metal and <u>it was discovered</u>
       A   B   C

    in 1789, <u>was named for</u> the plant Uranus.
             D

    ＜解答＞ C：which was discovered

577. The government troops <u>were very fortunate</u> than the rebels <u>in having</u>
                    A   B

    large numbers of <u>foot soldiers</u> <u>ready for</u> combat.
                  C   D

    ＜解答＞ A：were more fortunate

578. The Mayan priests, <u>who were not only</u> excellent mathematicians
                         A

but also outstanding scientists, calculated <u>the correct revolution</u> of several
<u>but also outstanding</u>
       B   C

planets and <u>even predict</u> eclipses.
                   D

＜解答＞ D：even predicted

579. One of <u>the most famous</u> men of ancient times <u>Socrates was</u>, <u>whose teachings</u>
                   A   B   C

<u>are reflected</u> in Plato's writing.
       D

＜解答＞ B：was Socrates

580. When archeologists <u>begin digging</u>, <u>they generally have</u> a good idea <u>of what</u>
                              A   B   C

they are looking for and where <u>they are like</u> to find it.
                                       D

＜解答＞ D：they are likely

581. In Mesopotamia kings <u>were regarded as</u> the servants <u>of the gods</u>, but in Egypt,
                                 A   B

<u>on the other hand</u>, the Tharaoh was thought <u>he was</u> divine.
       C   D

＜解答＞ D：to be

582. Sugar <u>provides man</u> with quick energy, but it has neither vitamins, minerals,
                 A

<u>and other</u> body-building material <u>necessary for</u> <u>an adequate</u> diet.
       B   C   D

＜解答＞ B：nor other

583. Although <u>tea drinking</u> is <u>a considerably old</u> custom in the Far East, this custom
                    A   B

first reached Europe <u>for the first time</u> <u>during</u> the seventeenth century.
                              C   D

<解答> C：cancel

584. The Mediterranean, a large sea <u>surrounded by land</u>, is <u>a mile deep</u>
                                     A   B

<u>on the average</u> and more than <u>2,000 miles length</u>.
       C   D

<解答> D：2,000 miles long

585. During the Middle Ages people <u>were willing </u>to pay <u>a great deal for</u> spices
                                    A   B

<u>because disguised</u> the bad taste of <u>spoiled</u> food.
       C   D

<解答> C：because they disguised

586. Many people enjoy <u>stamp collecting</u>, and they <u>will pay often</u> large sums for
                        A   B

stamps <u>on which</u> a mistake <u>was made</u>.
         C   D

<解答> B：will often pay

587. <u>Whether have individuals</u> served good or evil governments, these individuals
           A

<u>are remembered</u> if <u>their actions</u> have altered <u>historical events</u>.
       B   C   D

<解答> A：Whether individuals have

588. John Calhoun <u>objected to creating</u> a <u>federal strong govenment</u> because he
                          A   B

believed that each state <u>should</u> decide most issues <u>for itself</u>.
                            C   D

<解答> B：strong federal government

589. <u>Although violent</u>, tornadoes are small storms <u>which paths</u> <u>are not usually</u>
            A   B   C

more than a quarter of a mile <u>in width</u>.
D

<解答> B：whose paths

590. In 1954, the United States Navy <u>decided to add</u> the Nautilus, the first
A

submarine <u>to be</u> <u>driven for</u> atomic power, <u>to its fleet</u>.
B   C   D

<解答> C：driven by

591. <u>It is</u> <u>generally known</u> that the natural habitat of <u>these types</u> of monkeys <u>are</u> the
A   B   C   D

central and eastern forests of Africa.

<解答> D：is

592. Not only <u>did the Egyptians preserve</u> the dead bodies of important people, but
A

they also buried <u>with the dead person</u> <u>every which object</u> he <u>might possibly</u>
B   C   D

use in an afterlife.

<解答> C：every object which

593. We see lightning <u>before we hear</u> the thunder <u>it cause</u> becaus sound travels
A   B

<u>more slowly</u> than <u>light is</u>.
C   D

<解答> D：light does

594. With the <u>marriage of</u> Isabella and Ferdinand the rise <u>of Spain</u> began <u>and secured</u>
A   B   C

<u>a rich and extensive</u>.
D

<解答> C：and Spain secured

595. <u>West of</u> the Missouri River <u>there are</u> <u>vast, open grazing</u> lands, an area that
A   B   C

receives <u>little rain</u> than the farming region.
       D

<解答>　D：less rain

596. A book of many pages <u>would be needed</u> to <u>just list</u> <u>all the</u> animals <u>native to</u>
               A   B C   D

South America.

<解答>　B：just to list

597. Some of the land in that region is <u>so wet</u> and hot and <u>covered with</u> jungle that
              A   B

<u>a few people</u> live <u>there</u>.
   C   D

<解答>　C：few people

598. <u>Wealthy</u> people have always desired <u>and wear</u> precious stones because
   A   B

<u>their beauty</u> <u>is lasting</u>.
   C   D

<解答>　B：and worn

599. <u>While vistiting</u> a cotton plantation, Eli Whitney got the idea for the cotton gin,
   A

<u>which</u> soon helped <u>to increase</u> <u>the production cotton</u> throughout the South.
   B   C   D

<解答>　D：① the production of cotton ② the cotton production

600. Michelangelo's father <u>sent him</u> to school, <u>poping that</u> he <u>would be</u> a scholar,
              A   B   C

but the boy was fond <u>only in</u> sculpture.
           D

<解答>　D：only of

601. <u>From</u> its name, <u>one might guess</u> <u>that</u> meteorology is the study of meteors,
   A   B   C

but instead of, it is the study of weather.
      D

＜解答＞ D：but instead

602. Some mercury exists free in nature, most of it, however, is found
           A   B   C

in combination to sulfur.
      D

＜解答＞ D：in combination with

603. By 1910, other scientists had carried out experiments which were much
    A   B

like Mendel, and their results were the same as his.
      C   D

＜解答＞ C：① like Mendel's ② like those of Mendel

604. After exploring the coast for a month, the Pilgrims founded a new colony
     A   B   C

and named Plymouth.
    D

＜解答＞ D：and named it

605. Approximately one in every three marriages in America today end in divorce.
   A   B   C   D

＜解答＞ D：ends in

606. Most bothersome flies belong to the family Sacophagidae and are
             A

popular known as flesh flies because the larvae feed on flesh.
    B   C   D

＜解答＞ B：popularly known

607. The cheetah, the fastest of all land animals, can cover a mile in less than a
          A   B

minute, but the cheetah seems slow compared some birds.
           C   D

<解答> D：compared with some birds

608. <u>To say</u> the Ferdinand Magellan, the first European to <u>discover the Philippines,</u>
        A   B

did not actually circumnavigate the earth because he was killed

<u>before his famous</u> voyage <u>was completed</u>.
         C   D

<解答> A：It is said

609. Both solar energy <u>or nuclear energy</u> will supply most of America's <u>electrical</u>
                       A   B

power in the twenty-first century; <u>however,</u> giant windmills will abso dot
                                   C

the <u>coastal regions of New England</u> and the Middle Atlantic states.
                 D

<解答> A：and nuclear energy

610. <u>Close to</u> <u>73 percentage</u> of the United States' population <u>is concentrated in</u>
     A   B   C

metropoliten areas, <u>and more than</u> half the population lives in the South
                          D

and West.

<解答> B：73 percent

611. All Middle East people <u>believed in</u> life after death, but the Egyptians of ages
                        A

past <u>carried</u> this idea <u>further</u> than <u>any ancient civilization</u>.
     B   C   D

<解答> D：any other ancient civilization

612. <u>A collection of</u> Indian artifacts, <u>which was taken</u> from graves in the area and
       A   B

<u>it was lent</u> to Harvard University, will <u>be-returned</u> to the museum next week.
     C   D

<解答> C：lent

613. Caviar is generally <u>spread on</u> toast, flavored with <u>a few</u> drops of lemon juice,

                          A   B

and <u>eating as an</u> appetizer <u>with</u> various beverages.

            C   D

＜解答＞ C：eaten as an

614. The common notion <u>that</u> fish is an excellent food <u>for improving</u> the brain

                       A   B

is not <u>supported by</u> any available <u>scientist</u> information.

            C   D

＜解答＞ D：scientific

615. If <u>allowed to turn yellow</u> while still on the plant, bananas lose

              A

their <u>character-istically good</u> flavor, <u>the skin break open</u>, insects

                  B   C

<u>enter the inside</u>, and the fruit rots.

        D

＜解答＞ C：the skin breaks open

616. <u>During</u> a rainstorm, mud rivulets form <u>on the side of</u> a hill and thus <u>move</u>

     A   B   C

soil from one place to <u>other</u>.

                  D

＜解答＞ D：another

617. Naturalists say <u>that there is</u> evidence <u>to support</u> the assertion that anthropoids,

                   A   B

whether <u>in captive or</u> in the native state, sometimes <u>beat their breasts</u>.

            C   D

＜解答＞ C：in captivity or

618. No one took cable television <u>seriously</u> fifteen years ago, when it <u>has been</u>

                                    A   B

no more <u>than a way</u> for isolated towns to receive <u>television signals</u>.
　　　　　　 C　　　　　　　　　　　　　　　　　　 D

＜解答＞ B：was

619. <u>Despite the fact that</u> the South Pole is <u>as snow-covered</u> as the North Pole <u>is</u>,
　　　　　 A　　　　　　　　　　　　　　　 B　　　　　　　　　　 C

<u>is colder</u> than the North pole.
　　 D

＜解答＞ D：it is colder

620. Today, the peanut <u>is cultivated</u> commercially <u>in</u> the southern United States
　　　　　　　　　 A　　　　　　　　　 B

<u>from California to</u> Florida and <u>as far north</u> Washington, D.C.
　　　　 C　　　　　　　　　　　 D

＜解答＞ D：as far as north

621. <u>Depriving</u> of the financial means <u>to remain independent</u>, Samuel Johnson
　　　 A　　　　　　　　　　　　　　 B

was forced to <u>search for a job</u> <u>as a scribe</u>.
　　　　　　　 C　　　　 D

＜解答＞ A：Deprived

622. <u>Despite of</u> his limited <u>educational opportunities</u>, Abraham Lincoln <u>became</u>
　　 A　　　　　　　 B　　　　　　　　　　　　　　　 C

one of the greatest intellectuals <u>the world has ever known</u>.
　　　　　　　　　　　　　　　　 D

＜解答＞ A：① In spite of ② Despite

623. <u>In 1955</u>, a huge crowd gathered at the University of Michigan <u>to hear</u>
　　 A　　　　　　　　　　　　　　　　　　　　　　　　　 B

<u>scientists announce</u> that a vaccine against polio <u>had been developed</u> and
　　　　　　　　　　　　　　　　　　　　 C

<u>successful tested</u>.
　　 D

＜解答＞ D：successfully tested

624. <u>With</u> the possible exception of <u>the termite queen</u>, the cicada <u>is thought to be</u>
     A   B   C

the <u>longer-living</u> insect in the world.
          D

＜解答＞ D：longest-living

625. Both hard-and soft-shelled clams <u>have</u> a wedge-shaped foot that is <u>too fleshy</u>
                                  A   B

that they <u>can move easily</u> from <u>one place to another</u> by burrowing in the sand.
                C   D

＜解答＞ B：so fleshy

626. <u>Climatic</u> conditions <u>vary widely</u> from place to place and from season to season,
     A   B

but <u>there is</u> a recognizable order and pattern in this great diversity of
         C

<u>various climates</u>.
        D

＜解答＞ D：climates

627. Clouds hold water <u>that evaporates from</u> the land or the sea; later, <u>the water</u>
                          A   B

in clouds <u>returned</u> to the land <u>as rain or snow</u>.
          C   D

＜解答＞ C：returns

628. Cancer researchers <u>have done great</u> progress in the last decade; <u>however</u>,
                         A   B

scientists <u>still realize that</u> there are many aspects <u>that need to be</u> studied further.
               C   D

＜解答＞ A：have made great

629. <u>The most noticeable</u> feature of tarsiers, small animals <u>which look like</u>
         A   B

monkeys, <u>are their large eyes</u> that allow them <u>to see well</u> at night.
C　　　　　　　　　　　　　　D

　　＜解答＞　C：is their large eyes

630. People <u>who lose weight</u> with the help of behavioral techniques like
A

weighing themselves regularly and keeping records of <u>what do they eat</u>
B　　　　　　　　　　　　　　　　C

seem to need the same techniques to keep <u>the weight off</u>.
D

　　＜解答＞　C：what they eat

631. <u>In a report</u> issued by <u>United States Census Bureau</u>, the chemical industry
A　　　　　　　　　B

is investing <u>more than any other</u> United States manufacturing industry
C

<u>in fighting pollution</u>.
D

　　＜解答＞　B：the United States Census Bureau

632. <u>Throughout the history</u>, the mosquito has been not only a nuisance
A

<u>but a killer</u>, <u>carrying</u> some of the deadliest diseases <u>known to man</u>.
B　　　C　　　　　　　　　　　　　　　D

　　＜解答＞　A：Throughout history

633. Exploratory investigations reveal that Alaska is <u>capable to producing</u> 45 to 55
A

percent of <u>its own requirements</u> of <u>agricultural</u> products, instead of
B　　　　　　　　C

approximately 10 percent, <u>the quantity now produced</u>.
D

　　＜解答＞　A：capable of producing

634. The official name of <u>the capital of Mexico</u> is <u>Mexico</u>, D. F. , but most people
                                 A   B

    <u>call Mexico City</u> to distinguish it <u>from</u> the country.
        C   D

    ＜解答＞ C：call it Mexico City

635. The photograph revealed a group of mountain climbers who had <u>strung</u>
                                         A

    <u>twenty-feet</u> rope <u>between</u> two <u>particularly</u> dangerous peaks.
      B   C   D

    ＜解答＞ B：twenty-foot

636. <u>Only</u> in a few countries <u>do</u> the whole of the population <u>enjoy</u> <u>a</u> reasonable
    A   B   C D

    standard of living.

    ＜解答＞ B：does

637. One of the greatest factors hindering efficient farming and <u>proper agricultural</u>
                                                  A

    <u>development</u> in these countries since <u>the Second World War</u> <u>have been</u> the
                                            B   C

    lack of information concerning land capability, <u>utilization</u>, and availability.
                                         D

    ＜解答＞ C：has been

638. <u>Over the centuries</u>, women have developed <u>considerate</u> expertise in the
         A   B

    techniques of <u>adapting to men</u>, but that ability is not the same
              C

    <u>as truly understanding</u> male psychology.
         D

    ＜解答＞ B：considerable

639. The aperiodic compass is a magnetic compass <u>which its</u> needle is
                                     A

extremely stable under most flying conditions.
      B   C   D

＜解答＞ A：whose

640. The most Americans would benefit by doing more walking; in fact, physicians
          A   B   C

believe walking to be one of the best forms of exercise.
         D

＜解答＞ A：Most Americans

641. According to the corner's report, rock-music idol Elvis Presley died of a heart
                A   B

condition in August 16,1977, yet medical examiners later found evidence
        C   D

of an usually high concentration of dangerous drugs in his body.

＜解答＞ C：on

642. The duties of the secretary are to take the minutes, mailing the correspondence,
                       A B   C

and calling the members before meeting.
                     D

＜解答＞ B：taking

643. The valure of the dollar declines as the rate of inflation raises.
             A   B C   D

＜解答＞ D：rises

644. Anthropologists assert that many of the early American Plains Indians did not
  engage in planting crops but to hunt, living primarily on buffalo meat.
                A   B   C   D

＜解答＞ B：in hunting

645. the differential attractions of the sun and the moon have a direct effect in
                                              A   B

the rising and falling of the tides.
      C   D

<解答> B：on

646. Before TV, the common man <u>seldom never</u> <u>had</u> the opportunity to see and
                                             A   B

<u>hear</u> his leaders express <u>their</u> views.
  C   D

<解答> A：① never ② seldom

647. Psychology Today <u>is</u> <u>interesting</u>, informative, and <u>it is</u> easy to <u>read</u>.
                                 A   B   C   D

<解答> C：cancel

648. You have <u>to keep</u> a record of the <u>agreements</u> you have made the <u>salary</u> you pay
                   A   B   C

people, the <u>sales</u> you achieve.
             D

<解答> C：salaries

649. John Philip Sousa, <u>who</u> <u>many</u> people consider the <u>greatest</u> composer of
                         A   B   C

marches, wrote his music during the era <u>known</u> as the Gay 90s.
                                               D

<解答> A：whom

650. <u>Whoever</u> inspected <u>this</u> radio <u>should have</u> Put <u>their</u> identification number
   A   B   C   D

on the box.

<解答> D：his

651. The purpose <u>of</u> the United Nations, <u>broad speaking</u>, <u>is</u> to maintain peace
                   A   B   C

and security and <u>to encourage</u> respect for human rights.
                         D

<解答> B：broadly speaking

652. <u>Even though</u> Miss Colombia lost the beauty contest, she <u>was</u> still <u>more prettier</u>
     A   B   C

than the other girls in the pageant.

 D

<解答>　C：prettier

653. Although we are <u>concerned with</u> the problem of energy sources, we <u>must not</u>

          A   B

  fail <u>recognizing</u> the need <u>for</u> environmental protection.

      C   D

  <解答>　C：to recognize

654. Professor Baker recommended that we <u>are</u> present at the reception

                A

  <u>this afternoon</u> in order <u>to meet</u> the representatives <u>from</u> the Fubbright

    B   C   D

  Commission.

  <解答>　A：be

655. The information officer <u>at the bank</u> <u>told</u> his customers <u>that</u> <u>there was</u> several

            A B   C D

  different kinds of checking accounts available.

  <解答>　D：were

656. The Department of Fin Arts and Architecture <u>has</u> been criticized for

                   A

  <u>not having</u> <u>much</u> required courses scheduled <u>for</u> this semester.

    B   C   D

  <解答>　C：many

657. Although <u>no country</u> has exactly the same folk music <u>like</u> <u>that</u> of any other,

       A   B C

  it is significant that similar songs exist among <u>widely</u> separated people.

                   D

  <解答>　B：as

658. Never before <u>has</u> <u>so many</u> people <u>in</u> the United States been <u>interested in</u> soccer.

        A B   C   D

　　＜解答＞　A：have

659. <u>Not one</u> in one hundred children exposed to the disease <u>are</u> <u>likely</u> <u>to develop</u>
　　　A　　　　　　　　　　　　　　　　　　　　　B　　C　　　　D

　　symptoms of it.

　　＜解答＞　B：is

660. A catalytic agent <u>such as</u> platinum may be used <u>so</u> the chemical reaction
　　　　　　　　　　　　A　　　　　　　　　　　　　　B

　　<u>advances</u> more <u>rapidly</u>.
　　　C　　　　　　D

　　＜解答＞　B：so that

661. When a patient's blood pressure is <u>much</u> higher <u>than it</u> <u>should be</u>, a doctor
　　　　　　　　　　　　　　　　　　　A　　　　　B　　　C

　　usually insists that he <u>will not</u> smoke.
　　　　　　　　　　　　　　D

　　＜解答＞　D：not

662. First <u>raise</u> your right hand, <u>and then</u>, <u>you should</u> repeat <u>after me</u>.
　　　　　A　　　　　　　　　　　B　　　　C　　　　　　　D

　　＜解答＞　C：cancel

663. The examination <u>will test</u> your ability to understand <u>spoken</u> English, to read
　　　　　　　　　　A　　　　　　　　　　　　　　　　B

　　nontechnical language, and <u>writing</u> <u>correctly</u>.
　　　　　　　　　　　　　　　　C　　　　D

　　＜解答＞　C：to write

664. An organ <u>is</u> a group <u>of tissues</u> capable <u>to perform</u> some special function, as
　　　　　　A　　　　　B　　　　　　　C

　　<u>for example</u>, the heart, the liver, or the lungs.
　　　D

　　＜解答＞　C：of performing

665. Please send <u>me</u> information <u>with regard of</u> <u>insurance</u> policies available <u>from</u>
　　　　　　　　A　　　　　　　　B　　　　　　C　　　　　　　　　　　　D

company.

<解答> B：with regard to

666. If you <u>will buy</u> one box at the regular price, you would receive <u>another one</u>
  A   B   C

at <u>no</u> extra cost.
  D

<解答> B：bought

667. The bell <u>signaling</u> the end of the first period rang <u>loud</u>, <u>interupting</u> the
      A   B C

professor's <u>closing</u> comments.
       D

<解答> B：loudly

668. Neither of the two candidates <u>who</u> <u>had applied</u> for admission <u>to</u> the Industrial
            A   B   C

Engineering Department <u>were</u> eligible for scholarships.
          D

<解答> D：was

669. <u>Those</u> of us <u>who</u> smoke should have <u>their</u> lungs X-ray <u>regularly</u>.
  A   B   C   D

<解答> C：our

670. If Robert Kennedy <u>would have lived</u> <u>a little longer</u>, he <u>probably</u> would have
        A   B   C

<u>won</u> the election.
 D

<解答> A：had lived

671. The prices <u>at</u> The Economy Center <u>are</u> as reasonable, <u>if not more</u> reasonable,
     A   B   C

<u>as</u> those at comparable discount stores.
D

<解答> D：than

672. <u>Historically</u> <u>there</u> <u>has been</u> <u>only</u> two major factions in the Republican Party —
       A   B   C   D

the liberals and the conservatives.

＜解答＞ C：have been

673. The registrar has requested that each student and teacher <u>sign</u> <u>their name</u> on
                                      A   B

the grade sheet before <u>submitting</u> <u>it</u>.
                     C   D

＜解答＞ B：his name

674. The president, with his wife and daughter, <u>are</u> returning <u>from</u> a brief vacation
                                A   B

at Sun Valley in order <u>to attend</u> a press conference <u>this</u> afternoon.
                   C   D

＜解答＞ A：is

675. The more the relative humidity reading <u>rises</u>, <u>the worst</u> the heat <u>affects</u> <u>us</u>.
                           A   B   C D

＜解答＞ B：the worse

676. Lecture <u>for</u> the week of March 22-26 <u>will include</u> the <u>following</u>: The Causes of
       A   B   C

the Civil War, The Economy of the South, Battle Strategies, and <u>Assassinating</u>
                                            D

Lincoln.

＜解答＞ D：the assassination of

677. <u>As</u> every <u>other</u> nations, the United States <u>used to define</u> <u>its</u> unit of currency,
 A   B   C   D

the dollar, in terms of the gold standard.

＜解答＞ A：Like

678. <u>Until recently</u>, women <u>were</u> forbidden <u>by law</u> <u>from owning</u> property.
     A   B   C   D

＜解答＞ D：to own

679. John Dewey thought that children <u>will learn</u> <u>better</u> through participating in
                                             A   B

    experience <u>rather than</u> through <u>listening to</u> lecturer.
                        C   D

    ＜解答＞ A：would learn

680. <u>some</u> methods <u>to prevent</u> soil erosion <u>are</u> plowing parallel with the slopes
      A   B   C

    of hills, <u>to plant</u> trees on unproductive land, and rotating crops.
               D

    ＜解答＞ D：planting

681. .Interest <u>in</u> automatic data processing has <u>grown</u> <u>rapid</u> <u>since</u> the first large
            A   B   C   D

    calculators were introduced in 1950.

    ＜解答＞ C：rapidly

682. It is <u>interesting</u> <u>to compare</u> the early stylized art forms <u>of</u> ancient civilizations
            A   B   C

    <u>to</u> the modern abstract forms of today.
    D

    ＜解答＞ D：with

683. The plants that <u>they</u> <u>belong</u> to the family of ferns <u>are</u> quite varried in <u>their</u>
                  A   B   C   D

    size and structure.

    ＜解答＞ A：cancel

684. All of <u>we</u> students must <u>have</u> an identification card in order to check books
            A   B

    <u>out</u> <u>of</u> the library.
    C D

    ＜解答＞ A：us

685. This vase has <u>the same</u> design, but it is <u>different</u> <u>shaped</u> <u>from</u> that one.
                      A   B   C   D

<解答> B：differently

686. <u>It is</u> imperative that a graduate student <u>maintains</u> a grade point average
     A   B
     <u>of</u> " B " in <u>his</u> major field.
     C   D
     <解答> B：maintain

687. Economists have tried <u>to discourage</u> <u>the use</u> of the phrase " underdeveloped
                           A   B
     nation " and <u>encouraging</u> <u>the more</u> accurate phrase " developing nation "
                  C   D
     in order to suggest an ongoing process.
     <解答> C：to encourage

688. After he <u>had ran</u> <u>for</u> half a mile, he <u>passed</u> the stick to <u>the next</u> runner.
               A   B   C   D
     <解答> A：had run

689. A City University professor reported that he <u>discovers</u> a vaccine <u>which</u> has
                                                  A   B
     been 80 percent effective <u>in reducing</u> the instances of tooth decay <u>among</u>
                               C   D
     small children.
     <解答> A：discovered

690. When they <u>have been</u> <u>frightened</u>, as, for example, <u>by</u> an electrical storm,
               A   B   C
     daring cows may refuse <u>giving</u> milk.
                            D
     <解答> D：to give

691. <u>No other</u> quality is more important <u>for</u> a scientist to acquire <u>as</u> to observe
     A   B   C
     <u>carefully</u>.
     D

<解答> C：than

692. Fertilizers <u>are used</u> <u>primarily</u> to enrich <u>the soil</u> and <u>increasing</u> yield.
                 A   B   C   D

      <解答> D：to increase

693. The regulation requires that everyone <u>who</u> <u>holds</u> a non-immigrant visa
                                         A   B

   <u>reports</u> <u>his</u> address to the federal government in January of each year.
       C   D

      <解答> C：report

694. The statement <u>will be spoken</u> just one time; therefore, you must listen
                       A

   <u>very careful</u> in order <u>to understand</u> <u>what</u> the speaker has said.
        B   C   D

      <解答> B：very carefully

695. In the <u>relatively</u> short history of industrial <u>developing</u> <u>in the United States</u>,
              A   B   C

   New York City <u>has played</u> a vital role.
                   D

      <解答> B：development

696. For the first time in the history of the country the person <u>which</u>
                                                  A

   <u>was recommended</u> by the president <u>to replace</u> a <u>retiring</u> justice on the
       B   C   D

   Supreme Court is a woman.

      <解答> A：who

697. <u>Despite of</u> rain or snow <u>there are</u> always more <u>than</u> fifty thousand fans <u>at</u> the
     A   B   C   D

   OSU football games.

      <解答> A：① In spite of ② Despite

698. To see the Statue of Liberty and <u>taking</u> pictures <u>from</u> the top of the Empire
            A   B

 State Building <u>are</u> two reasons <u>for visiting</u> New York City.
       C   D

 ＜解答＞ A：to take

699. <u>Having chose</u> the topics for <u>their</u> essays, the students <u>were</u> instructed to make
   A   B   C

 <u>either</u> a preliminary outline or a rough draft.
  D

 ＜解答＞ A：Having chosen

700. If Grandma Moses <u>having</u> been able to continue <u>farming</u>, she might never
         A   B

 have <u>begun</u> to <u>paint</u>.
   C D

 ＜解答＞ A：have

701. <u>In response to</u> <u>question thirteen</u>, I enjoy <u>modern</u> art, classical music, and
   A   B   C

 to read.
  D

 ＜解答＞ D：literature

702. <u>In purchasing</u> a <u>winter coat</u>, it is <u>very</u> important <u>for trying</u> it on with heavy
   A   B   C   D

 clothing underneath.

 ＜解答＞ D：to try

703. I sometimes wish that my university <u>is</u> <u>as large as</u> State University because
            A B

 our facilities are <u>more</u> limited <u>than</u> theirs.
       C   D

 ＜解答＞ A：were

704. Although a doctor may be able <u>to diagnose</u> a problem <u>perfect</u>, he still may
                                              A   B

    not <u>be able to</u> find a drug <u>to which</u> the patient will respond.
               C   D

    ＜解答＞ B：perfectly

705. A turtle differs <u>from</u> all <u>other</u> reptiles in that it has its body encased in a
                 A   B

    protective shell of <u>their</u> <u>own</u>.
                   C D

    ＜解答＞ C：its

706. Professor Baker told her class that a good way to <u>improve</u> listening
                                                  A

    comprehension skills <u>is</u> <u>to watch</u> television, <u>especially</u> news programs
                        B   C   D

    and documentaries.

    ＜解答＞ B：was

707. Whoever turned in <u>the last</u> test did not <u>put</u> <u>their</u> name <u>on the paper</u>.
                        A   B C   D

    ＜解答＞ C：his

708. People with an <u>exceptionally</u> high intelligence quotient may not be <u>the best</u>
                A   B

    employee since they become <u>bored of</u> their work unless the job is constantly
                                   C

    <u>changing</u>.
       D

    ＜解答＞ C：bored with

709. The oxygen contend of Mars is not <u>sufficient enough</u> <u>to support</u> life <u>as</u> we
                                        A   B   C

    know <u>it</u>.
         D

<解答>　A：① sufficient ② enough

710. Those of us <u>who</u> have a family history of heart disease <u>should make</u> <u>yearly</u>
      A   B   C

 appointments with <u>their</u> doctors.
        D
 <解答>　D：our

711. <u>Living</u> in New York, apartments cost <u>more</u> to rent <u>than</u> they do in other, <u>smaller</u>
  A   B   C   D

 cities.
 <解答>　A：① Standing ② Built

712. The government requires that a census <u>be taken</u> <u>every ten years</u> <u>so</u> accurate
             A   B   C

 statistics <u>may be compiled</u>.
      D
 <解答>　C：so that

713. The flag is <u>risen</u> <u>in the morning</u> and taken down <u>at night</u> <u>by</u> the Boy Scouts.
      A   B   C D
 <解答>　A：raised

714. Frank Lloyd Wright <u>has been acclaimed</u> <u>by colleagues</u> <u>as</u> <u>the greater</u> of all
          A   B   C   D

 modern architects.
 <解答>　D：the greatest

715. There <u>have been</u> a tornado watch <u>issued</u> <u>for</u> Texas County <u>until</u> eleven
    A   B C   D

 o'clock tonight.
 <解答>　A：has been

716. Jane Addams had <u>already</u> established Hull House <u>in Chicago</u> and <u>began</u> her
         A   B   C

 work in the women's Suffrage Movement when she was <u>awarded</u> the Nobel
                         D

Prize for peace.

<解答> C：begun

717. Although <u>jogging</u> is a good way to lose weight and improve one's physical

　　　　　　　　　A

condition, <u>most</u> doctors recommend that the potential jogger begin

　　　　　　　　　B

<u>in a correct manner</u> by <u>getting</u> a complete checkup.

　　　　　　　C　　　　　　　　D

<解答> C：correctly

718. To the men <u>who</u> worked so <u>hard</u> on the project, the news <u>was</u> <u>profound</u>

　　　　　　　　　A　　　　　　　B　　　　　　　　　　　　C　　　D

disappointing.

<解答> D：profoundly

719. Because the solar tiles were very <u>secure fastened</u>, only <u>a few</u> became <u>detached</u>

　　　　　　　　　　　　　　　　　A　　　　　　　　　　B　　　　　　　C

when the Space Shuttle reentered <u>the earth's atmosphere</u>.

　　　　　　　　　　　　　　　　　　　　D

<解答> A：securely fastened

720. If biennials were planted this year, they <u>will be</u> <u>likely</u> <u>to bloom</u> <u>next year</u> and

　　　　　　　　　　　　　　　　　　　A　　　B　　　C　　　　D

every two years thereafter.

<解答> A：would be

721. Even though a member <u>has drank</u> <u>too much</u> the night <u>before</u>, the counselors

　　　　　　　　　　　　　A　　　　B　　　　　　　C

at Alcoholics Anonymous will try <u>to convince</u> him or her to sober up and stop

　　　　　　　　　　　　　　　　　D

drinking again.

<解答> A：has drunk

722. The neutron bomb provides the <u>capable</u> of a <u>limited</u> nuclear war <u>in which</u>

　　　　　　　　　　　　　　　　　A　　　　　　　B　　　　　　　　　C

buildings <u>would be preserved</u>, but people would be destroyed.

       D

 <解答>　A：capability

723.　<u>Despite of</u> the pills <u>which</u> are available, many people <u>still</u> have trouble <u>sleeping</u>.

  A   B   C   D

  <解答>　A：① Despite ② In spite of

724.　<u>If</u> it receives <u>enough</u> rain at the proper time, hay <u>will grow</u> quickly <u>as</u> grass.

  A   B   C   D

  <解答>　D：like

725.　<u>Before</u> she died, the daughter of Andrew Jackson <u>who</u> <u>lives</u> in the family

  A   B C

mansion <u>used to take</u> tourists through her home.

       D

  <解答>　C：lived

726.　Two <u>of the players</u> from the Yankees <u>has</u> been <u>chosen</u> <u>to participate</u> in the

      A   B   C   D

All Star game.

  <解答>　B：have

727.　In order for one to achieve the desired results in this experiment, it is

  necessary that <u>he</u> <u>work</u> as <u>fastly</u> <u>as</u> possible.

    A B   C D

  <解答>　C：fast

728.　The new model <u>costs</u> twice <u>more than</u> <u>last</u> <u>year's</u> model.

         A   B C D

  <解答>　B：as much as

729.　<u>It</u> is an <u>accepted</u> custom for one to say " excuse me " when <u>he</u> <u>sneezed</u>.

  A   B   C   D

  <解答>　D：sneezes

730.　<u>There have been</u> <u>little</u> change in the patient's condition <u>since</u> he <u>was moved</u>

      A   B   C   D

to the intensive care unit.

＜解答＞　A：There has been

731. <u>Because of</u> the movement of a glacier, <u>the form of</u> the Great Lakes was

　　　　A　　　　　　　　　　　　　　　B　　C

very <u>slow</u>.

　　　D

＜解答＞　B：formation

732. <u>The first</u> electric lamp had two carbon rods from <u>which</u> vapor <u>serves</u>

　　　A　　　　　　　　　　　　　　　　　　　B　　　　　C

<u>to conduct</u> the current across the gap.

　　　D

＜解答＞　C：served

733. <u>In order to</u> get married in this state, one must <u>present</u> a medical report

　　　A　　　　　　　　　　　　　　　　　　　B

<u>along with</u> <u>your</u> identification.

　　　C　　　　D

＜解答＞　D：① one's ② his

734. <u>Despite of</u> the Taft-Harthey Act which <u>forbids</u> unfair union practices, some

　　　A　　　　　　　　　　　　　　B

unions <u>such as</u> the air traffic controllers have voted <u>to strike</u> even though it

　　　　　C　　　　　　　　　　　　　　　　　　　　D

might endanger the national security.

＜解答＞　A：① In spite of ② Despite

735. The rest of the stockholders <u>will receive</u> <u>his</u> reports <u>in the mail</u> <u>along with</u>

　　　　　　　　　　　　　　　　A　　　　B　　　　　C　　　　D

a copy of today's proceedings.

＜解答＞　B：their

736. <u>There is</u> an unreasolved controversy as to <u>whom</u> <u>is</u> the real author of the

　　　A　　　　　　　　　　　　　　　　　　B　　C

Elizabethan plays <u>commonly</u> credited to William Shakespeare.

              D

＜解答＞ B：who

737. <u>From the airplane</u>, passengers are <u>able</u> <u>to clearly see</u> the outline <u>of</u> the whole
     A   B   C   D

island.

＜解答＞ C：to see clearly

738. Excavations in several mounds and village <u>on the east bank</u> of the Euphrates
                            A

River <u>have revealed</u> the city of Nebuchadnezzar, an ancient community that
     B

<u>had been laying</u> under <u>later</u> reconstructions of the city of Babylon.
    C   D

＜解答＞ C：had been lying

739. Located <u>in</u> the cranial cavity in the skull, <u>the brain</u> is the <u>larger</u> mass of nerve
      A   B   C

tissue in the <u>human body</u>.
        D

＜解答＞ C：largest

740. <u>Alike</u> other forms of energy, natural gas <u>may be used</u> <u>to heat</u> homes, cook
   A   B   C

food,and even <u>run</u> automobiles.
       D

＜解答＞ A：Like

741. Insulin, <u>it is</u> used <u>to treat</u> diabetes and <u>is</u> secured <u>chiefly</u> from the pancreas of
     A   B   C   D

cattle and hogs.

＜解答＞ A：is

742. Dairying <u>is</u> concerned not only <u>with</u> the production of milk, <u>but</u> with the
      A   B   C

manufacture of milk products <u>such as</u> butter and cheese.

　　　　　　　　　　　　　　　　D

　＜解答＞　C：but also

743. When he <u>was</u> a little boy, Mark Twain <u>would walk</u> along the piers, <u>watch</u>

　　　　　　　　　A　　　　　　　　　　　　　B　　　　　　　　C

the river boats, <u>swimming</u> and fish in the Mississippi, much like his famous

　　　　　　　　　　　　D

character, Tom Sawyer.

　＜解答＞　D：swim

744. <u>Upon reading</u> Innocents Abroad <u>by</u> Mark Twain, one begins <u>to understand</u>

　　　　A　　　　　　　　　　　　　　B　　　　　　　　　　　C

the value of <u>your</u> common sense.

　　　　　　　　D

　＜解答＞　D：① one's ② his

745. After the team of geologists had drawn diagrams in <u>their</u> notebooks and <u>wrote</u>

　　　　　　　　　　　　　　　　　　　　　　A　　　　　　　　B

explanations of the formations <u>which</u> they had observed, they returned to their

　　　　　　　　　　　　　　　　C

campsite <u>to compare</u> notes.

　　　　　　　　D

　＜解答＞　B：written

746. <u>It</u> was <u>her</u> <u>who</u> represented her country in the United Nations and <u>later</u> became

　A　　　B　　C　　　　　　　　　　　　　　　　　　　　　　　　D

ambassador to the United States.

　＜解答＞　B：she

747. <u>It is</u> <u>extremely</u> important <u>for</u> an engineer <u>to know</u> to use a computer.

　A　　B　　　　　　　　C　　　　　　　D

　＜解答＞　D：to know how

748. Whitman wrote Leaves of Grass as a tribute to the Civil War soldiers who

had laid on the battlefields and <u>whom</u> he <u>had seen</u> <u>while serving</u> as an

   A   B   C   D

army nurse.

    ＜解答＞ A：had lain

749. <u>The Chinese</u> were the first and <u>large</u> ethnic group <u>to work</u> on the construction <u>of</u>

      A   B   C   D

the transcontinental railroad system.

    ＜解答＞ B：largest

750. <u>Even</u> a professional psychologist may have difficulty talking <u>calm</u> and

    A   B

logically <u>about</u> <u>his own</u> problems.

               C   D

    ＜解答＞ B：calmly

751. The shore partrol <u>has found</u> the body of a man <u>who</u> they believe <u>to be</u> the

                A   B   C

<u>missing</u> marine biologist.

   D

    ＜解答＞ B：whom

752. <u>Despite of</u> <u>many</u> attempts <u>to introduce</u> a universal language, notably Esperanto

    A   B   C

and Idiom Neutral, the effort has met with very <u>little</u> success.

                                      D

    ＜解答＞ A：① Despite ② In spite of

753. It is necessary that one <u>met</u> with a judge <u>before signing</u> <u>the final papers</u>

                     A   B   C

<u>for a divorce</u>.

   D

    ＜解答＞ A：meet

754. <u>According</u> to the graduate catalog, student housing <u>is</u> <u>more cheaper</u> <u>than</u>

    A   B   C   D

housing off campus.

＜解答＞ C：cheaper

755. <u>In England</u> <u>as early as</u> the <u>twelfth century</u>, young boys enjoyed <u>to play</u> football.
      A   B   C   D

＜解答＞ D：playing

756. Vaslor Nijisky <u>achieved</u> world recognition <u>as</u> both <u>a dancer</u> <u>as well as</u> a
                      A   B   C   D

choreographer.

＜解答＞ D：and

757. <u>It is said</u> that Einstein felt <u>very</u> <u>badly</u> about the application of his theories <u>to</u>
      A   B C   D

the creation of weapons of war.

＜解答＞ C：bad

758. Columbus Day <u>is celebrated</u> <u>on</u> the <u>twelve</u> of October <u>because</u> on that day
                  A   B   C   D

in 1492, Christopher Columbus first landed in the America.

＜解答＞ C：twelfth

759. An unexpected <u>raise</u> in the cost of living <u>as well as</u> a decline in employment
                A   B

opportunities has <u>resulted in</u> the <u>rapid</u> creation by Congress of new
                            C   D

government programs for the unemployed.

＜解答＞ A：rise

760. <u>Because of</u> the approaching storm, the wind began <u>to blow</u> <u>hard</u> and the sky
      A   B   C

became dark <u>as</u> evening.
                  D

＜解答＞ D：like

761. A good artist <u>like</u> a good engineer learns <u>as</u> much from <u>their</u> mistakes as <u>from</u>
                  A   B   C   D

successes.

　　＜解答＞　C：his

762. <u>Regardless of</u> your teaching methord, class <u>should be</u> for the students
　　　　　A　　　　　　　　　　　　　　　　　　　　　B

　　<u>to practice</u> <u>speaking words</u>.
　　　　C　　　　D

　　＜解答＞　D：speaking

763. American baseball teams, <u>once</u> the only contenders for the world championship,
　　　　　　　　　　　　　　　A

　　are now <u>being</u> challenged <u>by</u> <u>either</u> Japanese teams and Venezuelan teams.
　　　　　　　B　　　　　　　　C　　D

　　＜解答＞　D：both

764. Miami, Florida, is <u>among</u> the few cities in the United States <u>which</u>
　　　　　　　　　　　A　　　　　　　　　　　　　　　　　　　　　B

　　<u>has been awarded</u> official status <u>as</u> a bilingual municipality.
　　　　　C　　　　　　　　　　　　　D

　　＜解答＞　C：have been awarded

765. After <u>the police</u> had tried <u>unsuccessfully</u> to determine to <u>who</u> the car belonged,
　　　　　　A　　　　　　　　　B　　　　　　　　　　　　　C

　　they towed <u>it</u> into the station.
　　　　　　　D

　　＜解答＞　C：whom

766. If the ozone gases of the atmosphere <u>did not filter out</u> the ultraviolet rays
　　　　　　　　　　　　　　　　　　　　　　　A

　　of the sun, life, <u>as</u> we know <u>it</u>, would not have evolved <u>on earth</u>.
　　　　　　　　B　　　　C　　　　　　　　　　　　D

　　＜解答＞　A：had not filtered out

767. <u>Every</u> man and woman <u>should vote</u> <u>for</u> the candidate of <u>their choice</u>.
　　　A　　　　　　　　　B　　C　　　　　　　　　D

　　＜解答＞　D：his choice

768. As the demand increases, manufacturers who <u>previously</u> produced only a
                                                    A

large,luxury car <u>is</u> compelled <u>to make</u> <u>a smaller model</u> in order to compete
                 B   C   D

in the market.

＜解答＞ B：are

769. A prism is used <u>to refract</u> white light <u>so</u> <u>it</u> spreads out in a continuous spectrun
                     A   B C

<u>of colors</u>.
   D

＜解答＞ B：so that

770. The prices of homes <u>are</u> <u>as</u> high that <u>most</u> people cannot afford to buy <u>them</u>.
                        A   B   C   D

＜解答＞ B：so

771. There <u>are</u> twenty species of wild roses in North America, all of which <u>have</u>
           A   B

prickly stems, pinnate leaves, and large flowers <u>which</u> usually smell <u>sweetly</u>.
                                                 C   D

＜解答＞ D：sweet

772. <u>Factoring</u> is the process of <u>finding</u> two or more expressions <u>whose</u> product
     A   B   C

is <u>equal as</u> a given expression.
   D

＜解答＞ D：equal to

773. Since infection <u>can cause</u> both fever <u>as well as</u> pain, it is a good idea <u>to check</u>
                    A   B   C

<u>his</u> temperature.
   D

＜解答＞ B：and

774. They asked us, Henry and <u>I</u>, whether we <u>thought</u> that the statistics

                                 A   B

    <u>had been presented</u> <u>fairly</u> and accurately.

                   C   D

<解答> A：me

775. <u>What happened</u> in New York <u>were</u> a reaction from city workers, <u>including</u>

        A   B   C

    firemen and policemen who had been laid off from <u>their</u> jobs.

                                                   D

<解答> B：was

776. Some executives insist <u>that</u> the secretary <u>is</u> responsible for <u>writing</u> all reports

                           A   B   C

    <u>as well as</u> for balancing the books.

         D

<解答> B：be

777. Although the Red Cross <u>accepts</u> blood from most donors, the nurses will not

                        A

    <u>leave</u> you <u>give</u> blood if you have just <u>had</u> a cold.

     B   C   D

<解答> B：let

778. Benjamin Franklin <u>was</u> the editor of <u>the largest</u> newspaper in the colonies,

                         A   B

    a diplomatic representative to France and later to England, and <u>he invented</u>

                                                             C

    <u>many</u> useful devices.

        D

<解答> C：the inventor of

779. <u>The most common</u> form <u>of</u> treatment <u>it</u> is mass inoculation and chlorination

                A   B   C

or <u>water sources</u>.

        D

＜解答＞　C：cancel

780. Neither the mathematics department <u>nor</u> the biology department at State

                       A

University requires that the students <u>must write</u> a thesis in order <u>to graduate</u>

                                         B   C

with a <u>master's degree</u>.

        D

＜解答＞　B：write

781. Students in the United States <u>often</u> support <u>themselves</u> <u>by</u> babysitting,

                            A   B   C

working in restaurants, or <u>they drive</u> taxicabs.

                        D

＜解答＞　D：driving

782. Although federal support <u>for</u> basic research programs <u>are</u> <u>much</u> less than <u>it</u> was

                               A   B C   D

ten years ago, more funds are now available from the National Foundation.

＜解答＞　B：is

783. <u>This</u> new model not only saves time but also <u>energy</u> by <u>operating</u> on two

  A   B   C

batteries <u>instead</u> of four.

         D

＜解答＞　B：① saves energy ② conserves energy

784. In 1975, <u>according to</u> the National Center for Health Slatistics, the average

             A

life expectancy for people <u>born</u> <u>during</u> that year <u>is</u> 72.4 years.

                            B   C   D

＜解答＞　D：was

785. When <u>the silkworm</u> gets through <u>to lay</u> <u>its</u> eggs, <u>it dies</u>.
                     A   B C   D

    ＜解答＞ B：laying

786. Scientists had <u>previously</u> estimated that the Grand Canyon in Arizona <u>is</u> ten
                       A   B

    million years old; but now, <u>by using</u> a more modern dating method, they agree
                                        C

    that the age is closer to <u>six million years</u>.
                              D

    ＜解答＞ B：was

787. Professor Baker, with six of his graduate students, <u>are</u> attending a conference
                                                    A

    in Boston <u>organized</u> <u>to compare</u> current business practices in the
                  B   C

    United States with <u>those</u> of other nations.
                    D

    ＜解答＞ A：is

788. If one had thought about the alternatives, <u>you</u> would not have <u>chosen</u> <u>such</u>
                                        A   B   C

    a difficult topic for a <u>term paper</u>.
                       D

    ＜解答＞ A：① one ② he

789. The flag of the <u>original first</u> colonies may or may not <u>have been made</u>
                    A   B

    <u>by Betsy Ross</u> <u>during the Revolution</u>.
        C   D

    ＜解答＞ A：original

790. The Indians of the southwestern United States <u>are</u> famous for their beautiful
                                                A

art work, <u>especially</u> hand made jewelry cast from silver, carved from stones,

　　　　B　　　　　C

or <u>decorations</u> with beads and feathers.

　　　　　D

＜解答＞　D：decorated

791. <u>The main</u> office of the factory can <u>be found</u> <u>in</u> Maple Street <u>in</u> New York City.

　　　A　　　　　　　　　　　　　B　　C　　　　　　D

＜解答＞　C：on

792. David is <u>particularly</u> <u>fond of</u> cooking, and he <u>often cooks</u> <u>really</u> delicious meals.

　　　　　　A　　　　　B　　　　　　　　C　　　　D

＜解答＞　D：very

793. Sandra has <u>not rarely</u> missed <u>a play</u> or concert <u>since</u> she <u>was seventeen years old</u>.

　　　　　　A　　　　　B　　　　C　　　　　D

＜解答＞　A：rarely

794. <u>There was a</u> very interesting news <u>on the</u> radio this morning <u>about</u> the

　　　A　　B　　　　　　　　　　C　　　　　　　　　D

earthquake in Italy.

＜解答＞　B：① cancel ② some

795. Having been beaten <u>by</u> the police <u>for striking an officer, the man</u>

　　　　　　　　　　A　　　　　　　B　　　　　C

<u>will cry out</u> in pain.

　　　D

＜解答＞　D：cried out

796. The bridge <u>was hitting</u> by a large ship <u>during</u> a <u>sudden</u> storm <u>last</u> week.

　　　　　　A　　　　　　　　　　B　　　C　　　　D

＜解答＞　A：was hit

797. The <u>taxi driver</u> <u>told the man</u> to don't allow his disobedient son <u>to hang out</u>

　　　　A　　　　B　　　　C　　　　　　　　　　　D

the window.

＜解答＞　C：not to allow

798. Harvey seldom <u>pays his bills</u> <u>on time</u>, and <u>his</u> brother <u>does too</u>.
                          A   B   C   D

<解答>　D：doesn't either

799. When <u>an</u> university formulates <u>new regulations,</u> <u>it</u> <u>must relay its</u> decision
          A   B   C   D

to the students and faculty.

<解答>　A：a

800. There <u>is</u> some <u>scissors</u> <u>in</u> the desk drawer <u>in</u> the bedroom if you need them.
            A   B C   D

<解答>　A：are

801. George is not <u>enough intelligent</u> <u>to pass</u> <u>this</u> <u>economics</u> class without help.
                        A   B   C   D

<解答>　A：intelligent enough

802. John lived <u>in</u> New York <u>since</u> 1960 to 1975, but he <u>is now living</u> <u>in</u> Detroit.
               A   B   C   D

<解答>　B：from

803. Mrs. Anderson bought <u>last week a new sports car;</u> <u>however,</u> she
                              A   B

<u>has yet to learn</u> <u>how to operate</u> the manual gearshift.
        C   D

<解答>　A：a new sports car last week

804. The officials object <u>to</u> <u>them</u> <u>wearing</u> long dresses for the inaugural dance
                      A B   C

<u>at the country club.</u>
        D

<解答>　B：their

805. He <u>knows</u> to repair <u>the</u> carburetor without <u>taking</u> the whole car <u>apart</u>.
           A   B   C   D

<解答>　A：knows how

806. She must <u>retyping</u> the report <u>before</u> she <u>hands it in</u> <u>to the</u> director of financing.
       A   B   C   D

  ＜解答＞　A：retyps

807. Each of the <u>students</u> <u>in the</u> accounting class has to type <u>their</u> <u>own</u> research
        A   B   C D

 paper this semester.

  ＜解答＞　C：his

808. They <u>are</u> going <u>to have to</u> <u>leave soon</u>, and <u>so do</u> we.
     A   B   C   D

  ＜解答＞　D：so are

809. Dresses, skirts, shoes, and <u>children's clothing</u> <u>are advertised</u> <u>at</u> <u>great</u> reduced
              A   B   C D

 prices this weekend.

  ＜解答＞　D：greatly

810. <u>A</u> lunch <u>of</u> soup and sandwiches <u>do</u> not <u>appeal to all of</u> the students.
 A   B   C   D

  ＜解答＞　C：does

811. Mr. Peters used to <u>think</u> of <u>hisself</u> <u>as the only</u> president <u>of the company</u>.
         A   B   C   D

  ＜解答＞　B：himself

812. Although both <u>of them</u> <u>are trying</u> <u>to get</u> the scholarship, she has the <u>highest</u>
       A   B   C   D

 grades.

  ＜解答＞　D：higher

813. The pilot <u>and the crew</u> <u>divided</u> the life preservers <u>between</u> the twenty
       A   B   C

 <u>frantic passengers</u>.
     D

  ＜解答＞　C：among

814. The <u>equipment</u> <u>in the office</u> <u>was badly</u> in need of <u>to be repaired</u>.
     A   B   C   D

 ＜解答＞ D：repair

815. We thought he <u>is</u> planning <u>to go on vaction</u> <u>after</u> <u>the first of</u> the month.
        A   B   C   D

 ＜解答＞ A：was

816. The president refuses <u>to accept</u> <u>either</u> of the four <u>new propsals</u> <u>made by</u> the
           A   B   C   D

 contractors.

 ＜解答＞ B：any

817. She wishes that we <u>didn't send</u> <u>her the candy</u> yesterday <u>because</u> she's <u>on</u> a diet.
         A   B   C   D

 ＜解答＞ A：hadn't sent

818. Today was <u>such beautiful</u> day that I could't bring <u>myself</u> <u>to complete</u> all
      A   B   C

 <u>my chores</u>.
   D

 ＜解答＞ A：such a beautiful

819. The artist tried <u>stimulate</u> <u>interest in</u> painting <u>by taking</u> his students <u>to the</u>
      A   B   C   D

 museums.

 ＜解答＞ A：to stimulate

820. Nancy said <u>that</u> she <u>went</u> <u>to</u> the supermarket before <u>coming home</u>.
      A   B C   D

 ＜解答＞ B：had gone

821. Each <u>of the</u> nurses <u>report</u> to the operating room when <u>his or her name</u> <u>is called</u>.
   A   B   C   D

 ＜解答＞ B：reports

822. Professor Duncan <u>teaches</u> <u>both</u> <u>anthropology</u> as well as sociology <u>each fall</u>.
       A   B   C   D

　　　　　　＜解答＞　B：cancel

823. I <u>certainly</u> appreciate <u>him</u> <u>telling</u> us about the delay in <u>delivering</u> the materials
　　　　A　　　　　　　　　B　　C　　　　　　　　　　　　　D

　　because we had planned to begin work tomorrow.
　　　　＜解答＞　B：his

824. Rudolph Nureyer <u>has become</u> one of the <u>greatest</u> <u>dancer</u> that the ballet world
　　　　　　　　　　　　　A　　　　　　　　B　　　C

　　had <u>ever known</u>.
　　　　　　D
　　　　＜解答＞　C：dancers

825. The town visited <u>was</u> a <u>four-days</u> journey from our hotel, so we <u>took</u> the
　　　　　　　　　　　A　　　　B　　　　　　　　　　　　　　　C

　　train instead <u>of the</u> bus.
　　　　　　　　　D
　　　　＜解答＞　B：four-day

826. The leader emphasized <u>the need</u> <u>for justice</u> and equality <u>between</u> his <u>people</u>.
　　　　　　　　　　　　　　　A　　　B　　　　　　　　　　C　　　　D
　　　　＜解答＞　C：among

827. Several people <u>have</u> <u>apparent</u> tried to change <u>the man's mind</u>, but he refuses
　　　　　　　　　　A　　　B　　　　　　　　　　　　C

　　<u>to listen</u>.
　　　　D
　　　　＜解答＞　B：apparently

828. The girl <u>were sorry</u> to <u>had missed</u> the singers <u>when</u> they <u>arrived at</u> the airport.
　　　　　　　A　　　　　　　B　　　　　　　　　C　　　　　D
　　　　＜解答＞　B：have missed

829. The harder he <u>tried</u>, the <u>worst</u> he <u>danced</u> before the <u>large</u> audience.
　　　　　　　　　　A　　　　B　　　C　　　　　　　D
　　　　＜解答＞　B：worse

830. <u>While searching</u> for <u>the</u> wreckage of <u>a</u> unidentified aircraft, the Coast Guard
            A   B   C

encountered <u>severe squalls at sea</u>.
              D

　＜解答＞ B：an

831. Since it was <u>so difficult for</u> American Indians <u>to negotiate</u> a peace treaty or
             A   B

declare war <u>in their native</u> language, they used a <u>universal</u> understood form
             C   D

of sign language.

　＜解答＞ D：univerally

832. While verbalization is <u>the most common form</u> of language in <u>existence</u>,
                     A   B

humans make use of many <u>others systems</u> and techniques to <u>express</u> their
                C   D

thoughts and feelings

　＜解答＞ C：other systems

833. Writers and media <u>personnel</u> sell <u>theirselves</u> best <u>by the</u> impression given in
             A   B   C

their verbal <u>expression</u>.
        D

　＜解答＞ B：themselves

834. <u>Stephen Cran's story</u> is <u>a</u> clinical portrayal <u>of man as an animal</u> trapped by
      A   B   C

<u>the fear</u> and hunger.
   D

　＜解答＞ D：fear

835. For a long time, <u>this</u> officials <u>have been known</u> throughout the country <u>as</u>
           A   B   C

political bosses and <u>law enforcers</u>.
D

　　＜解答＞　A：these

836. Air pollution, together <u>with</u> littering, <u>are</u> causing <u>many</u> problems <u>in our large</u>,
A　　　　　　B　　　　C　 .　　　　D

industrial cities today.

　　＜解答＞　B：is

837. Hummingbirds are <u>the only birds</u> capable <u>to fly</u> backward <u>as well as</u> <u>forward</u>,
A　　　　　　　B　　　　　C　　D

up, and down.

　　＜解答＞　B：of flying

838. Angie's bilingual ability and previous experience <u>were</u> the qualities <u>that which</u>
A　　　　　　　B

<u>helped her</u> get the job over all <u>the other</u> candidates.
C　　　　　　　　D

　　＜解答＞　B：① that ② which

839. They asked me <u>what did happen</u> <u>last night</u>, but I was <u>unable to</u> <u>tell them</u>.
A　　　　　B　　　　　　C　　　D

　　＜解答＞　A：what happened

840. <u>Our new</u> neighbors <u>had been living</u> in Arizona <u>since</u> ten years <u>before moving</u>
A　　　　　　B　　　　　　C　　　　　D

<u>to</u> their present house.

　　＜解答＞　C：for

841. We are <u>suppose to</u> read <u>all of chapter</u> seven and <u>answer</u> the questions
A　　　　　B　　　　　　C

<u>for tomorrow's class</u>.
D

　　＜解答＞　A：supposed to

842. <u>In the sixteenth century</u>, Spain <u>became involved in foreign</u> wars with
A　　　　　　　　　B

several other European countries and could not find the means of finance

    C   D

the battles that ensued.

＜解答＞ D：of financing

843. Neither of the girls have turned in the term papers to the instructor yet.

                 A   B   C   D

＜解答＞ B：has

844. The book that you see laying on the table belongs to the teacher.

          A   B   C   D

＜解答＞ C：lying

845. She is looking forward to go to Europe after she finishes her studies at the

        A   B   C   D

university.

＜解答＞ B：going

846. Mr. Anderson used to jogging in the crisp morning air during the winter

                     A   B   C   D

months, but now he has stopped.

＜解答＞ A：jog

847. I do not know where could he have gone so early in the morning.

                    A   B   C   D

＜解答＞ A：he could have

848. The professor was considering postponing the examination until the following

                   A   B   C

week because the students' confusion.

        D

＜解答＞ D：because of

849. The congressman, accompanied by secret service agents and aides, are

                              A   B

preparing to enter the convention hall within the next few minutes.

          C   D

<解答>　B：is

850. Lack <u>of sanitation</u> in restaurants <u>are</u> a major <u>cause of</u> disease <u>in some areas of</u>
　　　　　　　A　　　　　　　　　B　　　　　C　　　　　　　　D
the country.

<解答>　B：is

851. Malnutrition <u>is a major</u> cause of death <u>in those countries</u> where the cultivation
　　　　　　　　　　A　　　　　　　　　　　B
of rice <u>have</u> been impeded <u>by recurrent drought</u>.
　　　　　C　　　　　　　　　　D

<解答>　C：has

852. <u>Underutilized</u> species of fish <u>has been</u> proposed <u>as</u> a solution <u>to the famine</u>
　　　　A　　　　　　　　　　B　　　　　　C　　　　　　D
in many underdeveloped countries.

<解答>　B：have been

853. John's wisdom teeth <u>were troubling</u> him, so he went to a dental surgeon
　　　　　　　　　　　A
<u>to see about</u> having <u>them</u> <u>pull</u>.
　　　B　　　　　　　C　　D

<解答>　D：pulled

854. Suzy <u>had</u> better <u>to change</u> her study habits if she <u>hopes to be</u> admitted
　　　　　A　　　　B　　　　　　　　　　　　C
<u>to a good university</u>.
　　　D

<解答>　B：change

855. Some bacteria <u>are extremely</u> harmful, but <u>another</u> are <u>regularly</u> used in
　　　　　　　　A　　　　　　　　　　B　　　　C
producing cheeses, crackers, and <u>many other foods</u>.
　　　　　　　　　　　　　　　　　D

<解答>　B：others

856. <u>Most</u> Americans would not be happy <u>without</u> <u>a</u> color television, two cars,

      A   B   C

and <u>working</u> at an extra job.

          D

<解答>　D：cancel

857. <u>All</u> the scouts got <u>theirselves</u> ready for <u>the</u> long camping trip by spending

    A   B   C

their weekends <u>living</u> in the open.

                 D

<解答>　B：themselves

858. In 1927 Charles Lindbergh <u>was</u> the first <u>to fly</u> solo nonstop from New York

                                A   B

to Paris <u>in</u> <u>such short time</u>.

           C   D

<解答>　D：such a short time

859. When I <u>last</u> saw Janet, she <u>hurried</u> to her next class on <u>the other</u> side of

             A   B   C

the campus and <u>did not have</u> time to talk.

               D

<解答>　B：was hurrying

860. Patrick was very late <u>getting home</u> last night, and unfortunately <u>for him</u>,

                    A   B

the <u>dog</u> barking woke everyone <u>up</u>.

      C   D

<解答>　C：dog's

861. <u>After driving</u> for twenty miles, he suddenly <u>realized</u> that he <u>has been</u> <u>driving</u>

    A   B   C   D

in the wrong direction.

<解答>　C：had been driving

862. The Nobel prize winning candidate, accompanied <u>by</u> his wife and children,

                                                      A

<u>are</u> staying in Sweden <u>until</u> <u>after</u> the presentation.
  B   C   D

＜解答＞ B：is

863. <u>Those of</u> you who signed up <u>for</u> Dr. Daniel's anthropology class should get

      A   B

<u>their</u> books as soon <u>as possible</u>.
  C   D

＜解答＞ C：your

864. <u>Marta</u> being <u>chosen</u> as the <u>most outstanding</u> student on her campus

   A   B   C

<u>made her parents</u> very happy.
       D

＜解答＞ A：Marta's

865. <u>When Cliff was sick</u> with the flu, his mother made <u>him</u> <u>to eat</u> chicken soup

       A   B   C

and <u>rest</u> in bed.
     D

＜解答＞ C：eat

866. <u>The</u> geology professor showed <u>us</u> a sample <u>about</u> volcanic rock which dated

  A   B   C

<u>back</u> seven hundred years.
  D

＜解答＞ C：of

867. Ralph <u>has called</u> his lawyer last night <u>to tell</u> him about his problems,

         A   B

but was told <u>that</u> the lawyer <u>had gone</u> to a lecture.
            C   D

＜解答＞ A：called

868. <u>The</u> results of the test proved <u>to</u> Fred and <u>me</u> that we needed to study harder
  A   B   C

 and watch <u>less</u> movies on television if we wanted to receive scholarship.
      D

  <解答> D：fewer

869. Because there are <u>less</u> members present tonight <u>than</u> there <u>were</u> last night,
        A   B   C

 we must wait until the next meeting <u>to vote</u>.
              D

  <解答> A：fewer

870. The <u>progress</u> <u>made</u> <u>in space</u> travel <u>for</u> the early 1960s is remarkable.
     A   B   C   D

  <解答> D：since

871. <u>The</u> governor <u>has</u> not decided <u>how to deal with</u> the new problems <u>already</u>.
  A   B   C   D

  <解答> D：yet

872. The professor had already given <u>the homework assignment</u> when he
             A

 <u>had remembered</u> that <u>Monday</u> <u>was</u> a holiday.
    B   C   D

  <解答> B：remembered

873. This table is <u>not sturdy enough</u> <u>to support</u> a television, and <u>that one</u>
       A   B   C

 probably isn't <u>neither</u>.
       D

  <解答> D：either

874. <u>The company</u> representative sold <u>to the manager</u> a <u>sewing</u> machine <u>for</u>
   A   B   C   D

 forty dollars.

  <解答> B：the manager

875. These television are <u>quite</u> popular <u>in</u> Europe, but <u>those ones</u> <u>are</u> not.

                        A   B   C   D

    ＜解答＞ C：those

876. The <u>price</u> of crude oil used to be a <u>great</u> deal <u>lower</u> than now, <u>wasn't it</u>?

             A   B   C   D

    ＜解答＞ D：didn't it

877. Jim was <u>upset</u> last night <u>because</u> he <u>had to do</u> too <u>many homeworks</u>.

               A   B   C   D

    ＜解答＞ D：much homework

878. The Board of Realtors doesn't have any <u>informations</u> <u>about</u> the <u>increase</u>

                                         A   B   C

<u>in rent for</u> this area.

   D

    ＜解答＞ A：information

879. <u>There were</u> so <u>much</u> people trying to leave <u>the burning</u> building <u>that</u> the

        A   B   C   D

police had a great deal of trouble controlling them.

    ＜解答＞ B：many

880. The fire began <u>in</u> the <u>fifth</u> floor <u>of</u> the hotel, but it <u>soon spread</u> to

                A   B   C   D

adjacent floors.

    ＜解答＞ A：on

881. Janet is finally used to <u>cook</u> on an electric stove <u>after having</u> a gas <u>one</u>

                           A   B   C

<u>for so long</u>.

   D

    ＜解答＞ A：cooking

882. Stuart stopped <u>to write</u> his letter <u>because</u> he had to <u>leave</u> <u>for the hospital</u>.

                        A   B   C   D

    ＜解答＞ A：writing

883. How <u>much</u> times <u>did Rick and Jennifer have</u> to do the experiment before

         A   B

    they <u>obtained the results</u> they had <u>been expecting</u>.

                  C   D

    ＜解答＞ A：many

884. Mrs Steven, along <u>with her cousins from</u> New Mexico <u>are</u> planning <u>to attend</u>

                        A   B   C   D

    the festivities.

    ＜解答＞ C：is

885. All the <u>students</u> <u>are</u> looking <u>forward spending</u> <u>their</u> free time relaxing

              A   B   C   D

    in the sun this summer.

    ＜解答＞ C：forward to spending

886. Mary and <u>her sister</u> <u>just bought</u> <u>two new</u> <u>winters</u> coate at the clearance sale.

                A   B   C   D

    ＜解答＞ D：winter

887. Some of us <u>have to</u> study <u>their</u> lessons <u>more carefully</u> if we expect <u>to pass</u>

                A   B   C   D

    this examination.

    ＜解答＞ B：our

888. The instructor advised the students <u>for</u> the <u>procedures</u> to <u>follow</u> <u>in writing</u>

                                A   B   C   D

    the term paper.

    ＜解答＞ A：on

889. The new technique <u>calls</u> for <u>heat</u> the mixture before <u>applying</u> <u>it to the wood</u>.

                          A   B   C   D

    ＜解答＞ B：heating

890. <u>A</u> five-thousand-<u>dollars</u> reward <u>was offered</u> <u>for the capture</u> of the escaped

    A   B   C   D

    criminals.

　　　　　<解答>　B：dollar

891.　A liter is one of the metric measurements, aren't they ?
　　　A　　　　　　B　　　　　　　C　　　　　　D
　　　<解答>　D：isn't it

892.　There are a large supply of pens and notebooks in the storeroom to the left of
　　　　　A　　　　　　　　　B　　　　　　　　　　　C　　　　　D
　　　the library entrance.
　　　<解答>　A：is

893.　They are planning on attending the convention next month, and so I am.
　　　　　　　A　　　　　B　　　　　　　　　C　　　　　D
　　　<解答>　D：so am I

894.　While they were away at the beach, they allowed their neighbors use
　　　A　　　　B　　　　　　　　　　　　　　　　　B　　　　D
　　　their barbeque grill.
　　　<解答>　D：to use

895.　Mumpa are a very common disease which usually affects children.
　　　　　　　A　　　　　B　　　　C　　D
　　　<解答>　A：is

896.　Before she moved here, Arlene had been president of the organization since
　　　A　　　　　　　　　　　　　　　B　　　　　C　　　　　　D
　　　four years.
　　　<解答>　D：for

897.　The athlete, together with his coach and several relatives, are traveling to
　　　　　A　　　　　B　　C　　　　　　　　　　D
　　　the Olympic Games.
　　　<解答>　D：is

898.　My brother is in California on vacation, but I wish he was here so that he
　　　　　　　　A　　　　　　B　　　　　　　　　　C
　　　could help me repair my car.
　　　　　　　　D

<解答> C：were

899. The chemistry instructor explained the experiment <u>in</u> <u>such of a way</u> that it

                                          A   B

<u>was</u> <u>easily understood</u>.

  C   D

<解答> B：such a way

900. He has <u>less</u> friends in <u>his</u> classes now <u>than</u> he had last <u>year</u>.

        A   B   C   D

<解答> A：fewer

901. The influence of the <u>nation's</u> literature, art and <u>science</u> <u>have</u> captured

                    A   B   C

<u>widespread</u> attention.

      D

<解答> C：has

902. <u>Many</u> of the population in the <u>rural areas</u> is <u>composed of</u> manual <u>laborers</u>.

  A   B   C   D

<解答> A：Much

903. Keith is one of <u>the</u> <u>most</u> intelligent boys <u>of</u> the <u>science</u> class.

          A B   C   D

<解答> C：in

904. When Keith visited Alaska, he <u>lived</u> in <u>a</u> igloo in the winter <u>months</u> <u>as well as</u>

                              A   B   C   D

in the spring.

<解答> B：an

905. Although a number of police officers, <u>was guarding</u> the priceless <u>treasures in</u>

                                   A   B

the museum, the director worried that someone <u>would try to</u> <u>steal</u> them.

                                         C   D

<解答> A：were guarding

906. Louis Braille designed a form of communication <u>enabling</u> people <u>to convey</u>
A   B

and preserve their thoughts <u>to incorporate</u> a series of dots which <u>were read</u>
C   D

by the finger tips.

＜解答＞　C：by incorporating

907. The need <u>for</u> a <u>well-rounded education</u> was an idea <u>espoused</u> by the Greeks
A   B   C

<u>in time of</u> Socrates.

 D

＜解答＞　D：in the time of

908. <u>In the spirit</u> of the <u>naturalist</u> writers, the <u>author's</u> work portrays man's struggle
A   B   C

for <u>surviving</u>.

 D

＜解答＞　D：survival

909. Their silly, whiny conversation <u>on a child level</u> was meant <u>to create</u> tension
A   B

and <u>heighten</u> <u>Nancy's fears</u> and anxiety.
C D

＜解答＞　A：① on a childish level ② on a child's level

910. Nora hardly <u>never</u> misses <u>an</u> opportunity <u>to play</u> <u>in</u> the tennis tournaments.
A   B   C D

＜解答＞　A：ever

911. <u>Because of</u> the severe snow storm and the road blocks, <u>the</u> air force
A   B

<u>dropped food</u> and medical supplies <u>close the city</u>.
C   D

＜解答＞　D：close to the city

912. <u>The</u> news of the president's treaty negotiations with the foreign government

    A

    <u>were</u> <u>received with mixed emotions</u> by the citizens <u>of both governments</u>.

     B   C   D

    ＜解答＞　B：was

913. <u>Joel</u> giving up <u>smoking has</u> <u>caused him to gain</u> weight and <u>become irritable</u>

    A   B   C   D

    with his acquaintances.

    ＜解答＞　A：Joel's

914. The <u>test</u> administrator ordered <u>we</u> <u>not to open</u> our books until he

          A   B   C

    <u>told us to do so</u>.

          D

    ＜解答＞　B：us

915. I <u>would of </u>attened the meeting <u>of the planning</u> committee last week, but I

        A   B

    <u>had to deliver</u> a speech <u>at a convention</u>.

          C   D

    ＜解答＞　A：would have

916. The explanation that <u>our</u> instructor <u>gave us</u> was different <u>than</u> the one

                       A   B   C

    <u>yours gave you</u>.

          D

    ＜解答＞　C：from

917. <u>After studying</u> <u>all the new</u> materials, the student <u>was able</u> to <u>rise</u> his test

         A   B   C   D

    score by twenty-five points.

    ＜解答＞　D：raise

918. I suggest <u>that</u> he <u>goes</u> <u>to the doctor</u> as soon as he <u>returns from</u> taking the exam.

              A   B   C   D

<解答>　B：go

919. They said <u>that</u> the man <u>jumped</u> off <u>of</u> the bridge and <u>plunged into</u> the
             A　　　　　　　　B　　C　　　　　　　　　D

    freezing water.

    <解答>　C：cancel

920. <u>The volume</u> four of <u>our</u> encyclopedia set <u>has been missing</u> <u>for</u> two months.
        A　　　　　　B　　　　　　　　　　C　　　　D

    <解答>　A：Volume

921. The people tried <u>of defending</u> <u>their</u> village, but they were finally <u>forced</u>
                A　　　　B　　　　　　　　　　　　　C

    <u>to retreat</u>.
      D

    <解答>　A：to defend

922. <u>Having lost</u> the election, the presidential candidate intends <u>supporting</u>
      A　　　　　　　　　　　　　　　　　　　　　　　　　B

    the opposition <u>despite</u> <u>the objection of</u> his staff.
              C　　　　D

    <解答>　B：to support

923. <u>Because</u> the <u>torrential</u> rains that <u>had devastated</u> the area, the governor
      A　　　　　B　　　　　　　C

    sent the National Guard <u>to assist in</u> the clean-up operation.
                   D

    <解答>　A：Because of

924. <u>Had the committee members</u> considered the alternatives <u>more carefully</u>,
             A　　　　　　　　　　　　　　　　　　　　　　B

    they would have realized that the <u>second was</u> better <u>as the first</u>.
                     C　　　　　　D

    <解答>　D：than the first

925. The decision <u>to withdraw</u> <u>all support</u> from the activities of the athletes
            A　　　　　　B

are causing an uproar among the athletes, fans.

      C   D

＜解答＞ C：is causing

926. Because the residents had worked so diligent to renovate the old building,

     A   B   C   D

the manager had a party.

＜解答＞ C：diligently

927. Hardly he had entered the office when he realized that he had forgotten his

       A   B   C   D

wallet.

＜解答＞ A：Hardly had he

928. The teacher told the students to don't discuss the take-home exam

         A   B   C

with each other.

       D

＜解答＞ B：not to

929. The lion has long been a symbol of strength, power, and it is very cruel.

    A   B   C   D

＜解答＞ D：cruelty

930. Nobody had known before the presentation that Sue and her sister

        A   B

will receive the awards for outstanding scholarship.

    C   D

＜解答＞ C：would receive

931. Until his last class at the university in 1978, Bob always turns in all of his

   A   B   C

assignments on time.

       D

＜解答＞ B：turned

932. <u>Before we returned</u> from swimming in the river near the camp, someone
　　　　　　A

<u>had stole</u> our clothes, and we had to walk <u>back</u> with our towels around us.
　　B　　　　　　　　　　　　　　　　　C

＜解答＞　B：had stolen

933. He <u>has been hoped</u> for a raise for the <u>last</u> four months, but his boss is
　　　　　　A　　　　　　　　　　　　B

reluctant <u>to give</u> him <u>one</u>.
　　　　　　C　　　　D

＜解答＞　A：has been hoping

934. <u>The</u> Department of Foreign Languages <u>are</u> not located <u>in</u> the new builing
　　　A　　　　　　　　　　　　　　　B　　　　　　　C

<u>opposite</u> the old one.
　　D

＜解答＞　B：is

935. Neither <u>of the</u> scout leaders <u>know</u> how to trap wild animals <u>or</u> how to
　　　　　　A　　　　　　　B　　　　　　　　　　　　　　C

prepare them <u>for mounting</u>.
　　　　　　　　D

＜解答＞　B：knows

936. I put my new <u>book of zoology</u> here on <u>the</u> desk a few minutes <u>ago</u>,
　　　　　　　　A　　　　　　　　B　　　　　　　　　　C

but <u>I cannot seem to find it</u>.
　　　　　　D

＜解答＞　A：zoology book

937. Jane said she would <u>borrow</u> <u>me</u> her new movie camera if I <u>wanted</u> to use
　　　　　　　　　　　A　　B　　　　　　　　　　　　　　C

it <u>on my trip to Europe</u>.
　　　D

＜解答＞　A：① loan ② lend

938. My cousin <u>composes not only</u> the music, <u>but</u> also sings <u>the songs for</u> the <u>major</u>
                           A   B   C   D

Broadway musicals.

  ＜解答＞ A：not only composes

939. <u>The</u> girl <u>whom</u> my cousin married <u>was used</u> to be a chorus girl <u>for</u> the
     A   B   C   D

Rockettes in Radio City Music Hall in New York.

  ＜解答＞ C：used

940. Some bumper stickers <u>are</u> very funny and make us <u>laugh</u>, yet <u>another</u> can
                               A   B   C

make us angry because of their <u>ridiculousness</u>.
                                   D

  ＜解答＞ C：others

941. Buying clothes <u>are</u> often <u>a very time-consuming</u> practice <u>because those</u> clothes
                      A   B   C

that a person likes <u>are rarely the ones</u> that fit him or her.
                          D

  ＜解答＞ A：is

942. <u>There</u> television are <u>all too expensive</u> for <u>we to buy</u> at <u>this time</u>, but perhaps
     A   B   C   D

we will return later.

  ＜解答＞ C：us to buy

943. The next <u>important</u> question we have to <u>decide</u> is when <u>do we have to</u> <u>submit</u>
               A   B   C   D

the proposal.

  ＜解答＞ C：we haver to

944. John decided <u>to buy</u> <u>in the morning a new car</u>, but <u>in the afternoon</u>
                     A   B   C

<u>he changed his mind</u>.
        D

<解答> B：a new car in the morning

945. After George <u>had returned</u> <u>to his house</u>, <u>he</u> <u>was reading</u> a book.
                           A   B   C   D

<解答>D：read

946. <u>The food</u> that Mark <u>is cooking</u> in the kitchen <u>is smelling</u> <u>delicious</u>.
        A   B   C   D

<解答> C：smells

947. The manager <u>has finished</u> <u>working</u> <u>on the report</u> last night, and now she will
                       A   B   C

begin <u>to write</u> the other proposal.
        D

<解答> A：finished

948. Daniel said that <u>if he had to</u> do <u>another</u> homework tonight, he <u>would not be</u>
                  A   B   C

<u>able</u> <u>to attend</u> the concert.
        D

<解答> B：any more

949. We insist on <u>you</u> <u>leaving</u> the meeting <u>before</u> any <u>further outbursts</u> take place.
                A   B   C   D

<解答> A：your

950. Henry objects to <u>our buying</u> this house <u>without the approval</u> <u>of our attorney</u>,
                      A   B   C

and <u>John does so</u>.
        D

<解答> D：① John does too ② so does John

951. <u>After being</u> indicted <u>for</u> his part in a bank robbery, <u>the reputed</u> mobster
     A   B   C

decided <u>find</u> another attorney.
        D

<解答> D：to find

952. <u>The only</u> teachers <u>who were</u> required <u>to attend</u> the meeting were George, Betty,
　　　　A　　　　　　　　　B　　　　　　　　C

Jill, and <u>me</u>.
　　　　　D

　　＜解答＞ D：I

953. <u>The</u> President went <u>fishing</u> <u>after</u> he <u>has finished</u> with the conferences.
　　　A　　　　　　　　B　　　C　　　　D

　　＜解答＞ D：had finished

954. There <u>were</u> a time that I <u>used to swim</u> five laps every <u>day</u>, but now I do not
　　　　　　A　　　　　　　B　　　　　　　　　　　C

<u>have enough time</u>.
　　　D

　　＜解答＞ A：was

955. We <u>called</u> <u>yesterday our friends in Boston</u> <u>to tell</u> <u>them about</u> the reunion that
　　　　A　　　　　B　　　　　　　　　C　　　　D

we are planning.

　　＜解答＞ B：our friends in Boston yesterday

956. <u>Those</u> homework that your teacher <u>assigned</u> is due <u>on Tuesday</u> unless you
　　　A　　　　　　　　　　　　B　　　　　　C

<u>have made</u> prior arrangements to turn it in late.
　　　D

　　＜解答＞ A：That

957. <u>There are</u> ten <u>childs</u> playing in the yard near her house, but <u>your child</u> is not
　　　A　　　B　　　　　　　　　　　　　　　　C

<u>among them</u>.
　　　D

　　＜解答＞ B：children

958. He isn's <u>driving</u> to <u>the</u> convention <u>in March</u>, and <u>neither they are</u>.
　　　　　　A　　　B　　　　　　C　　　　　D

　　＜解答＞ D：① neither are they ② they aren't either

959. The company <u>has</u> <u>so little</u> money <u>that it</u> <u>can't hardly</u> operate anymore.
               A   B   C   D

    ＜解答＞ D：can hardly

960. The students <u>were</u> <u>interested</u> <u>in take</u> a field trip to The National History
               A   B   C

   Museum, but they <u>were not able to raise</u> enough money.
                            D

    ＜解答＞ D：in taking

961. <u>Us students</u> <u>would rather not attend</u> night classes in the summer, but <u>we</u> often
     A   B   C

   <u>have to</u>.
    D

    ＜解答＞ A：We

962. It was <u>him</u> <u>who</u> came running <u>into the classroom</u> <u>with the news</u>.
          A   B   C   D

    ＜解答＞ A：he

963. <u>Mary and her</u> sister <u>studied</u> biology <u>last year,</u> and <u>so does Jean</u>.
       A   B   C   D

    ＜解答＞ D：so did Jean

964. There's <u>a</u> <u>new</u> Oriental restaurant <u>in town,</u> <u>isn't it</u> ?
         A B   C   D

    ＜解答＞ D：isn't there

965. The professor <u>is</u> thinking <u>to go</u> to the conference <u>on aerodynamics</u> <u>next month</u>.
                 A   B   C   D

    ＜解答＞ B：of going

966. Children enjoy <u>telling and listening</u> to <u>ghosts stories</u>, <u>especially</u>
                 A   B   C

   <u>on Halloween night</u>.
         D

    ＜解答＞ B：ghost stories

967. No one would have <u>attended</u> the lecture if you <u>told</u> <u>the truth about</u> the
　　　　　　　　　　A　　　　　　　　　　B　　　　C

　guest speaker.
　　D
　＜解答＞ B：had told

968. <u>The</u> little boy's mother bought <u>him</u> a <u>five-speeds</u> racing bicycle <u>for his</u>
　birthday.
　A　　　　　　　　　　　　B　　　C　　　　　　　　D
　＜解答＞ C：five speed

969. <u>The Andersons</u> <u>just had</u> an enclosed <u>bricks patio</u> built <u>after fighting off</u> the
　　　　A　　　　　B　　　　　　　　　C　　　　　　　D

　insects for two months.
　＜解答＞ C：brick patio

970. <u>Although</u> the quantity <u>was</u> small, we had <u>supplies enough</u> to finish <u>the</u>
　　　A　　　　　　　　B　　　　　　　　　C　　　　　　　D

　experiment.
　＜解答＞ C：enough supplies

971. If Rudy <u>would have studied</u> German <u>in college</u>, he would not have found
　　　　　　　A　　　　　　　　　　B

　<u>the scientific</u> terminology <u>so difficult to understand</u>.
　　　C　　　　　　　　　　D
　＜解答＞ A：had studied

972. We wish today <u>was</u> sunny <u>so that</u> we <u>could spend</u> the day <u>in the country</u>
　　　　　　　A　　　　B　　　C　　　　　　D

　communing with nature.
　＜解答＞ A：were

973. Bess is used to <u>fly</u> after <u>having crossed</u> the continent <u>many times</u> during
　　　　　　　A　　　　　B　　　　　　　　C

　the <u>past decade</u>.
　　　D

<解答>　A：flying

974. Sam used to <u>living</u> in Oklaloma, <u>but</u> his company <u>had him transferred</u> to
　　　　　　　A　　　　　　　　　　B　　　　　　　　　　　C

a better position in Georgia.
<u>　　　　　　</u>
　D

<解答>　A：live

975. Hal's new <u>sports</u> car <u>costs</u> <u>much more</u> than his <u>friend Joel</u>.
　　　　　　　A　　　　B　　　C　　　　　　　　D

<解答>　D：friend Joel's

976. Sally <u>must have called</u> her sister last night, but she <u>arrived</u> home <u>too late</u>
　　　　　　A　　　　　　　　　　　　　　　　　　B　　　　　　C

to call <u>her</u>.
　　　D

<解答>　A：should have called

977. <u>Standing among</u> so many strangers, <u>the frightened</u> child began <u>to sob</u>
　　　A　　　　　　　　　　　　　　　B　　　　　　　　　　　C

<u>uncontrollable</u>.
　D

<解答>　D：uncontrollably

978. Whenever students asked <u>for help</u> or guidance, the counselor <u>would advise</u>
　　　　　　　　　　　　　A　　　　　　　　　　　　　　　　　B

<u>them or refer them</u> to someone who <u>will</u>.
　　　　C　　　　　　　　　　　　　　D

<解答>　D：would

979. The teachers and the administrators are having <u>such difficult</u> time <u>agreeing</u>
　　　　　　　　　　　　　　　　　　　　　　　　A　　　　　　B

on a contract for <u>the forthcoming year</u> that the teachers <u>may go on strike</u>.
　　　　　　　　　C　　　　　　　　　　　　　　　　D

<解答>　A：such a difficult

980. Our new television <u>came</u> with a <u>ninety-days warranty</u> <u>on all</u> <u>electrical</u>
                              A   B   C   D

components.
<解答>　B：ninety-day warranty

981. The director felt <u>badly</u> about <u>not giving</u> Mary the position <u>that</u> she <u>had sought</u>
                    A   B   C   D

with his company.
<解答>　A：bad

982. <u>The</u> political candidate talked as if she <u>has</u> already <u>been elected</u> <u>to the</u>
  A   B   C   D

presidency.
<解答>　B：had

983. <u>Even though</u> she <u>looks</u> very young, she is twice <u>older than</u> my <u>twenty-year-old</u>
     A   B   C   D

sister.
<解答>　C：as old as

984. I do not believe that I <u>have ever seen</u> as many expensive cars <u>than</u> <u>were</u> in
                      A   B C

<u>that shopping center</u>.
        D
<解答>　B：as

985. We thought our cameras were <u>the same</u>, but <u>his is</u> different <u>than</u> the one
                     A   B   C

that I <u>bought</u>.
        D
<解答>　C：from

986. <u>Having lived</u> here <u>for</u> seven years, my friend is used to <u>speak</u> English with
     A   B   C

<u>all her</u> classmates.
    D

<解答>　C：speaking

987. That novel is <u>definitely</u> a <u>dense-packed</u> narrative, but <u>one which requires</u>
       A   B   C

a vast knowledge of cultural background or <u>an</u> excellent encyclopedia.
                D

<解答>　B：densely packed

988. They <u>played</u> <u>so good game</u> of tennis last night <u>that</u> they surprised <u>their</u> audience.
    A B   C   D

<解答>　B：① so good a game ② such a good game

989. <u>Among us</u> students are <u>many foreigners</u> <u>who</u> attend <u>languages</u> classes at the
  A   B   C   D

south campus.

<解答>　D：language

990. That product that you <u>bought</u> at the lower price is <u>the more inferior</u> to the
       A   B

<u>one</u> that we sell at a <u>slightly</u> higher price.
 C   D

<解答>　B：inferior

991. <u>Writers</u> <u>like</u> William Shakespeare and Edgar Allan Poe <u>are</u> not only prolific
 A B   C

<u>but too interesting</u>.
   D

<解答>　D：but also interesting

992. Although Mark has <u>been cooking</u> for many years, he <u>still</u> doesn't <u>know</u>
       A   B   C

to prepare French foods <u>in the traditional manner</u>.
        D

<解答>　C：know how

993. <u>Visitors</u> were not permitted <u>entering</u> the park after dark <u>because of</u> the lack <u>of</u>
 A   B   C   D

security and lighting.

　　＜解答＞　B：to enter

994.　In spite Nellie's fear of heights, she decided to fly with a group of her
　　　　A　　　　　　　　　　　　　　　　　　B

　　　classmates to the Bahamas during the spring recess.
　　　　　　　　　　C　　　　　　D

　　＜解答＞　A：① In spite of ② Despite

995.　After rising the flag to commemorate the holiday, the mayor gave a long speech.
　　　　　　A　　　　　　B　　　　　C　　　　　　　　　D

　　＜解答＞　A：raising

996.　Louie got his sister read his class assignment, and then asked her to write the
　　　　　　　　　　　A　　　　　　　　　　　　　　　　　　　B

　　　report for him because he did not have enough time.
　　　　　　C　　　　　　　　　　　D

　　＜解答＞　A：to read

997.　News of Charles Lindergh's famous transatlantic flight in 1927 spread rapidly
　　　　A　　　　　　　　　　　　　　　　　　　　　　　　B

　　　despite of the lack of an international communication system.
　　　　C　　　　　　　D

　　＜解答＞　C：① despite ② in spite of

998.　The piano teacher requires that her student practices at least
　　　　　　　　　　　　　　A　　　　　B

　　　forty-five minutes every day in preparation for next week's recital.
　　　　C　　　　　　　　　　D

　　＜解答＞　B：practice

999.　If you set in that position for too long, you may get a cramp in your leg.
　　　　　A　　B　　　　　　　　C　　　　　　　D

　　＜解答＞　A：sit

1000.The conquerors stole not only the gold and silver that were needed to
　　　　　　　　　　　　　　　A　　　　　　　　B

replenish the <u>badly</u> depleted treasury but also the supplies that were vital

       C

to the colonists <u>as well</u>.

       D

<解答> D：cancel

1001. Did you <u>know how</u> that the actors' strike <u>will delay</u> the beginning <u>of the new</u>

      A   B   C

television season and <u>cause the</u> cancellation of many contracts ?

         D

<解答> A：know

1002. When we arrived <u>at the</u> store to <u>purchase</u> the dishwasher <u>advertise</u> in

       A   B   C

the newspaper, we learned that all the dishwashers had <u>been sold</u>.

                D

<解答> C：① advertised ② that had been advertised

1003. The director encouraged them <u>work</u> in committees <u>to plan</u> <u>a more effective</u>

          A   B   C

advertising campaign <u>for the new</u> product.

        D

<解答> A：to work

1004. Mr. Harris will <u>be divided</u> <u>the</u> biology class <u>into two-sections</u> to prevent

      A   B   C

<u>overcrowding</u> in his classroom.

    D

<解答> A：divided

1005. Maribel <u>has registered</u> for both the afternoon anthropology class <u>as well as</u>

      A   B

the evening <u>sociology lecture</u>.

   C   D

<解答> B：and

1006. The man, <u>of whom the</u> red car is <u>parked</u> in front <u>of our house</u>, <u>is a</u> prominent
                      A   B   C   D

     physician in this town.

     ＜解答＞ A：whose

1007. The proposal <u>has repealed</u> after a <u>thirty-minute</u> discussion and <u>a number of</u>
                       A   B   C

     objections <u>to its failure</u> to include our district.
                     D

     ＜解答＞ A：has been repealed

1008. <u>In spite of</u> the <u>tenant's objections</u>, the apartment manager decided <u>to rise</u>
    A   B   C

     the rent <u>by forty-dollars</u> per month.
                 D

     ＜解答＞ C：to raise

1009. The doctor <u>told Mr. Anderson that</u>, <u>because</u> of his severe cramps, he should
                        A   B

     <u>lay</u> in bed <u>for a few</u> days.
     C   D

     ＜解答＞ C：lie

1010. Dr. Harder, <u>which</u> is the professor for this class, <u>will</u> be absent <u>this week</u>
               A   B   C

     because <u>of illness</u>.
              D

     ＜解答＞ A：who

1011. This class <u>has cancelled</u> <u>because</u> <u>too few</u> students <u>had registered</u> before
               A   B   C   D

     registration closed.

     ＜解答＞ A：has been cancelled

1012. The problems that <u>discovered</u> <u>since</u> the initial research <u>had been completed</u>
                          A   B   C

caused the committee members <u>to table</u> the proposed temporarity.

D

<解答> A：were discovered

1013. Dr. Alvarez was <u>displeased</u> because the student <u>had turned in an</u> <u>unacceptable</u>

A   B   C

report, <u>so</u> he made him <u>to rewrite</u> it.

D

<解答> D：rewrite

1014. <u>Although</u> the danger that he might <u>be injured</u>, Boris <u>bravely centered the</u>

A   B   C

burning house in order to save the <u>youngster</u>.

D

<解答> A：① In spite of ② Despite

1015. <u>Despite Martha's attempts</u> <u>to rise</u> her test score, she did not receive

A   B

<u>a high enough</u> score <u>to be accepted</u> by the law school.

C   D

<解答> B：to raise

1016. When the tank car <u>carried</u> the <u>toxic</u> gas derailed, the firemen <u>tried</u> to isolate

A   B   C

the village <u>from</u> all traffic.

D

<解答> A：carrying

1017. If motorists do <u>not observe</u> <u>the</u> traffic regulations, <u>they</u> will be stopped,

A   B   C

ticketed, and <u>have to pay a fine</u>.

D

<解答> D：fined

1018. <u>A short time</u> before her operation <u>last</u> month, Mrs. Carlyle <u>dreams</u> of her

A   B   C

daughter who <u>lives overseas</u>.
$\qquad$ D

＜解答＞ C：dreamed

1019. <u>Now that</u> they have <u>successfully</u> passed the TOEFL, the students <u>were</u> ready

$\quad$ A $\qquad$ B $\qquad$ C

<u>to begin</u> their classes at the university.

$\quad$ D

＜解答＞ C：are

1020. Some <u>of the</u> people were <u>standing</u> in the street <u>watched</u> the parade, while

$\qquad$ A $\qquad$ B $\qquad$ C

<u>others</u> were singing songs.

$\quad$ D

＜解答＞ C：watching

1021. As soon as Pete <u>had arrived</u>, he told <u>us</u> that he <u>will be leaving</u> for London

$\qquad$ A $\qquad$ B $\qquad$ C

tomorrow after <u>the</u> board meeting.

$\qquad$ D

＜解答＞ C：would be leaving

1022. <u>The</u> teacher repeated the assignment <u>again</u> for the students, <u>since they</u> had

$\quad$ A $\qquad$ B $\qquad$ C

difficulty understanding what to do after he <u>had explained</u> it the first time.

$\qquad$ D

＜解答＞ B：cancel

1023. <u>When</u> you come after class this afternoon, we <u>discussed</u> <u>the</u> possibility of <u>your</u>

$\quad$ A $\qquad$ B $\quad$ C $\qquad$ D

writing a research paper.

＜解答＞ B：will discuss

1024. Having <u>finished</u> his term paper <u>before the</u> deadline, <u>it was delivered</u> to the

$\qquad$ A $\qquad$ B $\qquad$ C

professor <u>before</u> the class.
　　　　　　D

＜解答＞ C：he delivered it

1025. The new student's progress <u>advanced forward</u> with <u>such</u> speed <u>that all</u> his
　　　　　　　　　　　　　　　　　A　　　　　　　　B　　　　　C

teachers <u>were amazed</u>.
　　　　　　D

＜解答＞A：① advanced ② forwarded

1026. In the distance <u>could be seen</u> the <u>sleepy</u> little village with <u>their</u>
　　　　　　　　　　　A　　　　　　B　　　　　　　　　C

<u>closely clustered adobe houses</u> and red, clay-tile roofs.
　　　　　　　D

＜解答＞ C：its

1027. After she had dressed and <u>ate</u> breakfast, Lucy <u>rushed off</u> <u>to her</u> office for
　　　　　　　　　　　　　A　　　　　　　　　　B　　　　C

a meeting <u>with</u> her accountant.
　　　　　　D

＜解答＞ A：eaten

1028. The use <u>of videodisc</u> in the classroom, a <u>potentially powerful educational</u> tool,
　　　　　　A　　　　　　　　　　　　　　　　　　　B

<u>it will not</u> be widespread until <u>prices come down</u>.
　　C　　　　　　　　　　　　　D

＜解答＞ C：will not

1029. The <u>new more stringent</u> requirements <u>for obtaining</u> a driving license
　　　　A　　　　　　　　　　　B

<u>has resulted</u> in <u>traffic accidents</u>.
　　C　　　　　　D

＜解答＞ C：have resulted

1030. <u>Hearing</u> the <u>fire alarm sound</u>, the librarian requested <u>those reading</u> to leave
　　　A　　　　　B　　　　　　　　　　　　　　　C

their books <u>headed for the nearest exit</u>.

                    D

<解答> D：and head for the nearest exit

1031. Marcel Duchamp, <u>who died in 1969</u>, <u>is known</u> <u>as the artist</u> who <u>has abandoned</u>

               A   B   C   D

art for chess.

<解答> D：abandoned

1032. <u>After</u> two weeks of intensive computer training, the new recruits <u>were allowed</u>

  A   B

to <u>write a program</u> <u>theirselves</u>.

      C   D

<解答> D：themselves

1033. Meteorologists <u>have been using both</u> computers <u>or</u> satellites <u>to help make</u>

            A   B   C

weather forecasts <u>for two decades</u>.

            D

<解答> B：and

1034. <u>The Arctic ice pack</u> is <u>40 percent thin</u> and 12 percent less <u>in area</u> <u>than</u> it was

     A   B   C   D

a half century ago.

<解答> B：40 percent thinner

1035. <u>For nesting and shelter</u>, the sparrow <u>seeks out</u> the seclusion <u>and being secure</u>

       A   B   C

offered by tangled vines and <u>thick brushes</u>.

                     D

<解答> C：and security

1036. Aluminum, <u>which making</u> up about 8 percent of <u>the earth's</u> crust, <u>is</u>

         A   B   C

<u>the most abundant</u> metal available.

         D

　　＜解答＞　A：making

1037. Ms. Amelia Earhast, <u>like</u> many of the world's <u>greatest heroes</u>, sacrificed <u>their</u>
　　　　　　　　　　　A　　　　　　　　　　　　　　B　　　　　　　　C

life for the sake <u>of adventure</u>, glory, and country.
　　　　　　　　　　D

　　＜解答＞　C：her

1038. The organizers of the picnic thought <u>they</u> had put <u>enough</u> food <u>on</u> the basket,
　　　　　　　　　　　　　　　　　　　　　　A　　　　　　　B　　　　C

but there obviously was not enough <u>for</u> six hungry people.
　　　　　　　　　　　　　　　　　　　D

　　＜解答＞　C：in

1039. Welcoming the astronaut <u>to the community</u> <u>and prepare</u> a big banquet <u>were</u>
　　　　　　　　　　　　　　　　A　　　　　　　　　B　　　　　　　　　　　C

important responsibilities for the <u>newly formed</u> citizens group.
　　　　　　　　　　　　　　　　　　D

　　＜解答＞　B：and preparing

1040. Sacajawea, <u>the woman Indian</u> <u>who accompanied</u> Lewis and Clark
　　　　　　　　　　A　　　　　　　　B

<u>on their journey</u>, has been the inspiration for <u>countless romantic</u> legends.
　　C　　　　　　　　　　　　　　　　　　　　　　　D

　　＜解答＞　A：the Indian woman

1041. People who follow <u>the</u> pseudoscience astrology, <u>a false science</u>, <u>believe that</u>
　　　　　　　　　　　　A　　　　　　　　　　　　　B　　　　　　C

stars <u>govern</u> the fate of men.
　　　　　D

　　＜解答＞　B：cancel

1042. <u>Using</u> herbal medicines, <u>treat doctors</u> more <u>illness</u> for <u>less cost</u>.
　　　　A　　　　　　　　　　　B　　　　　　C　　　　　D

　　＜解答＞　B：doctors treat

1043. <u>Child labor</u> laws <u>were instituted</u> to protect the <u>neglected long rights</u>
       A   B   C

of <u>children</u>.
   D

＜解答＞ C：long neglected rights

1044. English, <u>is spoken</u> by <u>slightly more than</u> 8 percent of <u>the earth's population</u>,
            A   B   C

is <u>the most common</u> language after Chinese.
     D

＜解答＞ A：spoken

1045. Today's <u>playing cards</u> <u>who are modeled</u> after 18th century English design,
        A   B

trace <u>their</u> roots to <u>Turkey</u>.
   C   D

＜解答＞ B：which are modeled

1046. <u>Upon immigrants</u> arriving in America <u>at the turn</u> of the century, <u>most</u>
     A   B   C

immigrants <u>passed through</u> Ellis Island.
      D

＜解答＞ A：Upon

1047. <u>The</u> system of <u>time measured</u> in 24-hour days is <u>besed upon used</u>
 A   B   C

<u>in ancient Babylon</u>.
   D

＜解答＞ C：based upon the system used

1048. <u>Not able</u> to type accurately <u>would</u> hurt a graduate's chances of <u>finding</u>
   A   B   C

a suitable job <u>as a secretary</u>.
     D

＜解答＞ A：Not being able to

1049. When the government eliminated federal funds for day care centers,
　　　　A　　　　　　　　　　　B

　　many working parents are obliged to take part time jobs.
　　　　　　　　C　　　　　　D

　　＜解答＞　D：parents were obliged

1050. Dame Judith Anderson, an Australian actress, made his professional theater
　　　　　　　　　　　　　　　A　　　　　　　　　B

　　debut in sydney in 1915.
　　　C　　　　　D

　　＜解答＞　B：made her professional

1051. Trade relationships between the two countries have improved if their
　　　　　　　　　　　　A　　　　　　　　　　B　　　　C

　　respective leaders could agree on the propsed quotas.
　　　　　　　　　　　　　　　　　　　D

　　＜解答＞　B：have been improved

1052. Aristotle, the ancient Greek Philosopher, believed that any piece of matter
　　　　　　　　　　　　　　　　　　　　　　　　A　　　　B

　　could be indefinitely cut into smaller and smaller pieces without limit.
　　　　　　　　　　　　　　C　　　　　　　　　D

　　＜解答＞　D：cancel

1053. With all accounts, the defendant was innocent of the heinous crimes for which
　　　A　　　　　　　　　　　　　　　　　　B　　　　　　　　　　C

　　he was being tried.
　　　　D

　　＜解答＞　A：By

1054. High school students need to finish and complete courses in history and
　　　　　　　A　　　　　　　　B　　　　　　　　C

　　science before graduating.
　　　　　D

　　＜解答＞　B：cancel

1055. In postindustrial <u>society factories</u> became <u>less</u> places of <u>hard physics</u> labor
                              A   B   C

    and more places of <u>automated operation</u>.
                        D

    ＜解答＞　C：hard physical

1056. The Forest service <u>accertains that</u> no <u>more timber cut</u> in one year <u>than a single</u>
                        A   B   C

    year's growth <u>can replace</u>.
                  D

    ＜解答＞　B：timber is cut

1057. Fish flour must be proved <u>fit for</u> human <u>consumption</u> <u>although it</u> is
                          A   B   C

    <u>allowed to be</u> distributed to the public.
         D

    ＜解答＞　C：before it

1058. Parents, before <u>they are</u> moving to another state, <u>should consider</u>
                  A   B

    the effect <u>the move</u> may have on <u>their children</u>.
          C   D

    ＜解答＞　A：cancel

1059. Because of <u>the rising cost</u> of living, more families today <u>they are</u> discovering
                    A   B

    that <u>both husband</u> and wife <u>must work</u>.
         C   D

    ＜解答＞　B：are

1060. <u>After given</u> the award, <u>the recipient of</u> the Peace Prize made a short
       A   B

    acceptance speech <u>which was followed</u> by a <u>standing ovation</u>.
                  C   D

    ＜解答＞　A：After being given

1061. The cowboy epitomizes the belief <u>held by</u> many Americans <u>for rugged</u>

                                              A   B

<u>individualism</u> and <u>the frontier spirit</u>.

              C   D

<解答> B：in rugged

1062. <u>Recently</u> gasoline manufacturers have begun to develop <u>additives will reduce</u>

        A   B

the <u>harmful</u> emissions <u>from automobile engines</u>.

              C   D

<解答> B：additives which will reduce

1063. <u>As cooling</u> slows <u>the life</u> process, blood cells in the laboratory <u>is stored</u> at

       A   B   C

<u>low temperatures</u>.

              D

<解答> C：are stored

1064. Rectaurant patrons <u>who stay</u> after 11 o'clock will <u>have to drive, walk, or</u>

                       A   B

take a taxi home <u>unless the subway</u> stops <u>operating</u> then.

                         C   D

<解答> C：because the subway

1065. <u>During</u> the industrial revolution, the <u>birth rate</u> in Europe <u>declined</u>,

     A   B   C

<u>as the death rate</u>.

              D

<解答> D：as did the death rate

1066. Physics is <u>probably being</u> <u>the most</u> highly <u>organized</u> branch of <u>science</u> today.

                    A   B   C   D

<解答> A：probably

1067. People who <u>always</u> on time cannot understand the <u>seemingly</u> intentional

             A   B

tardiness of people <u>who</u> are always late.

        C   D

＜解答＞　A：are always

1068. Man can <u>cotrol changes</u> <u>in nature by</u> <u>imitating them</u>, by using them,

                           A   B   C

<u>and also man can inhibit them</u>, too.

                    D

＜解答＞　D：and by inhibiting them

1069. If <u>a hydrogen-filled</u> ballon is brought <u>near a flame</u>, <u>it exploded</u>.

        A   B   C   D

＜解答＞　D：it will explode

1070. <u>Outside of Japan seldom pottes are</u> regarded <u>as</u> anything more than <u>craftsman</u>.

            A   B   C   D

＜解答＞　B：potters are seldom

1071. <u>Getting used</u> to eating fast food <u>and traffic</u> jams are problems newcomers

        A   B

<u>have to face</u> <u>after arriving</u> in Los Angeles.

        C   D

＜解答＞　B：① and dealing with traffic ② and coping with traffic

1072. <u>A</u> world Health Organization survey <u>showed that</u> <u>incidence of eye</u> disease

A   B   C

along <u>the Nile three times</u> that along the Amazon.

             D

＜解答＞　D：the Nile is three times

1073. The <u>hippopotamus kills</u> <u>more men</u> each year <u>than lion</u> and the <u>elephant</u>

                 A   B   C   D

combined.

＜解答＞　C：than the lion

1074. The first sound at Groton is the great bell <u>in the school house tower</u>

                                                 A

tolling six times over the lawn that is the center at the school.
　　　　　　　　B　　　　　　　　　C　　　　　　　　　　　　D

＜解答＞　D：of the school

1075. Since first it being performed on a bare stage in the fifties, Wagner's Ring
　　　　　　　　　　A　　　　　　　　　　B　　　　　　　C

　　　Cycle has usually been done in minimalist conceptual decor.
　　　　　　　　D

＜解答＞　A：being

1076. Serious bird watchers must know not only the appearance nor the sounds
　　　　　　A　　　　　　　　　　　　　　　　　　　　　B

　　　of the 840-odd species that can be counted in North America.
　　　　　　　　　　　　　　　C　　　　　　　　　　D

＜解答＞　B：appearance but also the sounds

1077. Many sociologists believe that sports organized serve both a recreational and
　　　　　　　　　　　A　　　　　B　　　　　　　　　C

　　　a social function by reflecting the values of society.
　　　　　　　　　　D

＜解答＞　B：that organized sports

1078. Education on environmental issues it should include not only physical
　　　　A　　　　　　　　　　　　　　　B

　　　problems like pollution but also social problems caused by pollution.
　　　　　　　C　　　　　　　　　　　　　D

＜解答＞　B：should include

1079. Although some difficulty was expected, the extent of the problem was not
　　　　　　　　　　　A　　　　　　　　　　　　　　　　　　B

　　　known until the project completed and the final report was distributed.
　　　　　　　　C　　　　　　　　　　　　D

＜解答＞　C：project was completed

1080. To add distilled water, a large-gauge hollow needle inserted through a cork
　　　　　A　　　　　　　　　　　　B　　　　　C

in the base <u>made of</u> opaque material.
      D

 ＜解答＞ C：was inserted

1081. A stain <u>which has first been</u> soaked in solvent can then easily <u>removed</u>
      A   B

by <u>adding water</u> which has <u>been distilled</u>.
   C   D

 ＜解答＞ B：been removed

1082. The <u>well-known</u>, well-advertised <u>products developed</u> by major corporations
     A   B

have become an industry standard <u>to emulated</u> rather than improved upon.
  C   D

 ＜解答＞ D：emulated

1083. Risks which <u>are taking</u> by today's entrepreneurs ane <u>considerable</u> and,
     A   B

while <u>stimulating, pose threats</u> to their financial security.
  C   D

 ＜解答＞ A：are taken

1084. <u>The sugar</u> the cook left <u>on shelf</u> was eaten by <u>a mouse</u> as large as <u>a rat</u>.
   A   B   C   D

 ＜解答＞ B：on the shelf

1085. Some people prefer <u>hotels</u> to <u>apartment buildings</u>, but most like <u>the houses</u>
      A   B   C

the best of the <u>three</u>.
     D

 ＜解答＞ C：houses

1086. People who dislike concerts prefer listening to <u>records</u>, but musicians insist
               A

that <u>an orchestra</u> must be heard in person to appreciate <u>the strength</u> and
  B   C

subtleties of <u>a music</u>.

                          D

＜解答＞　D：music

1087. <u>The biology teacher</u> suggested <u>class</u> collect <u>sea shells</u>, rocks, wideflowers,

           A   B   C

of <u>fossils</u>.

     D

＜解答＞　B：the class

1088. <u>All travelers</u> should carry <u>change of clothes</u>, extra money, and their passport

           A   B

in <u>a small bag</u> that can be carried <u>on the plane</u>.

        C   D

＜解答＞　B：the change of clothes

1089. The days become <u>more long as</u> the sun moves into a <u>wider</u> orbit <u>farther</u>

                      A   B   C   D

from the earth.

＜解答＞　A：longer

1090. The <u>strange</u> sound that came <u>through</u> the thick walls separting <u>the two</u>

           A   B   C

buildings seemed to be as close <u>than</u> next door.

                              D

＜解答＞　D：as

1091. <u>The brave man</u> the city has ever seen was that <u>strong</u> fireman who worked

           A   B

<u>most of the night</u> saving lives from <u>the big fire</u> at the Ballingall Hotel.

        C   D

＜解答＞　A：The bravest man

1092. A <u>greater</u> member of doctors in <u>fewest</u> hospitals indicates another <u>significant</u>

           A   B   C

change in the status of health care for the <u>low</u> income family.

                                       D

<解答> B：fewer

1093. Before dental care became <u>more widespread</u> people looked <u>older</u> before their
                                A   B

time since so <u>many</u> lost their teeth at <u>an early age</u>.
              C   D

<解答> B：old

1094. If the terms <u>had been</u> better, the borrower <u>would accept</u> the bank's proposal
             A   B

<u>even though</u> he <u>disagreed</u> with some of the conditions.
    C   D

<解答> B：would have accepted

1095. <u>Had they known</u> the snowstorm <u>would</u> be so treacherous, the hikers
      A   B

<u>did not verture</u> into <u>it</u> without proper equipment.
     C   D

<解答> C：would not have ventured

1096. <u>If going</u> to that restaurant is Jeff's choice, <u>then</u> we automatic <u>vetoed</u>
    A   B   C

it because <u>he is consistently</u> too extravagant for out tastes.
        D

<解答> C：veto

1097. If the new student <u>followed</u> the rules as they <u>were explained</u> <u>to him</u>,
          A   B   C

he <u>would not</u> have been in such a predicament.
   D

<解答> A：had followed

1098. <u>If</u> the library is <u>closed</u> over the holidays, it <u>would be</u> very difficult <u>to finish</u>
A   B   C   D

the research project.

　＜解答＞　C：will be

1099. Mosquitos, which have a voracious appetite <u>and explosive</u> breeding rate, are

　　　　　　　　　　　　　　　　　　　　　　　　　　　　A

　　　<u>coutrolled neither</u> by the draining of <u>forest and swamp</u> areas <u>by the spraying</u>

　　　　　　B　　　　　　　　　　　　　　　　　　C　　　　　　　　　　D

　　　of pesticides.

　＜解答＞　B：controlled

1100. The cowboy turned <u>and rode</u> towards the sun, <u>but</u> neither the horse <u>or he</u>

　　　　　　　　　　　　　A　　　　　　　　　　　　B　　　　　　　　　　C

　　　knew the exact path home, <u>and</u> soon both were lost.

　　　　　　　　　　　　　　　　　　D

　＜解答＞　C：nor he

1101. Neither the photographer <u>and the reporter</u> witnessed <u>the event, but</u> they

　　　　　　　　　　　　　　　A　　　　　　　　　　　　　B

　　　<u>and their</u> editors prepared <u>both articles and</u> photos as if they had been there.

　　　　　C　　　　　　　　　　　　D

　＜解答＞　A：nor the reporter

1102. Rodney asked that we come <u>and help</u> him, <u>but</u> when we arrived, he had

　　　　　　　　　　　　　　　　A　　　B

　　　already finished <u>but left</u>, with neither a note <u>nor an apology</u> for us.

　　　　　　　　　　　　C　　　　　　　　　　　　　　D

　＜解答＞　C：leaving

1103. A study <u>released last week indicates</u> that college <u>students, particularly</u> men,

　　　　　　　　A　　　　　　　　　　　　　　　　　　　　　　B

　　　regard female teachers <u>as less</u> worthy <u>of male</u> teachers.

　　　　　　　　　　　　　　C　　　　　　　D

　＜解答＞　D：than male

1104. An <u>element</u> cannot be formed from simpler <u>substances</u>, not can

　　　　　　A　　　　　　　　　　　　　　　　　　B

it be decompose with simpler varieties of matter.

     C   D

  ＜解答＞ C：be decomposed

1105. Without entering the body and cause damage, the CT is far superior to

    A   B   C

  the X-ray or exploratory surgery.

        D

  ＜解答＞ B：causing

1106. In our society, where peer recognition is prized, those who join everything

        A   B

  often take spaces from those wanting to join.

      C   D

  ＜解答＞ D：who want to join

1107. I know that lying is bad and to cheat is too, but no one seems to have told them.

         A   B   C   D

  ＜解答＞ B：cheating

1108. We need to know the hour of your departure and the time you are arriving,

           A

  not where you have been or where you are going.

    B   C   D

  ＜解答＞ A：you are departuring

1109. The istructions in the manual state that the equipment must be placed in

        A   B

  a flat surface and in a climate-controlled room free of dust.

         C   D

  ＜解答＞ B：on

1110. We studied the Mayans, which had developed a system of writing, as well as an

    A   B   C D

  accurate calendar.

  ＜解答＞ B：who

1111. The students looking <u>through</u> their binoculars <u>saw to the</u> birds sitting <u>on</u> the
                                     A   B   C

branch <u>of</u> the cherry tree.
       D

<解答> B：saw the

1112. All <u>since</u> the night, the bandleader hoped for a clear sky <u>at</u> dawn, as his
       A   B

plans <u>for</u> the parade depended <u>on</u> it.
       C   D

<解答> A：cancel

1113. Recent studies show that <u>during</u> a volcanic eruption, ash spreads <u>by</u> the sky,
                             A   B

lava flows <u>down</u>, and hot winds travel <u>for</u> miles disturbing weather patterns.
         C   D

<解答> B：in

1114. Management and Data Systems, a course for business executives and <u>their</u>
                                                                        A

employees, offers <u>their</u> own approach to financial planning that class members
                       B

can learn what <u>they</u> need to know for <u>their</u> jobs.
                 C   D

<解答> B：its

1115. The manager insisted <u>that</u> there <u>wasn't</u> <u>no</u> reason for making the customers
                        A   B   C

<u>wait</u> so long.
   D

<解答> C：any

1116. <u>We</u> agreed that <u>hers</u> way was probably the easiest trail to <u>our</u> cabin for <u>them</u>
     A   B   C   D

to follow.

　　＜解答＞　B：her

1117. He told me that I would have to speak to herself.
　　　A　　　B　　　　　　　　　　C　　　　　　　　　　　D

　　＜解答＞　D：to her

1118. Each time I caught sight of he was standing with his back to me.
　　　　　　　　A　　　　　　　B　　　　　　　　　　C　　　　　D

　　＜解答＞　B：sight of him, he was

1119. The biennial review was published every six months by the pen and pencil
　　　　　A　　　　　　　　　　B　　　　　　　　　　　　　　　　C

committee of the Principals and Teachers Association.
　　　　　　　　　　　　　　　D

　　＜解答＞　A：cancel

1120. Each boy I speak with tells me about his mother, father, and parents and
　　　　　　　　A　　　　B　　　　　　　　C

wishes they could visit him at summer camp.
　　　　　D

　　＜解答＞　C：① his mother and father ② his parents

1121. It was the morning dawn that convinced us we had stayed up too late and
　　　　　　　　A　　　　　　　　　　　　　　　　　　　　　　　　B

talked too much, and would now get no sleep until the evening hours.
　　　　C　　　　　　　　　　　　　　　　　　　　　　　D

　　＜解答＞　A：cancel

1122. Chcikens and poultry furnish a large portion of the critical protein the body
　　　　　A　　　　　　　　　　　　　　B　　　　C

requires to maintain its many functions.
　　　　　　　　　　　　　　　D

　　＜解答＞　A：① Chickens ② Poultry

1123. Even in Ms. Wilson's poverty-stricken days she was always generous and
　　　　　　　　　　　　　A　　　　　　　　　　　　　　　　　　　B

giving, helping the <u>needy</u> as if they were <u>worse</u> off than she was.
　　　　　　　　　　　　C　　　　　　　　　　　　D

＜解答＞　B：① generous ② giving

1124. Splashing <u>water</u> from the shower <u>produces</u> negative charges in the room's air,
　　　　　　　　A　　　　　　　　　　　B

which promotes a <u>feeling of well-being</u>.
　　　C　　　　　　　D

＜解答＞　C：we promote

1125. Professor Janes had <u>told the class</u> repeatedly that <u>we has</u> no <u>business</u>
　　　　　　　　　　　　A　　　　　　　　　　　　　B　　　　　C

in that room <u>and should never</u> use it to study.
　　　　　　　　　D

＜解答＞　B：we have

1126. The <u>appearance</u> of fresh <u>molten</u> rock on a volcan's lava <u>dome indicates</u>
　　　　　　A　　　　　　　B　　　　　　　　　　　　　　C

that eruptions of new lava <u>flow is imminent</u>.
　　　　　　　　　　　　　　D

＜解答＞　D：flow imminent

1127. <u>Arms control</u> is a major <u>issue</u> of this decade since all of mankind <u>live</u> under
　　　　A　　　　　　　　B　　　　　　　　　　　　　　　C

the shadow of nuclear <u>war</u>.
　　　　　　　　　D

＜解答＞　C：cancel

1128. <u>Carrying</u> the equipment easily, <u>rounded</u> to corner and <u>entered</u> the
　　　A　　　　　　　　　　　B　　　　　　　　C

<u>restricted-access</u> laboratory.
　　　D

＜解答＞　B：we rounded

1129. The Communications Commission, usually in the news because of airwave arguments, <u>has issued</u> a <u>proposal could have</u> a <u>devastating</u> effect on

           A   B   C

<u>some landmark</u> districts.

          D

＜解答＞ B：① proposal which could have ② proposal that could have

1130. <u>Children who like</u> to read <u>usually read more</u> in the summer, and <u>those only</u>

          A   B   C

<u>read</u> for school assignments <u>can be persuaded</u> to read for fun in the summer

                             D

because there is no school pressure.

＜解答＞ C：those who only read

1131. Captain John Smith <u>found the</u> Potomac River <u>sparkling clean</u> and full of

                      A   B

<u>fish when sailed</u> upriver <u>to what is now</u> Washington, D.C., at the beginning

        C   D

of the 17th century.

＜解答＞ C：fish when he sailed

1132. <u>Eating and drinking</u>, the tourists <u>worked</u> their way through the historic inns

          A   B

<u>had read</u> about before <u>taking</u> the trip.

    C   D

＜解答＞ C：they had read

1133. Aaron <u>complained</u> that his colleague <u>was always correcting</u> his work without

        A   B

<u>paying attention</u> to the work <u>did herself</u>.

    C   D

＜解答＞ D：she did herself

1134. The book of formulas <u>it</u> was kept a <u>secret</u> for many years, and <u>no one</u>, not

          A   B   C

even the chemist in charge of the project, knew where <u>it was</u> hidden.

D

　　＜解答＞　A：cancel

1135. The <u>escalating</u> inflation <u>rate, which it has been</u> fodder for political <u>speeches</u>,

A　　　　　　　　　　B　　　　　　　　　　　　C

has shown <u>no sign</u> of stabilizing.

D

　　＜解答＞　B：rate, which has been

1136. <u>New computerized</u> technologies <u>have given</u> doctors diagnostic and surgical

A　　　　　　　　　　　　B

tools <u>offering</u> a precision which until recently <u>it was</u> only a tantalizing dream.

C　　　　　　　　　　　　　D

　　＜解答＞　D：was

1137. <u>Originally designed</u> to carry only cargo, the Alexandria, a 125-foot

A

<u>three-masted trading</u> <u>schooner built in</u> Sweden in 1927, <u>it has been refitted</u>

B　　　　　　　C　　　　　　　　　　　D

for passengers.

　　＜解答＞　D：has been refitted

1138. The <u>visiting delegation</u> <u>which inspected</u> the new <u>facilities was</u> surprised to

A　　　　　　　B　　　　　　　　　C

find the <u>building it was so large</u>.

D

　　＜解答＞　D：building was so large

1139. School counselors <u>are convinced</u> that <u>it</u> will be obligatory that all applicants

A　　　　　　B

<u>must have</u> computer training <u>to enter</u> the job market in the future.

C　　　　　　　　　　D

　　＜解答＞　C：have

1140. Educators are now <u>recommending</u> that reasoning skills <u>are emphasized</u> in
                                 A   B

the classroom since recent tests <u>indicate</u> that many teachers in the past
                                      C

<u>having ignored</u> these skills.
     D

<解答>　B：be enphaized

1141. The requirement that all students <u>must pay</u> an activities fee <u>was met</u> with
                                 A   B

protests from the students who <u>would not</u> benefit because they only <u>attended</u>
                                    C   D

classes at night.

<解答>　A：pay

1142. The lawyers for the <u>defense made</u> the recommendation to the judge that
                                 A

the trial <u>will be</u> <u>delayed</u> until the <u>missing witness was found</u>.
                B   C   D

<解答>　B：be

1143. It is the requirement of the personel director that the <u>applicant is a</u> college
                                                 A

graduate, even though <u>the director</u> <u>has never felt</u> the need <u>to go</u> to college
                               B   C   D

herself.

<解答>　A：applicant be a

1144. Lionel gave a <u>credulous</u> account of <u>how</u> he <u>had spent</u> so much money on his
                        A   B   C

<u>vacation</u>.
     D

<解答>　A：credible

1145. What needs the community and is actively looking for is a source of income
　　　　　　　A　　　　　　　　　　　　　B　　　　　　　C

not generated by local taxes.
　　D

　　　＜解答＞　A：What the community needs

1146. How much of the $96 billion advertising expenditures will be aimed at the
　　　　A　　　　　　　　　　　　　　　　　　　　　　　　　　B

new teen and university markets are an advertising executive's chief concern.
　　　　　　　　　　　　　C　　　　　　　　　　　　　　D

　　　＜解答＞　C：markets is

1147. Most urban professionals talk about how much they did exercise rather than
　　　　　　　　　　　　　　A　　　　　　　B　　　　　　C

how much money they earned.
　　　D

　　　＜解答＞　B：exercise they did

1148. The picture on this television set is much more clearer than on that one.
　　　　A　　　　　　　　　　　　B　　　　C　　　　　　　　D

　　　＜解答＞　C：much clearer

1149. I couldn't hardly believe my eyes when I saw a 90 on my geometry test;
　　　　A　　　　　　　　　　　　　　　B

I must have remembered the formulas better than I thought I would.
　　　　　C　　　　　　　　　D

　　　＜解答＞　A：could

1150. The exhibition, toured in major cities, has returned to the Boston
　　　　　　　　A

Museum, where it originated and where it will be on view for another month.
　　　　B　　　　　　　　　　　C　　　　　　　D

　　　＜解答＞　A：exhibition, which toured in major cities

1151. When Mr. Hayos calls on me in chemistry class, I can't help but feel
　　　　　　　　A　　　　　　　　　　　　　　　B　　　C

nervous and uncertain.

            D

　＜解答＞　C：feeling

1152. Restaurants <u>where</u> people smoke, parks where <u>people</u> play loud radios,

                A   B

<u>pools</u> that are too crowded, and grass <u>is</u> mowed annoy many people.

   C   D

　＜解答＞　D：that

1153. The <u>accountant is known</u> for his <u>honesty was</u> troubled by the

              A   B

<u>discrepancy which he</u> discovered in the <u>ledgers that he</u> examined.

          C   D

　＜解答＞　A：accountant who is known

1154. <u>If you want to find</u> additional information about Southlown, you <u>had ought</u>

 A   B   C

to go to <u>the</u> library.

          D

　＜解答＞　C：ought

1155. <u>Although a time</u> saving device, the computer is <u>difficult to operate</u> and,

           A   B

<u>when it not</u> functioning properly, <u>is impossible</u> to use.

      C   D

　＜解答＞　C：when it is not

1156. <u>When the electricity</u> came back on, the <u>power surge blew</u> the fuses, so the

           A   B

hospital <u>continued to rely</u> on the emergency generator <u>until the electrician</u>.

              C   D

　＜解答＞　D：until the electrician arrived

1157. <u>The rain had not stopped</u> the roads would have been inundated <u>and no</u>

             A   B

travelers, <u>unless they rode</u> in amphibious vehicles, <u>would be able to pass.</u>
C   D

<解答> A：Had the rain not stopped

1158. The first English settlers in New World quickly <u>established living patterns</u>
A

<u>based on their</u> various backgrounds, the conditions <u>they had left</u>, and those
B   C

In which they found themselves when <u>arrived</u>.
D

<解答> D：they arrived

1159. Cape Cod <u>Canal, is said</u> <u>to be</u> the widest sea level <u>canal anywhere</u>, is cluttered
A   B   C

during the summer season with as many as 300 or more pleasure craft a day,

<u>most coming</u> from Boston.
D

<解答> A：Canal, said

1160. The physical matter in a " black hole " in the galaxy is so <u>dense that it creates</u>
A

a gravitational <u>pull which strong</u> enough <u>to prevent anything</u>, even
B   C

<u>light, from escaping</u>.
D

<解答> B：pull strong

1161. The <u>flights were not being</u> allowed to take off until the control tower
A

<u>which monitoring</u> <u>the changing</u> weather felt <u>it was safe</u>.
B   C   D

<解答> B：which monitored

1162. The <u>delays are caused</u> by the <u>striking longshoremen</u> <u>cost the steamship</u>
A   B   C

companies millions every <u>day their ships were</u> not allowed to dock.

                             D

　＜解答＞　A：delays caused

1163. The <u>freezing rain</u> made <u>driving</u> dangerous, was <u>obliging many motorists</u>

           A   B   C

to <u>use public transportation</u>.

             D

　＜解答＞　C：and obliged many motorists

1164. Although <u>they frequently misinterpreted</u>, <u>these laws</u> apply, in part, to groups

                A   B

<u>seeking</u> redress for wrongs <u>without their having</u> to hire a lawyer.

    C   D

　＜解答＞　A：they are frequently misinterpreted

1165. <u>After signing it</u>, insurance policy covers illness <u>on or off</u> the company grounds,

       A   B

<u>where</u> most accidents are likely <u>to occur</u>.

    C   D

　＜解答＞　A：After signing

1166. While <u>be covered</u> by warranty <u>for</u> the next two years, the <u>product</u> is

          A   B   C

guaranteed <u>to be</u> free of defects.

             D

　＜解答＞　A：covered

1167. <u>Before design</u> the building the architect <u>studied</u> the <u>plans of</u> other buildings

      A   B   C

<u>built</u> near the site.

 D

　＜解答＞　A：Before designing

1168. <u>When they traveling</u> long distances, <u>tourists should reduce</u> caloric intake

             A   B   C

and <u>limit consumption</u> of alchohol.

          D

＜解答＞ A：When traveling

1169. Local transit <u>officials that</u> bus and rail <u>patronage</u> appears <u>to have</u> reached

              A   B   C

a <u>level last</u> recorded 10 years ago.

      D

＜解答＞ A：officials said that

1170. Whenever John <u>thinks</u> <u>about quitting work</u> and going back to school,

                 A   B

he becomes <u>worried that</u> he <u>won't able</u> to pay the rent.

              C   D

＜解答＞ D：won't be able

1171. <u>Keeping to a routine</u> <u>by establishing</u> <u>patterns useful</u> in <u>meeting deadlines</u>.

         A   B   C   D

＜解答＞ C：patterns is useful

1172. <u>Being that</u> she has passed <u>all</u> the tests, the is <u>a</u> likly candidate <u>for</u> the military

    A   B   C   D

academy.

＜解答＞ A：Since

1173. The <u>county school</u> board learned last night that local 10th graders <u>continuing</u>

      A   B

to score <u>higher than</u> the national <u>average on reading</u> tests.

        C   D

＜解答＞ B：are continuing

1174. During the fire, most of the injured <u>were been</u> trampled <u>or crushed</u> when the

                        A   B

<u>spectators raced</u> for <u>the exits</u>.

      C   D

＜解答＞ A：were

1175. The journalist, who <u>had not slept</u> for 36 hours, <u>was obliged</u> <u>to must drive</u>
                               A   B   C

    through the <u>fog to interview</u> the union leader.
                       D

    ＜解答＞ C：to drive

1176. <u>Music is</u> an international language and a way for <u>newly arrived immigrants</u>
        A   B

    <u>to be assimilate</u> themselves into the <u>cultural activities</u> of the community.
           C   D

    ＜解答＞ C：to assimilate

1177. Many service personnel <u>like being</u> plumbers and <u>repairmen charge</u> high
                           A   B

    prices <u>and do</u> an inadequate <u>job unworthy</u> of their qualifications.
           C   D

    ＜解答＞ A：like

1178. <u>Tokyo founded in</u> the 16th century, <u>is older</u> than New York, but because of
          A   B

    fires, earthquakes, and war destruction, much less <u>is remains</u> of old Tokyo
                                      C

    <u>than of old New York</u>.
          D

    ＜解答＞ C：remains

1179. My English grade, which for many <u>reasons was</u> not deserned, <u>were sent</u>
                           A   B

    to my parents, <u>who chose</u> not to <u>comment on it</u>.
           C   D

    ＜解答＞ B：was sent

1180. There <u>were</u> no clear-cut sides in the Civil War unless the local <u>stories which</u>
        A   B

<u>tend</u> to <u>propagate partition</u> <u>is considered</u>.
　　　　　　　　　　 C　　　　　　　 D

＜解答＞ D：are considered

1181. <u>Telling</u> ghost stories <u>is</u> one of my grandfater's favorite hobbies and when
　　　　 A　　　　　　　　 B

　　 he <u>begins</u> to whisper, it <u>send</u> chills up and down my spine.
　　　　　　 C　　　　　　　　 D

＜解答＞ D：sends

1182. The camel, <u>which shuffles</u> its feet and <u>nod its head</u>, <u>has been</u>, as the desert
　　　　　　　　　 A　　　　　　　　　　　 B　　　　 C

　　 <u>tribes know</u>, a true beast of burded.
　　　　　 D

＜解答＞ B：nods its head

1183. Violence at recent soccer matches <u>is causing</u> city officials <u>to reevaluate</u>
　　　　　　　　　　　　　　　　　　　 A　　　　　　　　　　　 B

　　 security <u>measures which</u> <u>has proven</u> ineffectual.
　　　　　　　 C　　　　　 D

＜解答＞ D：have proven

1184. My book <u>is having</u> three torn pages, which I <u>tried</u> <u>to tape</u> before I <u>left</u> home.
　　　　　　　 A　　　　　　　　　　　　　 B　 C　　　　　　 D

＜解答＞ A：had

1185. Knowing how long the test <u>would run</u>, the students who finished <u>settle</u>
　　　　　　　　　　　　　　 A　　　　　　　　　　　　　　 B

　　 back and <u>opened</u> their books to read while time <u>passed</u>.
　　　　　　 C　　　　　　　　　　　　　　 D

＜解答＞ B：settled

1186. A labor <u>survey revealed</u> that <u>less than</u> 4 or 5 percent of the labor force
　　　　　　 A　　　　　　　 B

　　 <u>is doing</u> its <u>work at</u> home last year.
　　　　 C　　　 D

　　＜解答＞　C：was doing

1187. Business <u>are looking</u> for software that they <u>can adapt</u> and <u>applied immediately</u>
　　　　　　　　　A　　　　　　　　　　　　　　B　　　　　　　　C

　　　to their own <u>accounting procedures</u>.
　　　　　　　　　　　　　　D

　　＜解答＞　C：apply immediately

1188. You ought <u>not</u> to have <u>left</u> her <u>drop</u> geometry <u>last year</u>.
　　　　　　　　　　A　　　　　B　　　　C　　　　　　　D

　　＜解答＞　B：let

1189. Our partner, being business <u>printed</u> <u>provided</u> us with the <u>information</u> we
　　　　　　　　　　　　　　　　A　　　　　B　　　　　　　　　C

　　　needed to start our own <u>commerce</u> venture.
　　　　　　　　　　　　　　　　D

　　＜解答＞　D：commercial

1190. The agent asked <u>politely</u> for the <u>wooded</u> case, but the clerk <u>adamantly</u> refused
　　　　　　　　　　　A　　　　　　　B　　　　　　　　　　　C

　　　to give it to her until she brought the <u>proper</u> authorization.
　　　　　　　　　　　　　　　　　　　D

　　＜解答＞　B：wooden

1191. The lecture <u>similingly</u> addressed the <u>massively</u> audience in the <u>city</u> auditorium
　　　　　　　　　A　　　　　　　　　　B　　　　　　　　　C

　　　without using her <u>numberous</u> notes.
　　　　　　　　　　　　D

　　＜解答＞　B：massive

1192. The major <u>investors</u> decided <u>without warn</u> to withdraw their large contribution
　　　　　　　　　A　　　　　　　B

　　　and <u>refused</u> to <u>elaborate</u> on the decision.
　　　　　　　C　　　　　D

　　＜解答＞　B：without warning

1193. The government's <u>obligation</u> to its <u>constiuency</u> prompted it to <u>resume</u> local
                       A   B   C

food distribution <u>immediate</u>.
                       D

    ＜解答＞ D：immediately

1194. The <u>new company</u> <u>develops and markets</u> a series of high-quality, inexpensive
               A   B

<u>products peripheral</u> for both <u>micro-and mini-computers</u>.
              C   D

    ＜解答＞ C：peripheral products

1195. A <u>particular natural event</u> <u>called a phenomenon</u> is used by scientists in
              A   B

<u>making guessess intelligent</u> <u>called hypotheses</u>.
              C   D

    ＜解答＞ C：making intelligent guessess

1196. The <u>brilliant star</u> that shone <u>that first night</u> was <u>barely visible</u> on the
              A   B   C

<u>clear evening next</u>.
         D

    ＜解答＞ D：next clear evening

1197. Even <u>granted extenuating circumstances</u>, the gardener <u>still might have</u>
                    A   B

managed to bring in the <u>fragile tree palm</u> and rose bush <u>before</u> the storm.
                              C   D

    ＜解答＞ C：fragile palm tree

1198. <u>A shrill horn</u> sounding by <u>my left ear</u> announced <u>the return triumphant</u>
        A   B   C

of the <u>exhausted football</u> team to the rain-soaked field.
                   D

    ＜解答＞ C：the triumphant return

1199. <u>Upon further examination</u> it was discovered that your shipment, which
               A

<u>late arrived</u>, was <u>incomplete</u> and <u>incorrectly</u> labeled.
    B   C   D

<解答>　B：arrived late

1200. <u>After</u> its owner <u>has been forced</u> <u>to leave</u>, the castle <u>was allowed</u>
     A   B   C   D

to fall into ruin.

<解答>　B：had been forced

1201. <u>Porcelain is distinguished</u> from other days in that <u>white it is</u>, <u>extremely creamy</u>
          A   B   C

in consistency, and <u>virtually free</u> of impurities.
                  D

<解答>　B：it is white

1202. <u>Prices agricultural</u> are <u>determined daily</u> in <u>large central markets</u> by the
        A   B   C

<u>laws of supply</u> and demand.
    D

<解答>　A：Agricultural prices

1203. <u>Illegally cars parked</u> will be towed <u>at the owner's expense</u> and <u>may not be</u>
        A   B   C

<u>retrieved</u> until the <u>following week</u>.
            D

<解答>　A：Cars parked illegally

1204. <u>Because</u> they had spent <u>too many</u> time <u>considering</u> the new contract, the
     A   B   C

students <u>lost the opportunity to lease</u> the apartment.
            D

<解答>　B：too much

1205. After she <u>had bought</u> <u>himself</u> a new automobile, <u>she sold</u> <u>her</u> bicycle.
                          A   B   C   D
<解答>　B：herself

1206. George <u>has not</u> completed <u>the assignment</u> <u>yet</u>, and Maria <u>hasn't neither</u>.
                          A   B   C   D
<解答>　D：hasn't either

1207. <u>Some of the plants</u> in this store require very <u>little care</u>, but this one needs
        A   B
<u>much more sunlight</u> than <u>the others one</u>.
          C   D
<解答>　D：① the others ② the other ones

1208. <u>Many</u> theories on conserving the purity of water <u>has been</u> proposed, but
    A   B
<u>not one has</u> been <u>as widely accepted</u> as this one.
    C   D
<解答>　B：have been

1209. After John <u>eaten</u> dinner, <u>he wrote</u> <u>several letters</u> and <u>went to bed</u>.
                 A   B   C   D
<解答>　A：had eaten

1210. <u>Because</u> Sam and Michelle <u>had done</u> all of the work <u>theirselves</u>, they were
    A   B   C
<u>unwilling to give</u> the results to Jean.
      D
<解答>　C：themselves

1211. After <u>to take</u> the medication, <u>the patient</u> <u>became drowsy</u> and more <u>manageable</u>.
        A   B   C   D
<解答>　A：taking

1212. It <u>has</u> been <u>a long time</u> <u>since</u> we have talked to John, <u>isn't it</u> ?
   A   B   C   D
<解答>　D：hasn't it

1213. Rita enjoyed <u>to be</u> <u>able to meet</u> <u>several</u> Congress members <u>during</u> her vacation.
                              A   B   C   D

  ＜解答＞ A：being

1214. Harry's advisor persuaded <u>his taking</u> several courses <u>which</u> did <u>not involve</u>
                                          A   B   C

much knowledge of mathematics.
                             D

  ＜解答＞ A：him to take

1215. The work performed <u>by these officers</u> <u>are</u> not <u>worth our paying</u>
                                A   B   C

them any longer.
                    D

  ＜解答＞ B：is

1216. Peter and Tom <u>plays</u> tennis <u>every</u> <u>afternoon</u> with <u>Mary and me</u>.
                              A   B   C   D

  ＜解答＞ B：play

1217. He <u>was drink</u> <u>a cup of</u> coffee <u>when</u> the telephone <u>rang</u>.
             A   B   C   D

  ＜解答＞ A：was drinking

1218. The children <u>were playing</u> <u>last night outdoors</u> when it <u>began</u> <u>to rain very hard</u>.
                          A   B   C   D

  ＜解答＞ B：outdoors last night

1219. Please <u>give me</u> <u>a few</u> coffee and <u>some donuts</u> <u>if you have any</u> left.
                   A   B   C   D

  ＜解答＞ B：a little

1220. <u>People</u> respected George Washington <u>because</u> he was <u>a honest man</u>, and he
     A   B   C

turned out to be <u>one of our greatest</u> military leaders.
                                D

  ＜解答＞ C：an honest man

1221. Catherine is <u>studying</u> <u>law</u> <u>at the university</u>, and <u>so does John</u>.

      A B   C   D

  ＜解答＞ D：so is John

1222. <u>My cousin</u> attends <u>an university</u> in the Midwest which <u>specializes</u> <u>in astronomy</u>.

   A   B   C   D

  ＜解答＞ B：a university

1223. <u>Because</u> they <u>have moved</u> away, they <u>hardly never</u> go <u>to the beach</u> anymore.

   A   B   C   D

  ＜解答＞ C：① hardly ever ② never

1224. The policeman ordered <u>the suspect</u> <u>to don't remove</u> <u>his handle</u> <u>from the</u>

             A   B   C   D

  hood of the car.

  ＜解答＞ B：not to remove

1225. <u>My brother</u> doesn't care how much <u>does the car cost</u> <u>because</u>

   A   B   C

  <u>he is going to buy</u> it anyway.

      D

  ＜解答＞ B：the car costs

1226. Pete had <u>already saw</u> that musical <u>before</u> he <u>read</u> the reviews <u>about it</u>.

      A   B   C   D

  ＜解答＞ A：already seen

1227. The government <u>has</u> decided <u>voting</u> <u>on the resolution</u> now <u>rather</u> than

       A   B   C   D

  next month.

  ＜解答＞ B：to vote

1228. His father <u>does not</u> approve of <u>him to go</u> to the banquet <u>without dressing</u>

       A   B   C

  <u>formally</u>.

   D

  ＜解答＞ B：his going

1229. At the rate the clerks were <u>processing</u> the applications, Hary figured that it
　　　　　　　　　　　　　　A

<u>will take</u> four hours for <u>his</u> <u>to be reviewed</u>.
　　B　　　　　　　　　C　　　D
＜解答＞ B：would take

1230. We had better <u>to review</u> this chapter <u>carefully</u> because we will have <u>some</u>
　　　　　　　　　　A　　　　　　　　　B　　　　　　　　　　C

questions <u>on it on our</u> test tomorrow.
　　　　　　D
＜解答＞ A：review

1231. <u>Despite</u> the time of the years, <u>yesterday's</u> temperature was <u>enough hot</u>
　　　　A　　　　　　　　　　　B　　　　　　　　　　C

<u>to turn on</u> the air conditioning.
　　D
＜解答＞ C：hot enough

1232. Danny spent <u>such enjoyable</u> vacation in Europe this summer <u>that he</u> plans
　　　　　　　　　A　　　　　　　　　　　　　　　　　　　B

<u>to return</u> as soon as he <u>saves enough money</u>.
　　D　　　　　　　　　D
＜解答＞ A：such an enjoyable

1233. Kurt had <u>so interesting</u> and creative <u>plans</u> that everyone <u>wanted</u> to work <u>on</u>
　　　　　　　A　　　　　　　　　B　　　　　　　　C　　　　　　D

his committee.
＜解答＞ A：such interesting

1234. I have to <u>depositing</u> this money in <u>my checking</u> account or else the check I
　　　　　　　A　　　　　　　　　B

<u>just wrote</u> <u>will bounce</u>.
　　C　　　　D
＜解答＞ A：deposit

1235. Paul did <u>so</u> well in his speech today <u>that</u> he <u>should have rehearsed</u> it many

           A   B   C

   times <u>this past week</u>.

            D

   ＜解答＞ C：must have rehearsed

1236. Our Spanish professor would like <u>us</u> <u>spending</u> more time <u>in the</u> laboratory

                                      A   B   C

   <u>practicing</u> our pronunciation.

        D

   ＜解答＞ B：to spend

1237. The bolder <u>the matador's</u> display <u>in the arena</u> became, <u>louder</u> the audience

                   A   B   C

   expressed <u>its</u> approval of his presentation.

        D

   ＜解答＞ C：the louder

1238. Max would rather <u>to be fishing</u> <u>from his boat</u> in the lake <u>than</u> sitting <u>at his desk</u>

                       A   B   C   D

   in the office.

   ＜解答＞ A：be fishing

1239. If crisis <u>would occur,</u> <u>those unfamiliar</u> with <u>the</u> procedures would not know

                  A   B   C

   <u>how to handle</u> the situation.

        D

   ＜解答＞ A：occurred

1240. The teacher <u>tried to make</u> the classes enjoyable experiences for the students

               A

   <u>so</u> they <u>would take a greater</u> interest <u>in the</u> subject.

   B   C   D

   ＜解答＞ B：so that

1241. Anybody <u>who plans</u> <u>to attend</u> the meeting <u>ought send</u> a short note <u>to the</u>

               A   B   C   D

chairperson.

＜解答＞ C：ought to send

1242. Mary <u>usually arrives</u> <u>at the office</u> at nine o'clock, but <u>because</u> the storm,

             A   B   C

she was two hours <u>late</u>.

                      D

＜解答＞ C：because of

1243. It is <u>difficult</u> to get used <u>to sleep</u> in a ten after <u>having</u> a soft, comfortable bed

           A   B   C

<u>to lie on</u>.

      D

＜解答＞ B：to sleeping

1244. Tom and Mark hope <u>go</u> skiing <u>in the mountains</u> this weekend <u>if the</u> weather

                     A   B   C

permits.

    D

＜解答＞ A：to go

1245. The salad tasted <u>so well</u> that my brother <u>returned to</u> the <u>salad bar for</u>

                 A   B   C

<u>another helping</u>.

      D

＜解答＞ A：so good

1246. <u>Despite</u> his <u>smiling</u> face, the <u>second-place contestant</u> is <u>more sadder</u>

   A   B   C   D

the winner.

＜解答＞ D：sadder than

1247. <u>The</u> members of the orchestra <u>had to arrived</u> an hour <u>prior to the performance</u>

   A   B   C

for a short rehearsal.
          D

＜解答＞ B：had to arrive

1248. If Monique had not attended the conference, she never would meet her old
                                  A   B

friend Dan, whom she had not seen in years.
                    C   D

＜解答＞ B：① never would have met ② would never have met

1249. No one in our office wants to drive to work any more because of there are
                           A   B   C

always traffic jams at rush hour.
                    D

＜解答＞ B：because

1250. Louise is the more capable of the three girls who have tried out for the part
                  A   B   C

in the play.
          D

＜解答＞ A：the most

1251. I would rather that they do not travel during the bad weather, but they insist
                    A   B   C

that they must return home today.
            D

＜解答＞ B：did not travel

1252. My book is different than yours because mine has a vocabulary section at the
                      A   B   C

bottom of each page, and yours has one in the hack.
                    D

＜解答＞ A：from

1253. After a carefully investigation, we soon discovered that the house was
                  A   B   C

infected with termites.
      D

<解答>　A：careful

1254. Jame's counselor recommended that <u>he should take</u> a foreign language
                                     A

<u>in his</u> freshman year instead of <u>watching</u> until <u>the following year</u>.
  B   C   D

<解答>　A：he take

1255. It is most important that <u>he</u> <u>speaks</u> to <u>the</u> dean before <u>leaving</u> for his vaction.
                         A   B   C   D

<解答>　B：speak

1256. I need <u>both fine</u> brown sugar as well <u>as</u> powdered sugar <u>to bake</u> a
            A   B   C   D

Hawaiian cake.

<解答>　A：cancel

1257. Let Nancy and <u>her</u> <u>to make</u> all the plans for the party, and you and I
                A   B

<u>will provide</u> <u>the refreshments</u> and entertainment.
     C   D

<解答>　B：make

1258. <u>The</u> general commanded <u>the officers' club</u> be <u>off limits</u> to <u>the new</u> recruits.
   A   B   C   D

<解答>　B：that the Officers' Club

1259. Marcy said that she <u>knew how</u> the procedures for doing the experiment, but
                            A

when we began <u>to work</u> in the laboratory, she found <u>that</u> she was <u>mistaken</u>.
                B   C   D

<解答>　A：knew

1260. It <u>was</u> suggested that Pedro <u>studies</u> the material <u>more thoroughly</u> before
     A   B   C

attempting to pass the exam.
              D

＜解答＞ B：study

1261. Marie's cousin is studied law at one of the ivy-league universities in the East.
                       A   B   C   D

＜解答＞ A：studying

1262. The president mentioned to the cabinet members he was going to negotiate
                           A   B   C

a new treaty with the foreign minister.
                    D

＜解答＞ B：that he

1263. Despite the roadblock, the police allowed us enter the restricted area to search
    A   B   C

for our friends.
              D

＜解答＞ B：us to enter

1264. We should have been informed Janis about the change in plans regarding
                       A   B   C

our weekend trip to the mountains.
              D

＜解答＞ A：have informed

1265. That manufacturer is not only raising his prices but also decreasing the
                              A   B   C

production of his product as well.
                    D

＜解答＞ D：cancel

1266. Jason's professor had him to rewrite his thesis many times before allowing
                             A   B   C

him to present it to the committee.
              D

<解答> A：rewrite

1267. <u>Hundreds of</u> houses and <u>other</u> building <u>were destroying</u> by the <u>raging</u> tropical
    A   B   C   D

  storm which later developed into a hurricane.

  <解答> C：were destroyed

1268. Food prices have <u>raised</u> <u>so rapidly</u> in the past few months <u>that</u> some families
        A B   C

  have been forced to alter <u>their eating habits</u>.
            D

  <解答> A：risen

1269. <u>Although</u> her severe pain, Pat decided <u>to come</u> to the meeting <u>so that</u> there
    A   B   C

  <u>would</u> be a quorum.
   D

  <解答> A：① Despite ② In spite of

1270. He is the <u>only</u> candidate <u>who</u> the faculty members voted <u>not to retain</u>
      A   B   C

  <u>on the list</u> of eligible replacements for Professor Kotey.
    D

  <解答> B：whom

1271. This class, <u>that</u> is a <u>prerequisite for</u> microbiology, is <u>so difficult</u> that
      A   B   C

  I <u>would rather drop it</u>.
     D

  <解答> A：which

1272. If you had <u>sat</u> the plant <u>in a cooler</u> location, <u>the leaves</u> would not <u>have burned</u>.
      A   B   C   D
  <解答> A：set

1273. After Allan <u>had searched</u> <u>for</u> twenty minutes, he realized that his jacket had
      A   B

been <u>laying</u> on the table <u>the entire time</u>.

    C   D

 ＜解答＞ C：lying

1274. The doctor suggested that he <u>lay</u> <u>in bed</u> for <u>several</u> days as a precaution against

           A B   C

further damage to the tendons.

   D

 ＜解答＞ A：lie

1275. The project director <u>stated he</u> believed <u>it was necessary</u> <u>to study</u> the proposals

          A   B   C

for several more months <u>before making a decision</u>.

            D

 ＜解答＞ A：stated that he

1276. <u>That these</u> students <u>have improved</u> their grades <u>because of their</u>

  A   B   C

<u>participation in</u> the test review class.

   D

 ＜解答＞ A：Those

1277. <u>That</u> Mr. Jones is not prepared to teach this course is not <u>doubted</u>; however,

  A   B

at this late date <u>it is not likely that</u> we will be <u>able finding</u> a replacement.

        C   D

 ＜解答＞ D：able to find

1278. <u>Some</u> Italian scholars <u>stressed</u> <u>the study of</u> grammar, rhetoric,

  A   B   C

<u>learning about history</u>, and poetry.

    D

 ＜解答＞ D：history

1279. While the boys were <u>ice skating</u>, they <u>slip</u> on the thin ice and <u>fell</u> <u>into</u> the

        A   B   C D

deep water.

　　＜解答＞　B：slipped

1280. Fred, who usually conducts <u>the choir rehearsals</u>, did not <u>show up</u> last
　　　　　　　　　　　　　　　　　　　A　　　　　　　　　　　　B

night because he <u>had</u> an accident <u>no his way to her practice</u>.
　　　　　　　　　C　　　　　　　　　D

　　＜解答＞　C：had had

1281. The atmosphere of friendliness <u>in Andalucia</u> is open, warm and
　　　　　　　　　　　　　　　　　　　A

<u>gives a welcome feeling</u> to all <u>who</u> have the <u>good</u> fortune to visit there.
　　　B　　　　　　　　　　　C　　　　　D

　　＜解答＞　B：welcoming

1282. Being <u>that he was</u> a good swimmer, John Jumped <u>into</u> the water and <u>rescued</u>
　　　　　　　A　　　　　　　　　　　　　　　　　　　B　　　　　　　C

the <u>drowing</u> child.
　　　D

　　＜解答＞　A：cancel

1283. <u>The</u> carpenters tried to <u>join together</u> the pieces <u>of the</u> broken beam,
　　　　A　　　　　　　　　B　　　　　　　　　　C

but <u>found it impossible</u> to do.
　　　　D

　　＜解答＞　B：join

1284. In Rome, Venice, and <u>other</u> cities, <u>there developed</u> an intellectual movement
　　　　　　　　　　　　　A　　　　　　　B

called humanism, which <u>is</u> the <u>basis of</u> the Renaissance.
　　　　　　　　　　　C　　　　D

　　＜解答＞　C：was

1285. <u>The way we react</u> to other people, the educational training we <u>received</u>,
　　　　A　　　　　　　　　　　　　　　　　　　　　　　　　　　　B

and the knowledge we display are all <u>part</u> of our <u>cultural heritage</u>.
           C   D

  ＜解答＞ B：receive

1286. Mantovanic <u>conducted</u> the orchestra gracefully and <u>with style</u> <u>to the delight</u>
      A   B   C

of his <u>appreciative</u> audience.
     D

  ＜解答＞ B：stylishly

1287. <u>After learning</u> all the details about the <u>project</u>, the contractor told <u>us them</u>
    A   B   C

at the <u>planning meeting</u>.
     D

  ＜解答＞ C：them to us

1288. After Mr. Peabody <u>had died</u>, the money from his estate reverted <u>back</u> to the
        A   B

company <u>which</u> he <u>had served</u> as president for ten yeaes.
     C   D

  ＜解答＞ B：cancel

1289. <u>After</u> the rain had <u>let out</u>, the Mitchells <u>continued</u> <u>their hike</u> up the mountain.
  A   B   C   D

  ＜解答＞ B：let up

1290. <u>Even though</u> the girls have <u>all ready</u> visited St. Augustine, <u>they</u> want
    A   B   C

<u>to return to</u> the Castillo de San Marco.
   D

  ＜解答＞ B：already

1291. <u>Knowing that</u> it would be <u>helpless</u> to continue <u>working</u> for a nearly bankrupt
    A   B   C

company, Louise decided to go away and find <u>another type</u> of employment.
                     D

<解答> B：useless

1292. John <u>always</u> arrives <u>lately</u> for his chemistry class even though he <u>leaves</u> his

          A   B   C

dormitory <u>in plenty of time</u>.

                         D

<解答> B：late

1293. The Nelsons asked <u>us</u> to <u>look over</u> their plants for them while they were

                              A   B

<u>away</u> <u>on vacation</u>.

  C   D

<解答> B：① look after ② take care of

1294. <u>According</u> the weatherman, <u>there is</u> a fifty percent chance of rain <u>forecast</u>

    A   B   C

for today and a greater chance for <u>over the weekend</u>.

                            D

<解答> A：According to

1295. My English teacher said we <u>should write</u> another composition for tomorrow

                            A

<u>related for</u> out experience <u>at</u> last <u>week's</u> workshop.

  B   C   D

<解答> B：related to

1296. Eric and his sister <u>won first prize</u> for the <u>most</u> elaborate <u>customs</u> they had

                  A   B   C

worn to <u>the Halloween</u> party.

          D

<解答> C：costumes

1297. <u>After checking out</u> the motor and the carburetor <u>for problems</u>, Jesse found

      A   B

that the noise <u>was caused</u> by <u>lose</u> fan belt.

          C   D

　　　　　＜解答＞　D：loose

1298. Because the committee was anxious to attend the celebration, the president

　　　　　　　　　　A　　　　　　　　　　　　　　　　　　　　　　　B

　　　dispensed to reading the minutes.

　　　　　　　　C　　　　D

　　　＜解答＞　C：with reading

1299. The coach was depending for his team to win the game so that they would

　　　　　　　　　　　A　　　　　　　　B　　　　　　　C

　　　have a chance to play in the Super Bowl.

　　　　　　　　　　　　　　D

　　　＜解答＞　A：depending on

1300. His highly imaginary composition won the judges' approve and the first prize

　　　　　A　　B　　　　　　　　　　　C　　　　　　　　　　　D

　　　in the high school essay contest.

　　　＜解答＞　B：imaginative

1301. Although Chyde is formally from Pennsylvania, he finds it difficult to

　　　　　　　　　　　A　　　　　　　　　　　　　　　　　　　　　　B

　　　get used to the cold winters we are having.

　　　　　C　　　　　　　　　　　　D

　　　＜解答＞　A：formerly

1302. Paris has been well know about its famous monuments, beautiful music,

　　　　　　　A　　　　　B　　　C

　　　and wonderful restaurants for over on hundred years.

　　　　　　　　　　　　　　　　　　　　　D

　　　＜解答＞　B：known for

1303. As a result his inconsistency in represent his consituents, the senator was

　　　　　A　　　　　　　　　　　　　B

　　　not reelected to the state legislature.

　　　　　　C　　　　　　D

　　　＜解答＞　B：in representing

1304. Excepting for the graduate students, everyone will have to take the tests on
     A   B   C   D

     the same day.

     ＜解答＞　B：Except for

1305. Soon after Mel has finished his thesis, he will leave for Boston, where he has
               A   B   C

     a job waiting on him.
                D

     ＜解答＞　D：for him

1306. The refuges are very much upset because they have been deprived to their
     A   B   C   D

     homeland and their families.

     ＜解答＞　D：deprived of

1307. The athlete was disqualified from the tournament for participating at an
     A   B   C   D

     illegal demonstration.

     ＜解答＞　D：in

1308. If it had not been for the computerized register tape from the grocery store,
          A   B

     I never would have been able to figure on my expanditures.
        C   D

     ＜解答＞　D：figure out

1309. Our new office building will be located downtown in the corner of Euclid
                     A   B   C

     Avenue and East Ninth Street.
            D

     ＜解答＞　B：on the corner

1310. The customer was interested to see one of those new pocket cameras with
     A   B   C

the <u>built-in</u> flash.

      D

    ＜解答＞ B：in seeing

1311. <u>Scientists</u> were <u>interested about</u> the radioactivity <u>emanating</u> <u>from</u> the nuclear

      A   B   C   D

power plant.

    ＜解答＞ B：interested in

1312. <u>Because it was faster</u>, John <u>insisted in</u> my <u>taking</u> the plane to Miami

        A   B   C

<u>instead of the train</u>.

      D

    ＜解答＞ B：insisted on

1313. The spring conference <u>will be held</u> in Milwaukee on three <u>successive</u> days,

                               A   B   C

<u>namely</u> May 15,16, and 17.

    D

    ＜解答＞ C：consecutive

1314. <u>Admittance for</u> the inauguration <u>ceremonies</u> was only <u>by</u> special invitation

        A   B   C

<u>of the</u> committee.

      D

    ＜解答＞ A：Admittance to

1315. Recent <u>studies done by</u> the Department of Labor <u>have shown</u> that

                     A   B

<u>nonsmoking are</u> more productive than those who <u>smoke</u>.

      D   D

    ＜解答＞ C：nonsmoking employees are

1316. <u>We all</u> thought the office <u>manager had</u> gone <u>too far</u>, but his staff

      A   B   C

did supported him.
　　　　D

＜解答＞　D：supported

1317. The scientific experiments <u>conducted</u> by the class <u>was</u> placed on <u>the</u> center
　　　　　　　　　　　　　　A　　　　　　　　B　　　　　　C

　　　table <u>for</u> the judges to evaluate.
　　　　　　D

＜解答＞　B：were

1318. The antrropologists reviewed <u>its</u> findings and discovered that <u>a fossil</u>
　　　　　　　　　　　　　　　A　　　　　　　　　　　　　　　　B

　　　previously <u>thought to date</u> from the Mesozoic period <u>was</u> a current forgery.
　　　　　　　　　C　　　　　　　　　　　　　　　　　D

＜解答＞　A：their

1319. <u>The general's</u> political judgment <u>or his ability</u> to analyze <u>a stituation accurately</u>
　　　　A　　　　　　　　　　　　B　　　　　　　　　C

　　　were both <u>as remarkable as</u> his military skill.
　　　　　　　　　D

＜解答＞　B：and ability

1320. The <u>freezing point and boiling</u> point of water <u>are standard</u> reference
　　　　　　　A　　　　　　　　　　　　　B

　　　<u>points used</u> in <u>calibrating thermometer</u>.
　　　　C　　　　　D

＜解答＞　D：① calibrating a thermometer ② calibrating the thermometer

1321. <u>Ceramic materials</u>, taken directly from the earth's crust <u>have used</u> as <u>building</u>
　　　　A　　　　　　　　　　　　　　　　　　　B　　　C

　　　stars <u>govern</u> the fate of men.
　　　　　D

＜解答＞　B：have been used

1322. The force of <u>gravity becomes</u> <u>least</u> as one goes <u>farther from</u> the center
　　　　　　　　A　　　B　　　　　　　C

of the earth.
   D

<解答> B：less

1323. Elizabeth Charlotte <u>provisions</u> through her bawdy <u>outspoken</u> letters
         A   B

<u>an unparalleled</u> <u>contemporary</u> view of the court of Louis XIV.
     C   D

<解答> A：provides

1324. <u>If</u> excess air <u>was pumped</u> into <u>an elastic</u> cylinder, <u>the cylinder</u> will explode.
 A   B   C   D

<解答> B：is pumped

1325. Many people, <u>physicians included</u>, <u>fail to appreciate</u> that <u>can bee stings</u>
       A   B   C

have <u>fatal results</u> in minutes.
     D

<解答> C：bee stings can

1326. The brain's left <u>hemisphere controls</u> <u>logic and language</u>, while the
         A   B

<u>right controlling</u> instuitive talents and musical <u>ability</u>.
   C   D

<解答> C：right controls

1327. Most <u>automobile engine</u> use <u>a liqid</u>, usually water, <u>to maintain the</u> engine
     A   B   C

at a constant <u>operating</u> temperature.
      D

<解答> A：automobile engines

1328. <u>Roman law had</u> became <u>the foundation for</u> law codes that <u>subsequently</u>
   A   B   C

<u>developed</u> in Europe <u>and in other</u> parts of the world.
          D

　　＜解答＞　A：Roman law

1329. The group of spectators was dispersed by the police who was at the scene
　　　　　　　　　　　A　　　　　　　　　　　　B　　　　　　C

　　　of the accident within minutes.
　　　　　　　　　　　　D

　　＜解答＞　C：who were

1330. Cities that highly polluted air show the effects of the weathering caused by
　　　　　　　　　　A　　　　　　　　　　　　B　　　　　　C

　　　acid rain on buildings, statues, and parks.
　　　　　　　　　　　D

　　＜解答＞　A：that have highly polluted air

1331. The appropriate action to take could not be decided on by either the
　　　　　　　　　　　　　　A　　　　　　B　　　C

　　　president nor the vice president.
　　　　　　　　　D

　　＜解答＞　D：or

1332. Jack London's tour of south Pacific was delayed by his illness and
　　　　　　　　　　　A　　　B　　　　　C

　　　the San Francisco earthquake of 1906.
　　　　　　　　　　　　D

　　＜解答＞　B：of the South Pacific

1333. By the year 2010, the earth will inhabit twice as many people as it is today.
　　　A　　　　　　　　　　　　　　　B　　　C　　　　　　　　　　D

　　＜解答＞　B：will be inhabited

1334. Working together, scientists and genetic researchers recently have made
　　　　A　　　　　　　　　　　　　　　　　　　　　　　　　B

　　　discoveries that are causing philosophical debates.
　　　　　　　　　C　　　　　　D

　　＜解答＞　B：have recently made

1335. <u>A hush</u> fell <u>over the concert</u> hall when <u>the well-known</u> classical guitarist in
       A   B   C

     the world <u>stepped onto</u> the stage.
                D

     ＜解答＞ C：the best known

1336. The honeysuckle bush, which smells <u>so sweetly</u> <u>when it blooms</u>, was
                                             A   B

     <u>originally brought</u> to the U.S. <u>from</u> Japan.
            C   D

     ＜解答＞ A：so sweet

1337. The <u>guests were</u> surprised by <u>their</u> host's <u>furniture was made</u> in Italy
            A   B   C

     <u>especially for</u> the new gallery.
         D

     ＜解答＞ C：furniture which was made

1338. Were <u>banks increase</u> <u>their</u> loans to businesses, <u>which</u> would use these funds
              A   B   C

     to increase their inventories, <u>investment</u> would increase.
                                D

     ＜解答＞ A：banks to increase

1339. A team <u>of specialists</u> <u>concluded that</u> the <u>patient's blindness</u> was <u>contemporary</u>.
               A   B   C   D
     ＜解答＞ D：temporary

1340. When <u>the Spanish</u> constructed <u>its missions</u> <u>in the New World</u>, they
            A   B   C

     incorporated <u>Moorish architectural festures</u>.
                      D

     ＜解答＞ B：their missions

1341. <u>Although the country's</u> military <u>budget</u> is insufficient, the army <u>be expected</u>
              A   B   C

to perform well in war.

        D

＜解答＞ A：Because the country's

1342. The archeologist believed which the tomb discovered in North Africa

    A   B   C

belonged to one of Hannibal's gemerals.

      D

＜解答＞ B：that the tomb

1343. There is a folk myth that the horsehair in a container of rainwater

    A   B

placed in the sunshine will develop into a snake.

           C   D

＜解答＞ B：a horsehair

1344. Crime prevention experts believe that if possession of small firearms were

            A   B   C

limited, crime and violence decreased.

            D

＜解答＞ D：violence would decrease

1345. The advent of calculators did fundamentally changed the teaching methods

    A   B   C

for mathematics.

      D

＜解答＞ B：fundamentally

1346. The screenwriter who provides the words for a film is acclaimed seldom,

          A   B   C

unlike the director and the actors and actresses.

           D

＜解答＞ C：is seldom acclaimed

1347. Most early immigrants are coming from an agricultural background find

    A   B   C

work <u>on farms</u>.

                  D

＜解答＞ B：coming

1348. <u>People, when</u> they sleep <u>less than</u> normal, <u>awake</u> more friendly

          A   B   C

<u>and more aggression</u>.

              D

＜解答＞ D：and more aggressive

1349. The lawyers for <u>the administration</u> <u>met</u> with the pepresentative of the

                    A   B

<u>students has been</u> occupying the building for <u>a week</u>.

        C   D

＜解答＞ C：students who had been

1350. The citizens, <u>who been</u> tolerant <u>of the mayor's</u> unsavory practices in the past,

            A   B

<u>finally impeached</u> the <u>amoral politician</u>.

        C   D

＜解答＞ A：who had been

1351. Psychologists <u>who study</u> sleep <u>habits believe</u> day dreaming is <u>an intrinsic and</u>

              A   B   C

essential part of <u>daily life</u>.

          D

＜解答＞ C：an

1352. Elizabeth I <u>of England</u> had <u>more wigs</u> in her wardrobe <u>than</u> hairs <u>in her head</u>.

            A   B   C   D

＜解答＞ D：on her head

1353. Greek <u>science preserved</u> for <u>posterity</u> by the Arabs, <u>who introduced</u> to

           A   B   C

science <u>the Arabic system of numbers</u>.

          D

<解答> A：science was preserved

1354. Hormones are chemical <u>substances are produced</u> in the body by
                                         A

structures known <u>as glands, such as</u> sweat <u>glands and</u> salivary glands.
        B   C   D

<解答> A：substances produced

1355. Tourists like <u>to travel</u> to <u>the</u> Eastern Shore <u>so the food is good</u>, the People
                A   B   C

are <u>friendly</u>, and the prices are reasonable.
        D

<解答> C：because the food is good

1356. <u>Today it is</u> almost impossible <u>to imagination</u> the <u>boredom and constrictions</u>
        A   B   C

of the <u>average middle-class woman's life</u> before World War II.
                        D

<解答> B：to imagine

1357. <u>In a recent ranking</u> of American cities, Rand Mcnally rated Pittsburgh,
        A

pennsylvania, as the most <u>livable</u> city <u>and</u> Yuba City, California, <u>as the less</u>.
                              B   C   D

<解答> D：as the least

1358. The Federal Art Project of 1935 supported some 5,000 <u>artists, enabling</u> <u>their to</u>
                                                        A   B

<u>work</u> all over America <u>rather than come</u> to New York <u>in search of a market</u>.
    C   C   D

<解答> B：them to work

1359. <u>Sophisticated</u> <u>communications have</u> taken the challenge <u>out of travel in</u>
        A   B   C

remote places <u>which are far away</u>.
                    D

<解答>　D：cancel

1360. <u>Because</u> the African tsetse is a <u>serious threat</u> to human health, <u>it helps</u>
    A   B   C

  maintain <u>the delicate balance</u> of nature.
        D

  <解答>　A：Although

1361. Rhodes Tavern, a quaint building over 200 years old <u>which it will</u> be torn
                  A

  down <u>soon</u>, <u>was considered</u> a historical monument <u>until</u> investors wanted it.
     B   C   D

  <解答>　A：which will

1362. Critics of television <u>commercials</u> would prefer <u>that advertisers conform</u>
         A   B

  to a strictes code of ethics <u>than was</u> currently <u>in effect</u>.
           C   D

  <解答>　C：that is

1363. Metal <u>must be hammered</u>, worked, <u>and cooled rapidly</u> <u>to relieve</u> internal
      A   B   C

  <u>stresses causing</u> by heating.
     D

  <解答>　D：stresses caused

1364. Theories and <u>laws applied to</u> phenomena to increase <u>understanding</u> of them
         A   B

  and to <u>adapt them</u> <u>in creating</u> products for man's use.
       C   D

  <解答>　A：laws are applied to

1365. Spacecraft <u>destined</u> for orbit will <u>be boosting</u> from low earth <u>orbit by</u>
      A   B   C

  <u>rockets developed</u> by a west coast engineering firm.
     D

<解答> B：he boosted

1366. The store front <u>being painted</u>, so the customers <u>were required</u>
                         A   B

    <u>to enter through</u> the alley <u>that ran behind</u> the building.
           C   D

<解答> A：was being painted

1367. Oil and gold, both of which <u>had an unparalleled</u> price increase in the 70's,
                                     A

    <u>have not been</u> popular recently and <u>not placed</u> on the <u>most favored</u> stock lists.
        B   C   D

<解答> C：have not been placed

1368. To design a <u>house</u> the architect needs only <u>a ruler</u>, a pencil, <u>piece of paper</u>
            A   B   C

    and <u>an eraser</u>.
        D

<解答> C：a piece of paper

1369. There are <u>103universities</u> in the Tokyo with more than <u>one-half million</u>
        A   B   C

    <u>students</u> from all parts <u>of Japan</u>.
          D

<解答> B：Tokyo

1370. <u>Television</u> replaced radio as <u>the most</u> widely enjoyed <u>from of</u> the <u>broadcasting</u>
    A   B   C   D

    in the United States.

<解答> D：broadcasting

1371. <u>The new doorman</u> has <u>the problem</u> remembering <u>the name</u> of the people
        A   B   C

    with offices <u>in the building</u>.
          D

<解答> B：a problem

1372. <u>A computer</u> with <u>a terminal</u> <u>monitor,</u> and printer is often refered to as

      A   B   C

<u>work station</u>.

      D

＜解答＞ D：a work station

1373. <u>Neither</u> the manager <u>nor</u> the two salespeople <u>was</u> prepared for the <u>number</u>

      A   B   C   D

of customers.

＜解答＞ C：were

1374. There <u>was</u> women, <u>as well as</u> men, <u>who</u> set out on the perilous journey <u>into</u>

        A   B   C   D

new territory.

＜解答＞ A：were

1375. I <u>am going to</u> note for <u>whomever</u> can <u>present</u> the best solution to

        A   B   C

<u>environmental</u> problems.

      D

＜解答＞ B：whoever

1376. The industrial community should be <u>closer enough</u> to the <u>crowed center</u>,

                                A   B

but <u>distant</u> enough to reduce <u>potential</u> hazards.

      C   D

＜解答＞ A：close enough

1377. The plane's instrument console, <u>one</u> of its <u>more</u> intricate design features, is

                                A   B

<u>lowest</u> in the compartment than usual, especially for those crew members

  C

<u>as well as</u> those doing the testing of the plane.

      D

＜解答＞ C：lower

1378. It is not impossible to overcome the difficulties of learning a new language if
　　　A　　　　　　　　　　　　　　　　　　　　B　　　　　　　C

　　　one will have the right attitude.
　　　　　D

　　　＜解答＞　D：has

1379. Realizing the extent of the skier's injuries, his companions would have left
　　　　A　　　　　　　　　　　　B　　　　　　　　　　C

　　　more comfortable if a doctor were present.
　　　　　　　　　　　D

　　　＜解答＞　D：① if a doctor had been ② had a doctor been

1380. If the resources of forest and water power were more fully developed, the
　　　　A　　　　　　　　　　　　　　　　　　　　　　　B

　　　economy would not have been so dependent on imports.
　　　　　　　　　　　C　　　　　　D

　　　＜解答＞　C：not be

1381. I think I would enjoy the movie we went to last night even more if I had read
　　　　A　　　　B　　　　　　　　　　　　　　　　　　　　C

　　　the book before seeing it.
　　　　　　　　　　D

　　　＜解答＞　B：would have enjoyed

1382. If all the members of the committee who are present would agree, the
　　　A　　　　　　　B　　　　　　　　　　　　　　　C

　　　proposal will go into effect immediately.
　　　　　　　　　　　　　　D

　　　＜解答＞　C：agree

1383. Project Oribis, a flying eye hospital or a DC-8 jet that is both a classroom
　　　　　　　　　　　　　　　A

　　　or a clinic, has visited 37 countries, performed 3,000 operations, and updated
　　　　B　　　　　　　　　C　　　　　　　　　　　　D

　　　the skills of at least 2,500 eye doctors.

＜解答＞　B：and a clinic

1384. The job requires that the <u>applicant not only</u> speak <u>both Spanish and</u> English
　　　　　　　　　　　　　　　　　　A　　　　　　　　　　　　　　B

　　　<u>but also be able</u> to type <u>but take</u> shorthand.
　　　　　　C　　　　　　　　　　　D

　　　＜解答＞　D：and take

1385. The musician could play neither modern melodies <u>nor</u> classical <u>works, but</u>
　　　　　　　　　　　　　　　　　　　　　　　　　　　　A　　　　　　　　B

　　　his performance of traditional folk tunes captivated <u>either</u> the parents and
　　　　　　　　　　　　　　　　　　　　　　　　　　　　　　C

　　　<u>the children.</u>
　　　　　D

　　　＜解答＞　C：both

1386. <u>Although</u> her grandfather was the person for <u>who</u> the town was named,
　　　　　A　　　　　　　　　　　　　　　　　　　　　B

　　　<u>she</u> <u>moved</u> away immediately after graduation.
　　　　C　　D

　　　＜解答＞　B：whom

1387. <u>Both</u> Mr. Parkinson <u>or</u> Ms. Stewart have <u>run and lost</u> that race <u>more than</u>
　　　　A　　　　　　　　　B　　　　　　　　　C　　　　　　　　　D

　　　anyone.

　　　＜解答＞　B：and

1388. Electric eels <u>use</u> charges to detect prey and also <u>stunning</u> them <u>before</u> <u>they</u>
　　　　　　　　　　A　　　　　　　　　　　　　　　　B　　　　　　　C　　D

　　　eat them.

　　　＜解答＞　B：stun

1389. I watched him <u>step off</u> the pavement <u>crossing</u> the road, <u>and disappear</u> <u>into</u>
　　　　　　　　　　A　　　　　　　　　B　　　　　　　　C　　　　　　　D

　　　the post office.

　　　＜解答＞　B：cross

1390. Catching crabs in the bay is <u>profitable,</u> but <u>to fish</u> for bass <u>in</u> the river is more
　　　　　　　　　　　　　　　　A　　　　　　　B　　　　　　　C

　　　<u>relaxing</u>.
　　　　D
　　　＜解答＞　B：fishing

1391. The stockholders <u>expect the</u> chairman of the board whom <u>they elected</u> to
　　　　　　　　　　　　A　　　　　　　　　　　　　　　　B

　　　organize, direct, <u>controlling and</u> <u>supervise the operations</u> of the company.
　　　　　　　　　　　　C　　　　　　　D
　　　＜解答＞　C：controll and

1392. <u>Telecommunication</u>, a phenomenon of this deacde, <u>is insignificant</u> compared
　　　　　　A　　　　　　　　　　　　　　　　　　　　　B

　　　to telepathic communication, <u>which is</u> a phenomenon <u>of the future</u>.
　　　　　　　　　　　　　　　　　C　　　　　　　　　D
　　　＜解答＞　C：cancel

1393. The hall was hung with flags draped <u>above</u> the ceiling, <u>from</u> the fireplaces,
　　　　　　　　　　　　　　　　　　A　　　　　　　B

　　　<u>around</u> the moldings, and even <u>along</u> the window ledges.
　　　　C　　　　　　　　　　　D
　　　＜解答＞　A：on

1394. My efforts to change the <u>procedures of the council</u> were not <u>met enthusiasm</u>
　　　　　　　　　　　　　A　　　　　　　　　　　　　　　B

　　　<u>by</u> my colleagues <u>on</u> the board.
　　　C　　　　　D
　　　＜解答＞　B：met with enthusiasm

1395. The music professor <u>from</u> the small midwestern school thought that <u>during</u>
　　　　　　　　　　　　A　　　　　　　　　　　　　　　　　　　　B

　　　the concert the violin opposite <u>from</u> her seat <u>in</u> the first row was not tuned
　　　　　　　　　　　　　　　C　　　　　D

　　　properly.

<解答> C：cancel

1396. My best student <u>of</u> my grammar class speaks <u>with</u> an accent, but she will
　　　　　　　　　　　　A　　　　　　　　　　　　　　B

have no <u>trouble getting</u> a job <u>with</u> her strong references.
　　　　　　　C　　　　　　　　D

<解答> A：is

1397. <u>In spite</u> <u>of the weather</u>, the <u>picnic on</u> the beach was <u>held the</u> usual spot.
　　　　A　　　　B　　　　　　　　C　　　　　　　　　D

<解答> D：held at the

1398. The district council and <u>its lawyers</u>, who met with the mayor, <u>they discussed</u>
　　　　　　　　　　　　　　　　　　　　　A　　　　　　　　　　　　　　　　B

the issue of pay increases <u>for themselves</u> but did not resolve <u>it</u>.
　　　　　　　　　　　　　　C　　　　　　　　　　　　　　D

<解答> B：discussed

1399. The computer case, <u>designed it</u> by two engineers for use in outer space,
　　　　　　　　　　　　A

satisfies <u>their</u> requirements that <u>it have</u> strength <u>and be light</u>.
　　　　　　B　　　　　　　　　C　　　　　　　D

<解答> A：designed

1400. The geologists used <u>their new instrument</u> to determine how deep the well
　　　　　　　　　　　　　A

was, but <u>its meter</u> proved unreliable <u>and they</u> <u>could not measure</u>.
　　　　　　B　　　　　　　　　　　C　　　　　D

<解答> D：could not measure it

1401. If <u>you</u> thought <u>about, you would</u> see <u>that I am</u> right <u>and he is</u> wrong.
　　　　A　　　　　　B　　　　　　C　　　　　　D

<解答> B：about it, you would

1402. <u>One's</u> reputation is entirely based <u>on your ability</u> to meet the expectations
　　　　A　　　　　　　　　　　　　　B

of your colleagues and your family.
             C   D

＜解答＞ A：Your

1403. Louise was unhappy to hear about the childless couple without children
                       A   B

who were still upset and angry over their treatment at the clinic where she
                  C

worked as an aide and part-time translator.
                       D

＜解答＞ B：the childless couple

1404. George asked us to copy all of everything in the book, but we thought it
                     A   B

would be better if he waited and got permission.
                  C   D

＜解答＞ B：everything

1405. I kept at the job persistently until I felt that I finally understood the
                   A   B

format and content required by the two people who were my bosses.
                  C   D

＜解答＞ A：cancel

1406. Generally, Mr. Jones usually goes to the store on Wednesday, as he has found
                     A   B

that on weekdays it is far less crowed and less frantic than on weekends.
                  C   D

＜解答＞ A：cancel

1407. The quarterly payments on the loan are due every three months at the
                   A

Savings and Loan located on the corner of North and Main.
                  B   C   D

＜解答＞ A：cancel

1408. The advent of <u>low cost, high-speed</u> <u>date processing</u> facilities <u>have provided</u>
         A   B   C

  school administrators with <u>resources not available</u> a few years ago.
               D

  ＜解答＞ C：has provided

1409. The law, <u>which is</u> in effect in 20 of the <u>50 states</u>, <u>safeguard against</u> tax <u>abuse by</u>
       A   B   C   D

  small corporations.

  ＜解答＞ C：safeguards against

1410. Banks in economically <u>depressed are as</u> <u>has demonstrated</u> their reluctance
             A   B

  to <u>extend the loans</u> <u>borrowers who have</u> not met their monthly payments.
       C   D

  ＜解答＞ B：have demonstrated

1411. Medical researchers <u>have discovered</u> a <u>way</u> in which the nervous systems
          A   B

  of <u>primates appears</u> <u>to communicate</u> with their immune systems.
      C   D

  ＜解答＞ C：primates appear

1412. This is an <u>idea</u> <u>researchers hope</u> will bring to them the <u>financial moral</u>
      A   B   C

  support <u>he desserves</u>.
       D

  ＜解答＞ D：they deserve

1413. Since <u>the 1830's have trekked</u> to Hot Springs and its 4,000-acre <u>park to bathe in</u>
       A   B

  143-degree mineral water, <u>enjoy the view</u> from the 216-foot observation
              C

  <u>towers, and sail</u> the nearly Diamond Lake.
     D

　　＜解答＞　A：the 1830's they have trekked

1414. Moved lightly up the steps that curved around the sides of the garden wall
　　　　A　　　　　　　　　　　　B

　　　topped by clusters of climbing roses.
　　　C　　　　　　　　D

　　　＜解答＞　A：They moved

1415. I have to go home and feed the cats, dust the furniture, take out the garbage,
　　　　　　　　　　　　　A　　　　　B　　　　　　C

　　　load the dishwasher, defrost the chicken, and etc.
　　　　　　　　　　　　　　　　　　　　　　D

　　　＜解答＞　D：etc

1416. This is the last time the Harrisons plan to go to the country sice grows cold
　　　　　　　　　　　　　　　　　　　A　　　　　　　　B

　　　in the fall, and heating the house becomes difficult.
　　　　　　　　　C　　　　　　D

　　　＜解答＞　B：since it grows

1417. The computer, it is a 20th century invention, has created starting technological
　　　　　　　　　A　　　　　　　　　B

　　　changes in the way we organize and produce information.
　　　C　　　　　　D

　　　＜解答＞　A：cancel

1418. Agreeing to the treaties, which they were signed early this morning, the two
　　　　　　　　　　　　　　A

　　　superpowers pledged not to reveal their contents to the press, who had been
　　　　　B　　　　　　　　　　　　C　　　　　　　　　D

　　　waiting at the door.

　　　＜解答＞　A：which were signed

1419. A square dance it is merely the act of going round and round in a circle of
　　　　　　　　　A　　　　　　　　　　　　　B　　　　　　　C

dancers <u>composed of four couples</u>.
　　　　　　　　　　　D

＜解答＞　A：is

1420. <u>Economics</u> a subject <u>which it has caused</u> many college students problems
　　　A　　　　　　　　　　B

in the <u>past, continues</u> to be one of the <u>least attended courses</u>.
　　　　　　　　C　　　　　　　　　　　D

＜解答＞　B：which has caused

1421. The <u>typewriter, whcih it is</u> one of the world's great <u>inventions, has</u> not yet
　　　　A　　　　B　　　　　　　　　　　　　　C

been <u>replaced by the word</u> processor.
　　　　　D

＜解答＞　B：cancel

1422. The suggestion that taxes <u>were cut</u> <u>was vetoed</u> by the mayor, who <u>foresaw</u>
　　　　　　　　　　　　　A　　　B　　　　　　　　　C

a defficit that <u>was</u> not yet public knowledge.
　　　　　　　D

＜解答＞　A：be cut

1423. The stubborn young man <u>did not follow</u> the advice that he <u>reflected on</u>
　　　　　　　　　　　A　　　　　　　　　　　B

his behavior since he <u>refused</u> to believe he <u>had done</u> anything wrong.
　　　　　　　　　C　　　　　　　　D

＜解答＞　B：reflect on

1424. After the man looking for work <u>completed</u> the application, he <u>was told</u>
　　　　　　　　　　　　A　　　　　　　　　B

that it <u>was</u> necessary that he <u>included</u> a resume.
　　　C　　　　　　　　D

＜解答＞　D：include

1425. Before renovation could <u>continue</u>, <u>it was</u> imperative that the owner
　　　　　　　　　　A　　　B

approve the work and <u>will suggest</u> additional improvements.

    C   D

＜解答＞ D：suggest

1426. The federal <u>government recommends</u> that local civic <u>groups will accept</u>

               A   B

the responsibility of <u>welfare disbursement</u> to <u>the</u> needy.

                      C   D

＜解答＞ B：groups accept

1427. The directions are <u>a lot</u> <u>less</u> complicated <u>then</u> they <u>first</u> seemed.

               A B   C   D

＜解答＞ C：than

1428. He <u>would</u> not have released the report <u>without</u> he <u>had</u> first <u>verified</u> his sources.

    A   B   C   D

＜解答＞ B：unless

1429. My sister has <u>more</u> cassettes <u>and</u> records <u>than</u> <u>anyone</u> in the family.

          A   B   C   D

＜解答＞ D：anyone else

1430. <u>That the mayor's</u> commission <u>has done an admirable job</u> of <u>protecting the</u>

    A   B   C

city's architectural <u>features are not</u> denied by the preservationists.

                  D

＜解答＞ D：features is not

1431. Where the <u>children play</u> is where <u>intend they</u> to put a food store, <u>but I</u>

           A   B   C

don't know <u>when</u> or how soon.

        D

＜解答＞ B：they intend

1432. <u>Miami</u>, which is known for its temperate <u>winters, has</u> become the home of

    A   B

many retired <u>citizens which left</u> their homes in the <u>North, where winters were</u>
　　　　　　　　　　　C　　　　　　　　　　　　　　　　D

too severe.

　　＜解答＞　C：citizens who left

1433. The metric system, <u>which introduced</u> in <u>England where</u> it met strong
　　　　　　　　　　　　　A　　　　　　　　　B

resistance, is a system of measurement <u>which uses</u> the unit <u>10 as a standard</u>.
　　　　　　　　　　　　　　　　　　　　C　　　　　　　D

　　＜解答＞　A：which was introduced

1434. <u>The officers who</u> were from the corporation <u>that it sponsored</u> the golf
　　　　A　　　　　　　　　　　　　　　　　　B

tournament felt that <u>announcing the name</u> of a <u>rival as the next</u> sponsor
　　　　　　　　　　　C　　　　　　　　D

of the tournament was inappropriate.

　　＜解答＞　B：that sponsored

1435. After the <u>Capulets,</u> party, Romeo stood in the garden <u>outside of</u> <u>Juliet's</u> room;
　　　　　　　A　　　　　　　　　　　　　　　　　B　　　C

they declared <u>their</u> love for one another.
　　　　　　　D

　　＜解答＞　B：outside

1436. Juliet <u>could hardly</u> bear to <u>let</u> Romeo go; nevertheless, she <u>hadn't ought to</u>
　　　　　A　　　　　B　　　　　　　　　　　　　　　C

have taken the <u>sleeping</u> potion.
　　　　　　　D

　　＜解答＞　C：shouldn't

1437. <u>Before</u> the motion was approved and <u>while</u> it was being debated, the
　　　A　　　　　　　　　　　B

opposition tried to influence the chairman <u>although</u> he had refused to hear
　　　　　　　　　　　　　　　　　　　C

arguments the motion was made.
          D

〈解答〉 D：arguments before the motion

1438. The merchandise arrived <u>before was expected</u>, and <u>since no one</u> was home,
                              A   B

the postman left it <u>in front of the door</u>.
     C   D

〈解答〉 A：before it was expected

1439. <u>Even though maintained</u> a united front, the migrant workers <u>quarreled among</u>
        A   B

themselves <u>until the strike</u> ended <u>and they returned</u> to work.
            C   D

〈解答〉 A：Even though they maintained

1440. The heavy rainclouds <u>and</u> the powerful winds <u>indicates</u> <u>that</u> <u>a</u> hurricane is
                            A   B   C D

approaching.

〈解答〉 B：indicate

1441. When the noise <u>died down and</u> <u>when order restored</u> to the lecture hall, the
                       A   B

<u>controversial speaker</u> began where <u>he had left off</u>.
     C   D

〈解答〉 B：the order restored

1442. The boys <u>who were</u> first in line <u>were given</u> the T-shirts <u>donating</u> by the
                 A   B   C

philanthropist <u>who has</u> always supported our charity.
                 D

〈解答〉 C：donated

1443. When the sun <u>rises</u>, I sometimes have difficulty <u>sitting</u> <u>aside</u> my cover and
                     A   B   C

<u>getting up</u>.

       D

＜解答＞ B：setting

1444. The <u>talks promote</u> the expansion of trade between the two neighboring

          A

<u>countries</u> were <u>discontinued</u> after certain protocol agreements <u>were violated</u>.

   B   C   C

＜解答＞ A：talks promoted

1445. <u>Muttering</u> to herself, the woman, being hot and <u>was weary</u>, <u>sat down</u> on a

     A   B   C

stump <u>next</u> to the road.

       D

＜解答＞ B：weary

1446. <u>Look on</u> <u>the other</u> side of any logs <u>laying</u> in the path to avoid <u>stepping</u>.

    A   B   C   D

＜解答＞ C：lying

1447. The extension services of the university, while <u>it is</u> providing an opportunity

                                          A

for the community <u>to take</u> courses, <u>offer</u> full-time students greater flexibility

                         B   C

<u>in arranging</u> their schedules.

     D

＜解答＞ A：cancel

1448. After <u>you testifying</u>, your statement and <u>that of</u> the officer will be sent to

         A   B

the court, <u>which</u> will hold both documents <u>until</u> the hearing.

          C   D

＜解答＞ A：testifying

1449. When <u>coming</u> to school, the children need <u>to think</u> before <u>they crossing</u>

         A   B   C

the streets <u>where</u> there is no crossing guard.
　　　　　　　D

　　＜解答＞ C：crossing

1450. <u>Conserving</u> heat in the winter and <u>reduce heat in</u> the summer, deciduous trees
　　　　A　　　　　　　　　　　　　　B

　　<u>planted at the west</u> and south parts of a house <u>are natural</u> energy savers.
　　　　　　C　　　　　　　　　　　　　　　D

　　＜解答＞ B：reducing heat in

1451. Since <u>they moving</u> to the east coast, the Parsons have not <u>been able</u> <u>to find</u>
　　　　　A　　　　　　　　　　　　　　　　　　　B　　　C

　　a home <u>large enough</u> for their family.
　　　　　　D

　　＜解答＞ A：moving

1452. The weather <u>has improved</u>, the game <u>was enjoyed</u> by players <u>and</u> spectators
　　　　　　　A　　　　　　　　B　　　　　　　C

　　<u>alike</u>.
　　　D

　　＜解答＞ A：having improved

1453. Cairo University, the Arab <u>world's first secular</u> university, <u>founded in 1925</u>
　　　　　　　　　　　　A　　　　　　　　　　B

　　<u>with seven main</u> faculties <u>and colleges</u>.
　　　　C　　　　　　　　D

　　＜解答＞ B：was founded in 1925

1454. The assistant manager <u>asked</u> the clerk <u>to help him</u> <u>move the supplies</u>, but
　　　　　　　　　　A　　　　　B　　　　C

　　the clerk <u>claimed he too</u> busy.
　　　　　　D

　　＜解答＞ D：claimed he was too

1455. <u>To catch</u> our colleague at home, you <u>must early</u> in the morning because
　　　A　　　　　　　　　　　　　B

he <u>leaves</u> at 7 a.m. <u>to go to</u> work.

      C   D

<解答> B：must come early

1456. Even though the guest did not like <u>sleeping</u> on a hard bed, she <u>managed</u>

                                            A   B

to fall <u>asleep</u> because <u>she so tired</u>.

              C   D

<解答> D：she was so tired

1457. <u>Thinking</u> through their plan thoroughly <u>did convinced</u> the committee they

         A   B

<u>were wrong</u> to bilieve that no one else <u>would find</u> fault with their logic.

         C   D

<解答> B：convinced

1458. Some <u>mammals that live</u> in the <u>wild have thick skins</u> or <u>hides which</u> <u>are protest</u>

                  A   B   C   D

them from the weather and their enemies.

<解答> D：protect

1459. In spite of recent <u>advances in</u> modern medicine, the <u>long-sought</u> cure for cancer

                        A   B

<u>has not been</u> found, and the incidence of the <u>disease is being increasing</u>.

       C   D

<解答> D：disease is increasing

1460. Working hard <u>may have been</u> good for the new recruit, but <u>it tired him</u>

                    A   B

out <u>so much</u> that <u>he was collapsed</u>.

         C   D

<解答> D：he collapsed

1461. Each of the owners of the building <u>had took</u> a look at the terrain

                                       A

before they agreed <u>to landscape</u> it and <u>put in</u> a road.

        B   C   D

<解答>　A：had taken

1462. We <u>learned</u> that it was <u>her</u> <u>who</u> <u>made</u> the first solo flight by a woman across

        A   B C D

the Atlantic.

<解答>　B：she

1463. The counselors from <u>the college feels</u> <u>it is unwise</u> for students to select a major

                        A   B

before <u>they have</u> <u>the opportunity to experience</u> different academic subjects.

        C   D

<解答>　A：the college feel

1464. Several authors <u>whose publishers rejected</u> their finished manuscripts

                 A

<u>and demanded</u> <u>they return</u> their advances <u>has prevailed</u>, in court in

    B   C   D

recent years.

<解答>　D：have prevailed

1465. The <u>pedestrian passing</u> the construction site <u>fell</u> in the hole where the crew

          A   B

<u>has been working</u> to replace the cover <u>that protect</u> the spot.

      C   D

<解答>　D：that protects

1466. The political power at <u>stake in</u> the upcoming <u>elections are</u> small, <u>considering</u>

                       A   B   C

that none of the three opposition <u>parties</u> is supporting a candidate.

                                  D

<解答>　B：elections is

1467. <u>In the skit</u>, Pygmalion <u>returned</u> from the festival of Venus, <u>him</u> and the

    A   B   C

statue <u>were</u> supposed to hug.

          D

＜解答＞ C：he

1468. The astronauts who <u>were not allowed</u> <u>to join</u> the shuttle mission for medical

                             A   B

reasons monitored <u>the orbits</u> of the Columbia from Houston after it <u>is launched</u>.

                           C   D

＜解答＞ D：was launched

1469. The chairman <u>will speak</u> to the crowd, which <u>did</u> not appear <u>to hear</u> him

                 A   B   C

even when he <u>raised</u> his voice.

                   D

＜解答＞ A：spoke

1470. The nurse's <u>aides will have learned</u> during their training last month that color

                             A

blindness <u>is</u> a condition <u>affecting</u> thousands with <u>varying</u> degress of severity.

                 B   C   D

＜解答＞ A：aides learned

1471. In those days there <u>were</u> no king in Israel, but every man <u>did</u> that <u>which</u> <u>was</u>

                         A   B   C   D

right in his own eyes.

＜解答＞ A：was

1472. The accountant <u>careful</u> looked over the <u>monthly</u> accounts, trying to find the

                     A   B

<u>terrible</u> error we had made <u>inadvertently</u>.

      C   D

＜解答＞ A：carefully

1473. To give <u>credit</u> where it is due, the assistant <u>loyal</u> supported his <u>superior</u>

                 A   B   C

even when seemed <u>hopeless</u>.
                               D
　＜解答＞　B：loyally

1474. <u>Given</u> the foul weather, the Coast Guard <u>strongly</u> urges all sailors to think
         A   B

<u>careful</u> about taking out <u>small</u> boats.
    C   D
　＜解答＞　C：carefully

1475. The journalist asked the <u>elected</u> official <u>presently</u> to make a statement, but
                                    A   B

he <u>refused</u> to <u>comment</u>.
      C   D
　＜解答＞　B：present

1476. For the <u>first time</u>, the <u>unpopular</u> regulations were <u>temporarily</u> <u>suspension</u>
              A   B   C   D

during the week-long celebration.
　＜解答＞　D：suspended

1477. <u>Strong winds</u> <u>flow naturally</u> from areas of <u>greater energy</u> concentration to
         A   B   C

areas of <u>concentration less</u>.
                  D
　＜解答＞　D：less concentration

1478. <u>Vanilla ice cream</u> was one of the <u>treats special</u> on the <u>Skylab menue</u> <u>provided</u>
         A   B   C   D

for the hardy astronauts.
　＜解答＞　B：special treats

1479. <u>The recently renovated</u> home is located in a <u>beautiful natural</u> <u>would setting</u>
              A   B   C

just minutes from a <u>local center shopping</u>.
                          D

<解答>　D：local shopping center

1480. <u>The simple charity</u> organized by the <u>patron wealthy</u> is now the <u>biggest</u> in
　　　　　　A　　　　　　　　　　　　　　　B　　　　　　　　　　C

　　　the state with hundreds of <u>loyal volunteers</u>.
　　　　　　　　　　　　　　　　　　　D

<解答>　B：wealthy patron

1481. The doctor, <u>unprepared for</u> the <u>difficult operation</u>, brought in <u>two special</u>
　　　　　　　　　　A　　　　　　　　　B　　　　　　　　　　　　　C

　　　assistants to help <u>in areas dangerous</u> where he was not an expert.
　　　　　　　　　　　　　　　　D

<解答>　D：in dangerous areas

1482. The <u>fast food trays</u> on the Space Shuttle <u>held not only</u> the food <u>in place</u>,
　　　　　　A　　　　　　　　　　　　　　　　　　　B　　　　　　　　　C

　　　but also served as <u>warning devices</u>.
　　　　　　　　　　　　　　　D

<解答>　B：not only held

1483. <u>Long after sewing</u> machines were ubiquitous <u>in American life</u>, <u>quilts continued</u>
　　　　　　A　　　　　　　　　　　　　　　　　　　　B　　　　　　C

　　　to be <u>by hand made</u>.
　　　　　　　D

<解答>　D：made by hand

1484. <u>Greatly the hotel strike</u> inconvenienced the <u>extremely</u> <u>elderly</u> patrons who
　　　　　　A　　　　　　　　　　　　　　　　　　　　B　　　　C

　　　<u>unwillingly and ungraciously made</u> their own beds.
　　　　　　　　　　　D

<解答>　A：The hotel strike greatly

1485. <u>Presumably</u> the espionage agent has <u>quietly</u> and <u>without delay</u> left the
　　　　　　A　　　　　　　　　　　　　　B　　　　　C

　　　country after his accomplices <u>forcibly were</u> apprepended.
　　　　　　　　　　　　　　D

<解答>　D：were forcibly

1486. Early man, to blunt the wind and conserve body heat, no doubt added
 　　　 A 　　　　　　　　　　　　　　　 B

 　　 the protective, insulating, hairy skins of other animals to his own
 　　　　　　　　　　　 C

 　　 thin one relatively.
 　　　　　 D

 　　 <解答>　D：relatively thin one

1487. The union delegates who are going to the convention in Miami Beach are
 　　　　　 A 　　　　　　 B 　　　　　　　　　　　　 C

 　　 Thompson, Steinmetz, and me.
 　　　　　　　　　　　　　 D

 　　 <解答>　D：I

1488. Us boys insist on your giving them what is theirs and us what is ours.
 　　 A 　　　　　 B 　　　　　　　　 C 　　　　　　　　 D

 　　 <解答>　A：We

1489. She wore a dress to the party that was far more attractive than the other girls.
 　　　　 A 　　　　　 B 　　　　　　　　 C 　　　　　　　　 D

 　　 <解答>　D：those of the other

1490. If he had laid quietly under the tree as he had been instructed to do, we
 　　　　　 A 　　　　　　 B 　　　　　　 C

 　　 would have found him.
 　　　　　　 D

 　　 <解答>　A：had lain

1491. Down the field have came the students of South High School: members of the
 　　　 A 　　　　　 B

 　　 newly organized, somewhat incompetent band; drum majorettes in white,

 　　 spangled skirts; and the team, muddy and wretched.
 　　　 C 　　　　　　　　　　　 D

 　　 <解答>　B：have come

1492. Between you and <u>I</u>, I <u>am convinced</u> that this painting by Dali shows greater
　　　　　　　　　　　A　　　　　B

<u>artistry</u> than <u>that</u> of Picasso.
　　C　　　　　　D

<解答>　A：me

1493. <u>Being that</u> you <u>are interested</u> in the outcome of the election, <u>let us</u> wait
　　　　A　　　　　　　　B　　　　　　　　　　　　　　　　　　C

until the final tally <u>has been made</u>.
　　　　　　　　　　　　D

<解答>　A：Since

1494. The <u>millenmium</u> <u>will have arrived</u> when parents give <u>appropriate</u>
　　　　　A　　　　　　　　B　　　　　　　　　　　　　C

responsibilities to <u>we</u> teenagers.
　　　　　　　　　　D

<解答>　D：us

1495. The crisis <u>in</u> the countries of the <u>Middle East</u> <u>have been discussed</u> at our
　　　　　A　　　　　　　　　　　B　　　　　　C

<u>weekly</u> forums.
　　D

<解答>　C：has been discussed

1496. The trouble <u>with</u> a good many people in our country is that they have <u>vested</u>
　　　　　　A　　　　　　　　　　　　　　　　　　　　　　　　　B

interests ─ <u>that is</u>, they are concerned with <u>theirselves</u> first and foremost.
　　　　　　　C　　　　　　　　　　　　D

<解答>　D：themselves

1497. There <u>seem</u> <u>nowadays</u> to be little of the optimism that <u>imbued</u> our ancestors
　　　　　A　　B　　　　　　　　　　　　　　　　　C

<u>with</u> courage and hope.
　　D

<解答>　A：seems

1498. Since it was an <u>unusually</u> warm day, the dog <u>laid</u> under the tree all <u>afternoon</u>
                   A   B   C

    without barking at <u>passersby</u>-something he usually does.
                             D

    ＜解答＞ B：lay

1499. The Chairman <u>of the Board</u> of Directors made it <u>clear</u> at the meeting that he
                   A   B

    <u>will not</u> step down from his position <u>as chairman</u>.
      C   D

    ＜解答＞ C：would not

1500. <u>These kind</u> of peopls who have little education, who have no desire for cultural
      A

    pursuits, and whose sole purpose <u>is acquiring</u> wealth, are not the <u>type</u> I wish
                              B   C

    <u>to associate with</u>.
        D

    ＜解答＞ A：These kinds

1501. Neither Sam Atkins <u>nor</u> Henry Miller, sales representatives for the company,
                   A

    presented <u>their</u> summories of sales <u>before</u> the deadline <u>for doing so</u>.
             B   C   D

    ＜解答＞ B：his

1502. The reason <u>her</u> and her cousin decided <u>to take</u> the train instead of the plane
             A   B

    was that <u>there was</u> a forecast over the radio about an <u>impending</u> storm.
           C   D

    ＜解答＞ A：she

1503. Jimand <u>him</u>, after spending several hours trying to ascertain the <u>whereabouts</u>
        A   B

of the missing children, <u>finally</u> discovered them in their <u>aunt's</u> house.
                              C   D

　＜解答＞ A：he

1504. Each of the <u>hotel's</u> 500 rooms <u>were equipped</u> with <u>high</u> quality <u>air conditioning</u>
                 A   B   C   D

and television.

　＜解答＞ B：was equipped

1505. <u>On</u> any <u>given</u> weekend-especially holiday <u>weekends</u>-the number of highway
   A   B   C

deaths <u>are</u> predictable.
        D

　＜解答＞ D：is

1506. Of the two cars that the Smiths <u>have</u> the Plymouth is, <u>without any question,</u>
                                A   B

the <u>cheapest</u> <u>to run</u>.
      C   D

　＜解答＞ C：cheaper

1507. Man <u>cannot</u> live <u>by bread</u> alone, <u>or</u> can he <u>live</u> without bread.
         A   B   C   D

　＜解答＞ C：nor

1508. <u>Having swam</u> <u>two thirds</u> of the distance <u>across</u> the English Channel, Dixon
      A   B   C

<u>could not give up</u> now.
        D

　＜解答＞ A：Having swum

1509. In the discussion, one speaker <u>held</u> that since we live in <u>money-orinted</u> society,
                                  A   B

the average individual cares <u>little</u> about solving <u>anyone's else</u> problems.
                             C   D

　＜解答＞ D：anyone else's

1510. We requested the superintendent of the building <u>to clean</u> up the storage room
                                                     A

    <u>in</u> the basement <u>so that</u> the children <u>had</u> enough space for their bicycles.
    B   C   D

    ＜解答＞ D：would have

1511. Namath played a <u>real</u> fine game <u>in spite of</u> the fact that the Jets lost <u>by</u> a
                      A   B   C

    touchdown <u>which</u> the opposing team scored in the last minute of play.
                D

    ＜解答＞ A：really

1512. Stores were <u>jammed</u> with <u>last-minute</u> Christmas shoppers, but the festive
                 A   B

    spirit was <u>slight</u> disrupted by homemade bombs that <u>exploded</u> at two
                 C   D

    department stores.

    ＜解答＞ C：slightly

1513. Nixon <u>has stated</u> that he <u>has always had</u> a great <u>interest and</u> admiration for
               A   B   C

    the <u>work</u> of the British economist Keynes.
          D

    ＜解答＞ C：interest in and

1514. Sharon planned to pay <u>around</u> a hundred dollars <u>for</u> a new spring coat but
                        A   B

    when she saw a gorgeous coat <u>which sold</u> for two hundred dollars, she
                            C

    decided <u>to buy</u> it.
           D

    ＜解答＞ A：about

1515. Members of the staff <u>of the District Attorney</u> made more than $100,000 from
                        A

a <u>get-rich-quick</u> scheme in which investors <u>bilked</u> of about <u>$1-million</u>.
　　　　　　B　　　　　　　　　　　　　　C　　　　　　　D

<解答> C：were bilked

1516. <u>Besides</u> <u>to be</u> an outstanding student, he is <u>also</u> a leader in school government
　　　　A　　　B　　　　　　　　　　　　　　C

and a <u>trophy-winner</u> in school sports.
　　　　　　D

<解答> B：being

1517. The dean <u>of the college</u>, together <u>with</u> some other faculty members, <u>are</u>
　　　　　　　　A　　　　　　　　B　　　　　　　　　　　　C

planning a conference tor the purpose of <u>laying</u> down certain regulations.
　　　　　　　　　　　　　　　　　　　D

<解答> C：is

1518. <u>Now</u> that the stress of examinations and interviews <u>are</u> over, we can <u>all</u> <u>relax</u>
　　A　　　　　　　　　　　　　　　　　　B　　　　　　C　D

for awhile.

<解答> B：is

1519. The American standard of living <u>is</u> still <u>higher</u> <u>than</u> <u>most</u> of the <u>other countries</u>
　　　　　　　　　　　　　A　　　　B　　　C　　　　　　D

of the world.

<解答> C：than that of most

1520. <u>Due to</u> the failure of the air-cooling system, many in the audience <u>had left</u> the
　　　A　　　　　　　　　　　　　　　　　　　　　　　　　B

meeting <u>before</u> the principal speaker <u>arrived</u>.
　　　　C　　　　　　　　　D

<解答> A：Because of

1521. <u>After waiting</u> in line <u>for three hours</u>, <u>much to our disgust</u>, the tickets <u>had been</u>
　　　A　　　　　　　B　　　　　　C　　　　　　　D

sold out when we reached the window.

<解答> C：the tickets had, much to our disgust, been-----

1522. <u>Sharp</u> advances last week in the wholesale price of beef <u>is</u> a strong indication
      A   B

    of higher meat <u>costs</u> to come, but so far retail prices continue <u>favorable</u>.
                  C   D
    ＜解答＞ B：are

1523. The supervisor <u>was advised</u> to give the assignment to <u>whomever</u> <u>he believed</u>
                  A   B   C

    had a strong sense of responsibility, and the courage <u>of</u> his conviction.
                                                 D
    ＜解答＞ B：whoever

1524. <u>When</u> the movie <u>was</u> over, Joe and <u>me</u> went for a <u>quick</u> walk.
      A   B   C   D
    ＜解答＞ C：I

1525. Michael <u>himself</u> could not <u>gone</u> to the concert, <u>which</u> <u>was held</u> at the school,
          A   B   C   D

    so he gave his sister his tickets.
    ＜解答＞ B：go

1526. Alice was <u>having</u> trouble controlling the children <u>because</u> <u>there</u> <u>was</u> so many
             A   B   C   D

    of them.
    ＜解答＞ D：were

1527. <u>Having seen</u> the <u>children's</u> work, Miss Adams <u>approves</u> <u>their requesting</u>
        A   B   C   D

    to go home.
    ＜解答＞ D：their request

1528. <u>Tom calling</u> Marie made <u>her</u> angry, <u>so</u> she <u>hung up</u> him.
        A   B   C   D
    ＜解答＞ A：Tom's calling

1529. Mary and Joe <u>want to go</u> to the shore <u>this summer</u>, <u>which</u> sounds like a
              A   B   C

good idea <u>to me</u>.

                            D

　＜解答＞　C：that

1530. My counselor <u>suggested</u> that I make my professor <u>to change</u> my grade <u>since</u>

                        A   B   C

I was sick <u>the day of the exam</u>.

                  D

　＜解答＞　B：change

1531. Martha <u>on violin</u>, accompanied by Saul on piano, <u>were</u> a great hit

          A   B

<u>at the annul recital</u> <u>last week</u>.

               C   D

　＜解答＞　B：was

1532. Freddy and Bill went to <u>his apartment</u> <u>for drinks</u>, <u>and then</u> drove <u>across town</u>

                                    A   B   C   D

to pick up their girl friends.

　＜解答＞　A：their apartment

1533. <u>As soon as</u> I saw the smoke, <u>I called</u> the fire department, but <u>they haven't</u>

          A   B   C

arrived <u>already</u>.

              D

　＜解答＞　D：yet

1534. <u>To</u> the finalists, <u>Bob and I</u>, the last high jump was the most exciting <u>as well as</u>

  A   B   C

the <u>most difficult</u>.

              D

　＜解答＞　B：Bob and me

1535. <u>To get a scholarship</u>, the bursar's office <u>called</u> Jaime in <u>to discuss</u> <u>his</u>

               A   B   C   D

application.

〈解答〉 A：Because of Jaime's getting a scholarship

1536. <u>By this time</u> next week, Randy <u>not only</u> <u>will have memorized</u> the words,
　　　　　A　　　　　　　　　　　　　B　　　　　　C

　　　but he <u>will also learn</u> the melody of the new song.
　　　　　　　　　　D

　　〈解答〉 D：will also have learned

1537. If we here in America <u>cannot live</u> <u>peaceably</u> and happily <u>together</u>, we connot
　　　　　　　　　　　　　　　　A　　　　B　　　　　　　　　C

　　　hope that nations which have different living conditions-different economic

　　　standards, different aspirations, different mores, different interests- <u>to live</u>
　　　　　　　　　　　　　　　　　　　　　　　　　　　　　　　　　　　　D

　　　peaceably with us.

　　〈解答〉 D：will live

1538. Every man, woman, and child <u>in this community</u> <u>are</u> now aware of the
　　　　　　　　　　　　　　　　　　　　　A　　　　　　　B

　　　<u>terrible consequences</u> <u>of the habit</u> of smoking.
　　　　　　　C　　　　　　　　　D

　　〈解答〉 B：is

1539. The question <u>arises</u> <u>as to who</u> <u>should go out</u> this morning in this below-zero
　　　　　　　　　　　A　　　B　　　　　C

　　　weather to clean the snow from the garage entrance, you or <u>me</u>.
　　　　　　　　　　　　　　　　　　　　　　　　　　　　　　　D

　　〈解答〉 D：I

1540. <u>Had I have been</u> in my <u>brother's position</u>, I would have <u>hung up</u> the phone
　　　　　　A　　　　　　　　　　B　　　　　　　　　　　　　C

　　　<u>in the middle</u> of the conversation.
　　　　　D

　　〈解答〉 A：Had I been

1541. The company is planning a <u>series</u> of lectures for <u>their</u> excutives <u>so that</u>
　　　　　　　　　　　　　　　　A　　　　　　　　　B　　　　　　　C

they may be aware of how to deal with racial problems that may occur

<u>from time to time</u>.

        D

  ＜解答＞　B：its

1542. <u>To implement</u> the new laws <u>may not be</u> easy, <u>but if</u> everyone does <u>their</u> part

        A   B   C   D

we will succeed.

  ＜解答＞　D：his

1543. When Columbus <u>discovered</u> America, he thought that he <u>arrived</u> <u>in India</u>,

                   A   B   C

so he called the people he met " <u>Indians</u> ".

                           D

  ＜解答＞　B：had arrived

1544. <u>Either</u> the carpenter or the electrician can store <u>their</u> tool <u>in the shed, but</u>

   A   B   C

<u>there is not room</u> for both sets.

        D

  ＜解答＞　B：his

1545. Since I <u>have eaten</u> before I <u>boarded</u> the plane, I was not hungry <u>when</u> the

           A   B   C

stewardess <u>brought</u> dinner.

        D

  ＜解答＞　A：had eaten

1546. Ferdinand and Isabella <u>journeyed</u> <u>to the south of Spain, and Granada was</u>

                                A   B   C   D

<u>besieged by them</u>.

  ＜解答＞　D：and besieged Granada

1547. We <u>need</u> an <u>unusual gifted</u> chemist <u>to solve</u> this sensitive problem

         A   B   C

without creating any hazards.
         D

＜解答＞ B：unusually gifted

1548. If you want a particular book, the person to see is the librarian
    A   B   C

she is wearing glasses.
        D

＜解答＞ D：who is wearing glasses

1549. Although Alice has been to the mountains many times before, she still loves it.
                A   B   C   D

＜解答＞D：them

1550. The mist raised from Lake Leman as we watched, reminding us of Brigadoon
         A   B   C

and other magical places.
        D

＜解答＞ A：rose

1551. In the yard there was a rake, a shovel, and a hoe, all getting rusty in the rain,
        A   B

but no one would run out to put them away.
     C   D

＜解答＞ A：there were

1552. Joan decided that she did not like the girl eating an ice cream cone on the
        A   B

bus after she yelled at her little brother.
        C   D

＜解答＞ C：Joan

1553. With his mother away, he had to prepare his own supper, but that upset
        A   B   C

him so much that he could not do his homework.
        D

<解答> C：cooking

1554. I <u>intend to move</u> that our committee <u>appoints</u> Tom as chairman, and <u>I hope</u>
           A   B   C

that you <u>will second</u> my motion.
           D

<解答> B：appoint

1555. His dog <u>having barked</u> a warning, the watchman who <u>had been assigned</u>
                A   B

to guard the valuable truckload of chemicals pulled out his gun <u>quick</u> and
                                                                C

proceeded <u>to search out</u> a possible intruder.
                D

<解答> C：quickly

1556. Popular impressions <u>about</u> slang are often erroneous; <u>their</u> is no necessary
                              A   B

connection, <u>for example</u>, <u>between</u> what is slang and what is ungrammatical.
                          C   D

<解答> B：there

1557. <u>Nor</u> has the writer even the satisfaction of calling his reader a fool for
    A

misunderstanding him, since he seldom hears <u>of</u> it, it is the reader who calls
                                                B

the writer a fool <u>for</u> not being able to express <u>hisself</u>.
                C   D

<解答> D：himself

1558. I appreciate <u>you</u> helping me <u>to do</u> the dishes, but I wish you would <u>lay</u> them
                  A   B   C

down on the table more <u>carefully</u>.
                    D

<解答> A：your

1559. <u>No sooner</u> had he <u>begun</u> to speak <u>when</u> an ominous muttering <u>arose</u> from
   A   B   C   D
  the audience.
  ＜解答＞　C：than

1560. Ellen <u>tried to tell</u> me <u>that</u> all the things <u>Bob said</u> <u>is</u> true.
       A   B   C D
  ＜解答＞　D：are

1561. <u>Either</u> Carol <u>or</u> Grace <u>are coming</u> to the recital, but one <u>of them</u> has to stay
   A   B   C   D
  home.
  ＜解答＞　C：is coming

1562. Between <u>you and I</u>, I don't <u>approve</u> of the way <u>in whcih</u> Frank is <u>handling</u>
      A   B   C   D
  the situation.
  ＜解答＞　A：you and me

1563. <u>Hoping</u> she would not <u>be seen</u>, Mary rushed in, <u>picking up</u> her purse, and
   A   B   C
  <u>rushed out</u>.
     D
  ＜解答＞　C：picked up

1564. After they <u>have eaten</u> lunch, the boys ran <u>outside</u> <u>to play</u> <u>with their</u> friends.
       A   B C   D
  ＜解答＞　A：had eaten

1565. A <u>red-hair</u> boy <u>is needed</u> to play <u>the part of Alfred</u> in <u>this</u> new comedy.
    A   B   C   D
  ＜解答＞　A：red-haired

1566. Mike is <u>so lazy</u> that <u>he has laid</u> <u>in the</u> hammock <u>since</u> lunch.
      A   B   C   D
  ＜解答＞　B：he has lain

1567. John is always <u>worried about</u> being late, <u>so</u> he leaves <u>early</u> than <u>anyone else</u>.
　　　　　　　　　　　　　A　　　　　　　　　B　　　　　C　　　　　　D

　　＜解答＞　C：earlier

1568. The <u>psychology</u> professor <u>arrived late</u> for his lecture <u>on promptness</u>, <u>which</u>
　　　　　　A　　　　　　　　B　　　　　　　　　　　　　C　　　　　D

made everyone laugh.

　　＜解答＞　D：his lecture

1569. We <u>will not be</u> <u>effected</u> by John's decision, but he <u>will not become aware</u>
　　　　　A　　　B　　　　　　　　　　　　　　　　　C

of that fact <u>for seceral</u> weeks.
　　　　　　　D

　　＜解答＞　B：affected

1570. The opinions of the crowd <u>exerts</u> <u>more</u> influence <u>on</u> her <u>than</u> they should.
　　　　　　　　　　　　　　　　A　　B　　　　　　　C　　　　D

　　＜解答＞　A：exert

1571. Each student <u>may</u> leave the room whenever <u>they</u> <u>may</u> desire <u>to do so</u>.
　　　　　　　　　A　　　　　　　　　　　　　　B　　C　　　　　D

　　＜解答＞　B：he

1572. We finished our climb <u>by</u> sighting the <u>mountain</u> top <u>then</u> we <u>prepared</u> the
　　　　　　　　　　　　　　A　　　　　　　B　　　　C　　　　D

evening meal.

　　＜解答＞　C：and then

1573. Proud his skill <u>in serving</u> liquor, he <u>poured</u> some of the wine into his own
　　　　　　　　　　　A　　　　　　　　B

glass first <u>so that</u> <u>he would get the cork and not the lady</u>.
　　　　　　　C　　　　　　　D

　　＜解答＞　D：he, not the lady, would get the cork

1574. Everyone <u>is expected</u> <u>to attend</u> the afternoon session <u>but</u> the field supervisor,
　　　　　　　A　　　　B　　　　　　　　　　　　　　C

the sales manager, and <u>I</u>.

               D

　＜解答＞　D：me

1575. Manslaughter <u>is where</u> a person <u>is killed</u> <u>unlawfully</u> <u>but without</u> premeditation.

               A   B   C   D

　＜解答＞　A：occurs when

1576. <u>Its</u> not <u>generslly known</u> that the word " buxom " <u>originally</u> came from the

A   B   C

<u>Old English</u> verb meaning " to bend. "

       D

　＜解答＞　A：It's

1577. Developed by the <u>research</u> engineers of Dupont, <u>by the government is</u>

                 A   B

<u>considered the new explosive</u> a <u>sure</u> deterrent <u>to war</u>.

                         C   D

　＜解答＞　B：the new explosive is considered by the government

1578. Baseball, football, and soccer have <u>all</u> been approved as <u>extracurricular</u>

                           A   B

activities. From <u>either</u> of them a coach can earn several <u>hundreds</u> of dollars

               C   D

each season.

　＜解答＞　C：any one

1579. Most of the citizens have <u>no doubt</u> that the <u>Mayor taking</u> a firm stand in the

                     A   B

matter of <u>clamping down</u> on drug peddlers will bear immediate results in

               C

<u>ridding the city</u> of these vermin.

       D

　＜解答＞　B：Mayor's taking

1580. None of the crew members who <u>flied</u> with me <u>over</u> Hanoi is happy today

           A   B

<u>about</u> the destruction <u>caused</u> in that bombing mission.

  C   D

  <解答> A：flew

1581. We, <u>as</u> parents who are interested in the welfare of our son, are <u>strongly</u>

   A   B

opposed to <u>him</u> associating with individuals who <u>do not seem</u> to have

     C   D

moral scruples.

  <解答> C：his

1582. <u>It</u> was very nice of the <u>Rodriguezes</u> to invite my husband, my mother,

  A   B

and <u>I</u> to their New <u>Year's</u> Eve party.

   C   D

  <解答> C：me

1583. When one <u>leaves</u> his car <u>to be repaired</u>, he <u>assumes</u> that the mechanic will

      A   B   C

repair the car <u>good</u>.

      D

  <解答> D：well

1584. <u>Amy</u> modern novelist <u>would be thrilled</u> to have <u>his</u> stories compared

  A   B   C

<u>with Dickens</u>.

  D

  <解答> D：those of Dickens

1585. Many people in the United States <u>don't</u> scarcely know <u>about</u> the terrible

              A   B

hardships that the Vietnamese <u>are experiencing</u> in their <u>war-ravaged</u> country.

              C   D

　　＜解答＞　A：cancel

1586. The automobile industry <u>is experimenting</u> with a new <u>type of a</u> motor that

　　　　　　　　　　　　　　　　　A　　　　　　　　　　　　　B

will consume <u>less</u> gasoline and <u>cause</u> much less pollution.

　　　　　　　　C　　　　　　　　D

　　＜解答＞　B：type of

1587. Sitting <u>opposite</u> my sister and <u>me</u> in the subway were <u>them</u> same men

　　　　　　　　A　　　　　　　　　B　　　　　　　　　C

who walked <u>alongside</u> us and tried to pinch us on Fifth Avenue.

　　　　　　　　　D

　　＜解答＞　C：those

1588. The <u>youth</u> of today are <u>seemingly</u> more sophisticated than were <u>they're</u>

　　　　　A　　　　　　　　B　　　　　　　　　　　　　　　　C

parents <u>at</u> the corresponding age.

　　　　　D

　　＜解答＞　C：their

1589. The lilaces in my <u>Uncle Joe's</u> garden smell <u>sweetly</u> <u>at</u> this time <u>of the year</u>.

　　　　　　　　　　　A　　　　　　　　　　　B　C　　　　　　D

　　＜解答＞　B：sweet

1590. <u>Being that</u> the United States has a food surplus, it is <u>hard to see</u> why

　　　A　　　　　　　　　　　　　　　　　　　　　　　B

<u>anyone</u> in our country <u>should</u> go hungry.

　　C　　　　　　　　　D

　　＜解答＞　A：Since

1591. A series <u>of debates</u> <u>between</u> the major condidates <u>were</u> scheduled for the

　　　　　　A　　B　　　　　　　　　　　　C

Labor Day <u>weekend</u>.

　　　　　　　D

　　＜解答＞　C：was

1592. We <u>did</u> the job as <u>good</u> as we <u>could</u>; however, it did not <u>turn out</u> to be
　　　　A　　　　　　B　　　　　C　　　　　　　　　　　　　D
satisfactory.
　　　＜解答＞　B：well

1593. If I <u>would have had</u> more time, I <u>would have written</u> a much <u>more</u> interesting
　　　　　　　　A　　　　　　　　　　　B　　　　　　　　　C
and a <u>far</u> more through report.
　　　　D
　　　＜解答＞　A：had had

1594. Morphine and other <u>narcotic drugs</u> are voaluable <u>medically</u>; if missused,
　　　　　　　　　　　　　A　　　　　　　　　　　　　B
however, <u>it</u> can cause <u>irreparable</u> damage.
　　　　　　　C　　　　　　　D
　　　＜解答＞　C：they

1595. Though you may not <u>agree</u> the philosophy of Malcolm X, you must admit
　　　　　　　　　　　　　A
that he <u>not only</u> had- but <u>continues</u> to have- tremendous influence <u>over</u>
　　　　　　B　　　　　　　　　C　　　　　　　　　　　　　　　D
a great many followers.
　　　＜解答＞　A：agree with

1596. After being wheeled <u>into</u> the <u>infirmary</u>, <u>by the nurse asked me several</u>
　　　　　　　　　　　　A　　　　B　　　　　　　C
<u>questions</u> <u>at the desk</u>.
　　　　　　　　　D
　　　＜解答＞　C：I was asked several questions by the nurse

1597. We hear <u>dissent</u> from a young man <u>whom</u>, we firmly believe, is not about
　　　　　　　A　　　　　　　　　　　B
<u>to pay</u> compliments to our political leaders <u>or</u> to the local draft board.
　　　C　　　　　　　　　　　　　　　　　　D
　　　＜解答＞　B：who

1598. Controversial matters <u>involving</u> the two groups <u>were discussed</u>; nevertheless,
A   B

<u>most</u> of the representatives <u>remaining calm</u>.
C   D

＜解答＞ D：remained calm

1599. If one reads a <u>great many</u> articles in Elementary English, <u>you</u> will become
A   B

<u>familiar with</u> the problems of the <u>beginning</u> teacher of reading.
C   D

＜解答＞ B：one

1600. <u>If</u> I <u>would have been</u> there, I certainly would have taken <u>care</u> of the problem
A   B   C

<u>in a hurry</u>.
D

＜解答＞ B：had been

1601. He <u>believes</u> in witchcraft, but he <u>doubts</u> that <u>they</u> ride <u>on</u> broomsticks.
A   B   C   D

＜解答＞ C：witches

1602. The <u>retreat</u> of the enemy soldiers into caves and tunnels <u>are deceiving</u>
A   B

the <u>oncoming</u> <u>infrantrymer</u>.
C   D

＜解答＞ B：is deceiving

1603. <u>In contrast</u> to <u>Arnold's</u> intellectual prowess <u>was</u> his <u>slovenly</u> appearance
A   B   C   D

and his nervous demeanor.

＜解答＞ C：were

1604. I <u>wouldn't</u> be interested in buying this <u>here</u> farm <u>even</u> if you <u>were</u> to offer
A   B   C   D

it to me for a hundred dollars.

<解答>　B：cancel

1605. There is no sense in <u>getting</u> angry with <u>them</u> radicals <u>just</u> because they

　　　　　　　　　　　　　　　A　　　　　　　　　　B　　　　　　C

disagree <u>with</u> you.

　　　　　　D

<解答>　B：those

1606. The high school graduate, if <u>he</u> is eighteen or nineteen, <u>has</u> these <u>alternatives</u>:

　　　　　　　　　　　　　　　　　A　　　　　　　　　　　　B　　　　C

attending college, finding a job, <u>or the army</u>.

　　　　　　　　　　　　　　　　　D

<解答>　D：or joining the army

1607. There <u>was</u> only an apple and three pears <u>in the refrigerator</u> when we

　　　　　A　　　　　　　　　　　　　　　　　　　B

<u>came home</u> after a <u>weekend</u> in the country.

　　C　　　　　　　D

<解答>A：were

1608. Although Hank was the captain of our high school track team, and

<u>was hailed</u> as the fastest man on the team, I have <u>no doubt about</u>

　　A　　　　　　　　　　　　　　　　　　　　　　B

<u>my being able</u> to run faster than <u>him</u> today.

　　C　　　　　　　　　　　D

<解答>　D：he

1609. <u>Whether</u> the sales <u>compaign</u> succeeds <u>probably not be known</u> for at least

　　　A　　　　　　　B　　　　　　　C

year, but it is clear now that the stakes <u>are</u> high.

　　　　　　　　　　　　　　　　D

<解答>　C：will probably not be known

1610. A recent poll <u>has indicated</u> that Harold is considered <u>brighter</u> than

　　　　　　　　A　　　　　　　　　　　　　　　　B

any student in the <u>senior calss</u> at the South Palmetto High School.

      C   D

＜解答＞ C：any other student

1611. <u>Though</u> Seaver Pitched <u>real</u> well, the Orioles <u>scored</u> four runs in the ninth

    A   B   C

inning <u>as a result</u> of two Met errors.

       D

＜解答＞ B：really

1612. <u>After</u> the oritics see the two plays, they <u>will</u>, as a result of <u>their</u> experience

   A   B   C

and background, be able to judge which is the <u>most</u> effective and moving.

                               D

＜解答＞ D：more

1613. A textbook <u>used</u> in a college class <u>usually always</u> <u>contains</u> an introduction,

           A   B   C

a glossary, and <u>an annotated</u> bibliography.

         D

＜解答＞ B：① usually ② always

1614. Since one of <u>their</u> members was a prisoner of war in Vietnam, the

      A

family felt <u>badly</u> when they heard <u>over the radio</u> that the peace talks

       B   C

<u>were to be discontinued</u>.

       D

＜解答＞ B：bad

1615. <u>Have you read</u> in the Columbia Spector that <u>Jeff's</u> leg <u>was broken</u>

    A   B   C

<u>while playing football</u> ?

     D

＜解答＞ D：while he was playing football

1616. George Foreman did <u>like</u> he said when he <u>forecast</u> that he would <u>knock out</u>

                           A   B   C

Joe Frazier <u>to win</u> the world's heavyweight championship.

            D

    ＜解答＞　A：as

1617. <u>Due to</u> the meat boycott, the butchers <u>were doing</u> about <u>half of</u> the

      A   B   C

business that they were doing <u>previous to</u> the boycott.

                           D

    ＜解答＞　A：Because of

1618. <u>Lidocaine's</u> usefulness as a local anesthetic was discovered by two Swedish

       A

chemists <u>whom</u> <u>repeatedly tested</u> the <u>drug's</u> effects on their bodies.

               B   C   D

    ＜解答＞　B：who

1619. You <u>may not</u> realize <u>it</u> but the weather in Barbados <u>during Christmas</u> is

           A   B   C

<u>like New York</u> in June.

           D

    ＜解答＞　D：like that of New York

1620. The teacher did not encourage the student <u>any</u> even though the boy

                                          A

began <u>to weep</u> when he <u>was told</u> that his poor marks would likely <u>hold up</u>

           B   C   D

his graduation.

    ＜解答＞　A：in any way

1621. <u>According</u> to the most recent estimates, Greater Miami <u>has more than</u>

      A   B

45,000 <u>Spanish-speaking</u> residents, of <u>who</u> about 400,000 are Cubans.

           C   D

<解答>　D：whom

1622. Had Lincoln <u>have been</u> alive during World War II, he <u>would have regarded</u>
　　　　　　　　　　　A　　　　　　　　　　　　　　　　　　　B

　　　the racial <u>situation in </u>the armed forces as a <u>throwback</u> to pre-Civil war days.
　　　　　　　　　　　　C　　　　　　　　　　　　　　　D

　　　<解答>　A：been

1623. The reason <u>that</u> Roberto Clemente, the great baseball star, was on the
　　　　　　　　　　A

　　　plane that <u>crashed</u> was <u>because</u> he was <u>on his way</u> to help the victims
　　　　　　　　　　　B　　　　　　C　　　　　　　D

　　　of the earthquake.

　　　<解答>　C：that

1624. If any singer of the Constitution <u>was</u> to return to life <u>for a day</u>, his opinion
　　　　　　　　　　　　　　　　　　　　A　　　　　　　　　　　B

　　　<u>of</u> our amendments <u>would be</u> interesting.
　　　C　　　　　　　　　　D

　　　<解答>　C：that

國家圖書館出版品預行編目資料

TOEFL 托福文法與構句／李英松著. --初版. --
新北市：李昭儀，2022.10
　　冊；　公分
ISBN 978-957-43-9951-2（中冊：平裝）
ISBN 978-957-43-9952-9（下冊：平裝）
1.CST: 托福考試 2.CST: 語法
805.1894　　　　　　　　　　111004270

TOEFL托福文法與構句　中冊

作　　者　李英松
發 行 人　李英松
出　　版　李昭儀
　　　　　Email：lambtyger@gmail.com
設計編印　白象文化事業有限公司
　　　　　專案主編：李婕　　經紀人：徐錦淳
經銷代理　白象文化事業有限公司
　　　　　412台中市大里區科技路1號8樓之2（台中軟體園區）
　　　　　出版專線：（04）2496-5995　　傳真：（04）2496-9901
　　　　　401台中市東區和平街228巷44號（經銷部）
　　　　　購書專線：（04）2220-8589　　傳真：（04）2220-8505
印　　刷　普羅文化股份有限公司
初版一刷　2022 年 10 月
定　　價　420 元